Lunatics

Dave Barry in Cyberspace

Dave Barry's Complete Guide to Guys

Dave Barry Is Not Making This Up

Dave Barry Does Japan

Dave Barry's Only Travel Guide You'll Ever Need

Dave Barry Talks Back

Dave Barry Turns 40

Dave Barry Slept Here

Dave Barry's Greatest Hits

Dave Barry's Homes and Other Black Holes

Dave Barry's Guide to Marriage and/or Sex

Dave Barry's Bad Habits

Claw Your Way to the Top

Stay Fit and Healthy Until You're Dead

Babies and Other Hazards of Sex

The Taming of the Screw

OTHER BOOKS BY ALAN ZWEIBEL

Clothing Optional: And Other Ways to Read These Stories

The Other Shulman: A Novel

Bunny Bunny: Gilda Radner—A Sort of Love Story

Our Tree Named Steve (children's book)

North

Dave Barry
and
Alan Zweibel

G. P. PUTNAM'S SONS

NEW YORK

Lunatics

PUTNAM

G. P. PUTNAM'S SONS
Publishers Since 1838
Published by the Penguin Group
Penguin Group (USA) Inc., 375 Hudson Street, New York,
New York 10014, USA • Penguin Group (Canada), 90 Eglinton Avenue East,
Suite 700, Toronto, Ontario M4P 2Y3, Canada (a division of Pearson Penguin
Canada Inc.) • Penguin Books Ltd, 80 Strand, London WC2R 0RL, England •
Penguin Ireland, 25 St Stephen's Green, Dublin 2, Ireland (a division of Penguin
Books Ltd) • Penguin Group (Australia), 250 Camberwell Road, Camberwell,
Victoria 3124, Australia (a division of Pearson Australia Group Pty Ltd) •
Penguin Books India Pvt Ltd, 11 Community Centre, Panchsheel Park,
New Delhi–110 017, India • Penguin Group (NZ), 67 Apollo Drive, Rosedale,
North Shore 0632, New Zealand (a division of Pearson New Zealand Ltd) •
Penguin Books (South Africa) (Pty) Ltd, 24 Sturdee Avenue, Rosebank,
Johannesburg 2196, South Africa

Penguin Books Ltd, Registered Offices: 80 Strand, London WC2R 0RL, England

ISBN 978-0-399-15869-8

Printed in the United States of America
1   3   5   7   9   10   8   6   4   2

BOOK DESIGN BY BRIAN MULLIGAN

This is a work of fiction. Names, characters, places, and incidents either are the
product of the authors' imagination or are used fictitiously, and any resemblance to
actual persons, living or dead, businesses, companies, events, or locales is entirely
coincidental.

While the authors have made every effort to provide accurate telephone numbers and
Internet addresses at the time of publication, neither the publisher nor the authors
assume any responsibility for errors, or for changes that occur after
publication. Further, the publisher does not have any control over and does not
assume any responsibility for author or third-party websites or their content.

ALWAYS LEARNING   PEARSON

We dedicate this book to our wives,

Michelle and Robin,

who, if we had discussed the idea with them ahead

of time, would definitely have discouraged us.

A D V I S O R Y

Dave Barry and Alan Zweibel have both written books for children.
This is definitely not one of them.

Before we explain how it all happened, we'd like to take this opportunity, from the get-go, to apologize.

What do you mean "we"?

I thought we agreed that we would take responsibility for . . .

Whoa whoa whoa. I agree that YOU should take responsibility. No way in hell am I apologizing for something I didn't do. Because none of this, no, let me correct that, NONE of this, would ever have happened if you knew the goddam rules of the game of socc . . .

Okay, let's not get into that again . . .

I'll get into whatever I want to get into, you douchebag.

The point is, dear reader, that mistakes were made, and things got out of hand, and we, I should say *I'm*, very sorry for any mental anguish, financial loss, destruction of property, or serious physical injury that may have been caused to anyone, including my loving wife and children, my friends, my community, innocent bystanders, the brave and dedicated men and women of the New York Police Department, the staff and patients of Lenox Hill Hospital, the fine officers, crew and passengers aboard the SS *Windsong*, the Port-au-Prince Duffel Bag Company, Charo, and the U.S. armed forces—in particular the Coast Guard. I also apologize to all three branches of the United States government, Arnie and Sue Kogen, and to both the General Assembly and Security Council of the United Nations for any role we may have played—and I assure you it was completely inadvertent—in exacerbating world tensions. And on a more personal note, let me say that, as a passionate lifelong lover and protector of animals, I deeply regret any of our actions that endangered any of the helpless, vulnerable creatures of the Central Park Zoo.

HELPLESS? Those things had teeth like fucking steak knives.

Finally, on the advice of legal counsel, I want to stress that nothing in the account that you are about to read is meant to suggest or imply that there is now, or has ever been, a connection between any international terrorist organization and the Chuck E. Cheese restaurant chain.

Chuck E. Cheese can bite me.

CHAPTER 1

Philip

What a wonderful day! One of those magical Sundays that punctuate the end of a great week with a huge exclamation point!

My name is Philip Horkman, and I own a pet shop called The Wine Shop—a modest store I opened fifteen years ago with money my in-laws, Lillian and Gerald Wine, loaned me on the condition that I name the place after them.

"But won't that be confusing?" I asked at the time. "Customers will think I sell liquor."

"Then sell liquor," they said.

"But I want to sell pets."

"Then borrow money from people named Pets."

Hungry to strike out on my own and desperate for funds, I acceded and opened The Wine Shop in a mini-mall a stone's throw from the George Washington Bridge. Things were slow at first. Painfully slow. But after months of bewildered looks and torrents of invective hurled from those seeking a merlot instead of an iguana, word slowly got out that we indeed sold animals. And the misnomer emblazoned on our sign eventually changed from being a source of scorn to a magnet attracting pet lovers who applauded our originality and found our wit refreshing.

Seven days a week, I worked in that store, and it is no exaggeration when I say that I loved every minute of it. Not only because it was so darned rewarding to see the glee on the faces of children whose folks treated them to a dog, a cat, a bird or colorful fish—but it had also allowed me to provide my family with a comfortable home and middle-class lifestyle in suburban New Jersey. We had two cars. Went skiing every winter. The kids took dancing lessons. Life was good, with promises to get even better, because I'd spent that Saturday morning at the bank signing what seemed like a thousand pages of loan documents so The Wine Shop could expand to a second location the following spring.

The next day was Sunday and I did what I always did on Sundays. I refereed soccer games for our town's AYSO league. I'm sure a lot of folks found that odd, as both of our children were well into their teens and hadn't played in this league for some time. That said, after being cooped up in a store all week, I still enjoyed refereeing, as nothing helped me unwind better than to be outdoors breathing the crisp autumn air while running up and down a grass field. Plus, I found it invigorating to be amongst such spirited children whose enthusiasm was fanned by their parents and friends who came out to cheer their favorite ten-year-old players on.

But that Sunday's game was set on an even bigger stage, as the winners of the two divisional playoffs were playing each other for the league championship. It was a special day. The crowd was bigger, the local press and their papers' photographers were on hand, and the kids rose to the occasion, playing their hearts out in a 1–0 nail-biter. And with the exception of one overzealous father who shouted his displeasure when I ruled his daughter offside after she kicked what would have been the tying goal, a great time was had by all, and the rest of the parents thanked me afterward for a job well done.

That glory of that Sunday continued that evening when I took my family to our favorite restaurant to celebrate the new store, returned home, watched our favorite movie (*The Sound of Music*) in HD on the flat screen, went upstairs, and fell asleep spooning my wife, Daisy.

I'm not a religious man. Yet I've always considered myself blessed. And though life presents us with challenges that test our resolve along the way, it's a positive attitude that's granted me the strength to handle any situation adeptly, cope with it, and move forward. I've always been the kind of person who, when given the choice, chooses to err on the side of being grateful.

Jeffrey

I'll be honest: I wanted to kill the asshole.

That was the first thing I said to my wife, Donna, after I temporarily stopped yelling at the asshole for calling offside on Taylor when there was NO WAY it was offside.

"I want to kill that asshole" were my exact words.

"Jeffrey," she said, looking around at the other parents, who were making a point of not looking at me. "Language."

"Right, sorry," I said. "I want to kill that *fucking* asshole." Now some of the parents were actively edging away from me. But I'm sorry. My daughter kicks the tying goal in the league championship, and this asshole calls offside? When it clearly was not? And I'm supposed to *not notice*?

It happens to be my job to notice things. It's my *profession*. I'm a forensic plumber. And before you laugh, you might be interested to know that forensic plumbing is a growing, high-demand field, with its own national association, which I happen to be on the board of directors of. You might also be interested to know that a top forensic plumber can command $300 per hour plus expenses, and that the expert testimony of forensic plumbers has proven to be crucial in several high-profile court cases, including one in which a man was found guilty of murdering his wife by holding her facedown in their master-bedroom toilet. He claimed she committed suicide, but the forensic plumber, testifying for the prosecution, was able to show the jury, by means of a dramatic courtroom reenactment, that with that particular model commode there was no way the victim could have reached the flush lever and still got that level of facial suction.

I'm not saying I've been involved in anything that glamorous. I mostly handle insurance work. But I make a good living, and the reason is that I have a highly organized mind and an eye for detail, which is how I know there was no fucking way Taylor was offside.

After the game, I confronted the ref. Donna was tugging on my sleeve, telling me not to embarrass Taylor. Like THAT was the issue, embarrassing Taylor, when the issue was that this asshole is out there making a complete mockery of the girls ten-and-under league championship. Which is what I told him to his face, and you know what he said? He said—and this should give you an idea of the mindset I was dealing with—"I'm sorry you feel that way, but she definitely looked offside to me."

Asshole.

So I told him that she probably looked offside to Ray Charles and Little Stevie Wonder, too, but anybody with working eyeballs could see she wasn't.

That was when Taylor started tugging on my other sleeve, saying, "Dad, forget about it." This is something I need to work on with her. As a player, she has all the physical tools, but she doesn't have the fire, the *fight* you want to see. If she doesn't turn that around, she's going to get killed when she moves up to the twelve-and-under division. Those girls will rip your throat out.

So anyway, we left. The last thing I saw was the asshole ref talking to some parents, and they were smiling. Parents from *our side*, I'm talking about. *Smiling.*

You wonder what has happened to this nation.

As you can imagine, I was in a pretty bad mood when we got home, so I ate some lasagna in the media room and watched *Silence of the Lambs*, and I felt a little better. I was still thinking about writing an email to the league, using my official stationery, Jeffrey A. Peckerman, C.F.P., so these people would know who they were dealing with. The only thing I was second-guessing myself about was that I mentioned both Ray Charles *and* Stevie Wonder. It wasn't racist. I was just going for blind guys, and in the heat of the moment no white blind guys came to mind. There don't seem to be that many famous ones. In a way, you could argue that what I said was actually kind of a tribute to African-Americans, but you just know the asshole ref would be the kind to twist things around. So I finally decided, reluctantly, that I wasn't going to pursue the matter any further.

And I probably wouldn't have, except for Oprah. She has this thing where she announces that everybody should read a certain book, and her zombie army of women followers go out and buy millions of copies of it. One of them is my wife, who belongs to a group of Oprah women who all buy the book and then meet in somebody's house to drink wine and discuss it, although mostly they drink wine because they haven't read the actual book.

So anyway, the next day I was driving home, coming from an inspection of an eighteen-unit apartment building whose landlord had hired me to find out which of his tenants was flushing metal balls down the toilet that were totally screwing up the plumbing. So far I had determined that the balls were from a game called Pétanque, which was invented by the French, so my next step in the investigation was to find out if any of the tenants were either French or known to exhibit French behavior such as scarves.

But the point is, I was driving home by an unusual route that took me near the George Washington Bridge, and Donna called my cell to tell me the Oprah zombie group was meeting at our house that night and could I stop and pick up some wine. I was just telling her that I was in an unfamiliar area and didn't know where a liquor store was, when I happened to glance to my right and see a strip mall with a sign listing the stores, including one called The Wine Shop.

So I put on my blinker and turned in.

Philip

I heard him before I saw him.

It was the day after that game, and I was in the back room of The Wine Shop counting canaries. A shipment had just arrived, and it was important that there were exactly twenty-four of the little tweeters, because that's how many I was donating to the kids in the obesity clinic over at Children's Hospital. It was the annual drive, and local merchants were asked to contribute to the department of their choice. And since one of our children has a propensity for being overweight, I am particularly sensitive to the plight of those boys and girls in the midst of that heartbreaking battle. So I planned on sending them a check as well as those canaries to hopefully cheer them up.

Counting birds of any kind is a challenge, but canaries are more active and tend to flit about the crates they're shipped in more so than others. So it requires total focus as you transfer them into individual boxes, at the same time making sure that none of them have watery eyes, puffed bellies, or any other telltale signs of disease.

One bird concerned me. A multi-colored Spanish Timbrado that appeared to be too thin and nowhere as lively as the others. I picked the little fellow up and held him to my ear. The Spanish Timbrado belongs to a species commonly referred to as "song canaries" for their unique chattering sounds and metallic tones. But when this bird opened his little mouth, I heard nothing—either because it was unable to sing or because his chirps were drowned out by the outburst coming from the front of the store.

"Are you fucking kidding me!"

I had left Hyo, a sixteen-year-old Korean American who worked for me after school and on weekends, to mind the register and assist customers. And while Hyo, who was saving up to buy a car when he got his driver's license the following year, was an affable lad capable of handling even the most difficult pet buyers, what came next turned my head.

"Please don't yell, sir. It scares the animals," said Hyo.

"And I wouldn't be yelling if these fucking animals weren't here and you sold what your sign says you're selling, or is 'wine shop' the way you say 'pet shop' in China or Japan or whatever rice-gobbling country you swam here from!"

While I couldn't place it at first, that voice was familiar. I knew I'd heard it. Recently. And when I stepped into the doorway that separated the back room from the front of the store to see what the commotion was about, I recognized the belligerent customer as the belligerent parent who dressed me down the day before at the soccer field. Once again, his rage was palpable. Red face, heaving chest, eyes bulging like a sick Yorkshire Canary. So I opted to remain calm and try to defuse things without incident.

"There's a liquor store about a mile from here. Would you like me to call to see if they're still open?"

He turned in my direction and immediately remembered me.

"You? This is your place?"

"It is," I nodded.

"Makes perfect sense."

"What does?"

"That the same idiot who can't see that a player is not offside also can't see why this is a ridiculous store. You can't see *anything*, can you?"

"I guess not," I answered, shaking my head. "Pretty much like Ray Charles and Stevie Wonder."

Hyo, who'd been silent up to this point, chose this moment to speak up.

"That's a pretty racist remark," he said, looking at me with a combination of surprise and disappointment.

"I know it is. I was just quoting what he said to me yesterday."

"I knew you'd never say such a thing," said Hyo, visibly relieved.

"It's not racist, goddammit! I only mentioned them because there are no famous blind white people!" shouted you-know-who.

"Oh, really?" I countered. "How about Helen Keller? And Galileo? And Joseph Pulitzer who created the Pulitzer Prize? Or Brian McKeever, the Olympic cross-country skier? Or Louis Braille, the man who invented Braille? Would you like me to continue?"

"Are you out of your fucking mind? Your blind white people couldn't shine my blind black people's shoes. My God, look at the joy Ray Charles's and Stevie Wonder's music have brought to millions of people. These are great men who just so happened to be blind. Not like your guys who made a fucking business out of it. The only reason Braille invented Braille was so he could read because other people got tired of telling him what he was missing. And what the hell did Helen Keller do except *be* blind? And she's on a stamp? Why would they put a person who couldn't even find the post office on a stamp?"

"She was also deaf and mute," I told him.

"Which means that even if she did find the post office, she couldn't tell the clerk she wanted to buy her own stamps or hear how much they cost. What bullshit!"

I was going to respond. Was going to explain that overcoming her handicaps was a laudable achievement itself and an inspiration to so many others similarly afflicted. But before I had a chance, the silence was broken by a faint chirp from the sickly Spanish Timbrado I'd been holding since I came in from the back room. So I looked down and started to gently stroke its head.

"What the hell is that?" he asked.

"A canary," I answered.

"We're donating two dozen of them to Children's Hospital," Hyo added. "As incentives for the boys and girls in the obesity program."

"That's very nice," he said.

It caught me off guard. Those were the first humane words he'd uttered in the two days he'd been a new, unwanted entry into my life.

"That's very, very nice," he continued.

Perhaps this is the real person, I wondered. Maybe this is who the guy really is and the maniac I'd been dealing with was merely him acting out other frustrations in his life. Understandable. Repulsive, but understandable. I'm wired to instinctively give people the benefit of the doubt. To focus on their inherent good. My wife Daisy has always claimed that was what attracted her to me. My desire to stress the positive. So I decided that I'd focus on the man who stood before me now and start anew.

"Yes," I said, with a smile. "They'll get them as rewards for reaching certain goal weights."

"That's wonderful," he said, nodding. "But if they don't reach their goal weights, how much you want to bet that those fat turds eat those fucking canaries?"

As I reached for the broken pole from a birdcage stand I kept behind the counter to fend off dangerous intruders, flashes of my own child's weight struggle—the tears, the object of name-calling, and the Saturday nights spent in a bedroom, uninvited to parties—I prayed I'd get in one good swing before he was out the door.

Jeffrey

It was totally self-defense.

I know how it might look in hindsight. But as the saying goes, hindsight is in the eye of the beholder. And at that moment, what I was beholding was an asshole—a *large* asshole—holding a broken pole from a birdcage stand, which can be a lethal weapon, in a threatening manner.

I had no way of knowing what this asshole was going to do. But I had reason to believe that he was mentally unstable, because, Exhibit A, he calls his store "The Wine Shop" and he's selling fucking parakeets in there, him and his little Jap sidekick, calling me a racist because I can't off the top of my head name seventeen famous blind white people. And for the record, how famous is a *cross-country skier*? Even if he is famous, which I doubt, I bet he has people skiing behind him yelling "Turn left! Turn right!" or else he's going to ski into a fucking tree. So while I admire his determination, no way is he in the same blindness league as Ray Charles and Stevie Wonder, who never had anybody standing behind them at the keyboard shouting, "Move your right hand to the left a little! Make an F-sharp!" Or whatever.

But my point is, this fucking unstable lunatic is coming at me in a threatening manner with a Louisville Slugger, and in that situation, legally—and bear in mind that I have spent many hours in a court of law—you have the right to defend yourself by whatever means necessary. So I grabbed the first thing I saw, which it turned out was a cage. My plan was to hold it between me and the lunatic while I backed out the door.

You should have seen his face when I picked up the cage. Jesus. His face turned the color of Hawaiian Punch, and his eyeballs got the size of fried eggs, and he's waving his broken pole from a birdcage stand and yelling "PUT DOWN THAT LEMUR!!"

I'll be honest: At the time I didn't know what a lemur was. Later I found out from Wikipedia that they were the little furry animals with the big eyes in *Madagascar*, which I have on DVD, but at the time all I knew was, I was not going to put down the cage and have nothing between me and the lunatic with the broken pole from a birdcage stand. So I backed up, got the door open, and took off running.

Fortunately I parked close by, and I was in the car and got the doors locked before the lunatic reached me. He was waving the broken pole from a birdcage stand and screaming, and all I wanted to do was get out of there, so I started the car, threw it into gear and stomped on the gas. Maybe I brushed him a little going past, but as I said earlier, this was clearly a self-defense situation.

Looking back, maybe I should have dropped the cage before I got into the car. But everything was happening so fast, plus if I dropped the cage it might have injured the lemur, which I later found out was endangered. So the argument could be made from an ecology standpoint that I actually *rescued* this valuable animal, which the unstable lunatic had placed in a potentially hazardous situation vis-à-vis he was swinging a broken pole from a birdcage stand in its vicinity. I'm not saying that is my main legal position. My main legal position is that I was totally within my rights to defend myself.

As you can imagine, by this point I was pretty upset, so I drove straight home. I have to say, as a person who just almost got his skull crushed, I was disappointed in Donna's reaction.

"A *lemur*?" she said. "I ask you to bring home wine and you BRING HOME A LEMUR?"

"It was self-defense," I said.

"Can we keep it?" said Taylor.

"NO WE CANNOT KEEP IT!" said Donna, who gets excited (she is Italian). "I have SEVENTEEN WOMEN coming here in a half hour to discuss *Freedom* by Jonathan Franzen, and they will be expecting to drink WINE, so your father is going to TAKE THE LEMUR BACK TO WHEREVER HE GOT IT FROM and BRING HOME SOME WINE LIKE I ASKED HIM TO or he is going to spend the REST OF HIS LIFE SLEEPING IN THE GARAGE."

"Mom, you're scaring the lemur," said Taylor.

"I can't take it back," I said.

"Yay!" said Taylor.

"Why not?" said Donna.

"Because the guy it belongs to tried to kill me," I said.

"And why would he do that?" said Donna.

"Well, partly because I took his lemur."

Donna rubbed her face with her hands, starting high and then pulling down, so her mouth got all stretched out. It's not an attractive look for her, but I have learned over the years not to point this out.

"All right," she said. "Taylor, you will put the lemur in the base-ment . . ."

"Yay!" said Taylor.

". . . for *now*. Tomorrow your father will get rid of the lemur."

"But *Mom* . . ."

"Your father will GET RID OF THE LEMUR, and I do not care

how he does it. But right now he will GO GET SOME WINE. He will get a LOT of wine."

Which is what I did. There is no point arguing with Donna when she is being that Italian. I thought about mentioning to her that the lemur owner was the same asshole who called the offside, but I decided it was probably better if she didn't know that. I figured she was never going to find out, because I had no intention of ever coming into contact with that lunatic again.

CHAPTER 5

Philip

I loved that lemur more than I loved my father-in-law.

I try my best not to get emotionally involved with the animals in my pet shop. Through the years, I've learned that it will only lead to heartbreak due to the inevitability that sooner or later they will leave the store—either by way of a sale or (as in the case of that sickly Spanish Timbrado that I accidentally dropped and crushed with my heel when I grabbed the broken pole from a birdcage stand and took off after that racist maniac) feet first.

So try as I may to maintain a purely professional relationship with all that crawl, hop, fly, lope, slither, or swim and regard them as mere inventory, there was something about that lemur that made me break my own rule. Why? Because it was endangered? Well, yes and no. Of course my heart goes out to any species that borders on extinction. I feel that way about polar bears, giant pandas, sunset frogs, Bengal tigers, Hawaiian monk seals, Egyptian vultures, Serpent Island centipedes, and Malagasy Giant Jumping Rats. But since I've never forged a personal relationship with any of them, I regret their impending demise but lose little or no sleep over it.

With that baby lemur, however, from the moment it came into The Wine Shop, I felt an immediate connection. Perhaps it was his size (just 2.1 oz.) or the fact that its thumbs were only pseudo-opposable, which made its hands less than perfect at grasping objects, that I felt the desire to care for it. Feed it. Nurse it. It was delivered about an hour before closing on a Saturday evening and, because of its special needs, I was reluctant to leave it unattended until the store reopened Monday morning. So I took it home, brought it downstairs to our finished basement, put it in a corner next to a heat lamp and hand-fed it dry leaves, which I left in a bowl next to the cage for his next feeding.

Daisy's folks were in town and I found her note saying that she, her mom, and the kids had gone to a movie. And that my father-in-law, who'd opted not to join them, was napping in the downstairs spare bedroom in the finished basement—about fifteen feet away from the lemur. Wanting to take full advantage of the quiet, I went upstairs to the family room to watch a game I'd TiVoed (*Wheel of Fortune*) when, not ten minutes later, the smell of something burning was followed by the sound of our smoke detector, which was followed by the sound of my father-in-law's incessant pounding of his fists on the door to the downstairs bedroom that he'd accidentally locked himself in. Apparently, I'd put the heat lamp too close to the dry leaves, so when I got down to the basement, I grabbed the cage and brought the frightened lemur up to the safety of our kitchen and cuddled it before grabbing the small fire extinguisher we kept inside the pantry, went back downstairs to the now smoke-filled basement, put the fire out, heard the sounds of my father-in-law's somewhat softer pounding on the spare bedroom door, went back upstairs, grabbed the spare key we kept inside a kitchen drawer, went back downstairs, opened the door to the spare bedroom, and carried my unconscious father-in-law up the stairs and outside for fresh air, where he was revived by oxygen-toting firemen who'd pulled up just as I was laying him down on our front lawn.

And now this very same lemur had been stolen. Kidnapped. Endangered in the hands of someone oblivious to or, even worse, uncaring about its delicacy. So I told the policeman that I knew who the perpetrator was and that I wanted him arrested and punished to the fullest extent of a law. I said "a" law and not "the" law because I really didn't care which law it was, just as long as its punishment was cruel and unusual. I told him this in the emergency room at Children's Hospital—where Hyo had driven me after that lunatic's car knocked me down and ran over my ankle as he sped away.

"What's his name?" asked the humorless policeman whose name-plate identified him as Officer H. Pepper from the local Fort Lee precinct.

"I have no idea," I answered.

"But you just told me that you know who this guy is."

"I do. But I don't know his name. All I can tell you is that he's number fourteen's father."

"Excuse me?" asked Officer Pepper, who was now looking at me with the same expression traditionally seen on the faces of people who are talking to idiots. "What could that possibly mean?"

"His daughter plays in the AYSO league that I'm a referee in. So all you have to do is get your hands on the roster for the Princess Daffodils in the ten-and-under division, see which player is number fourteen, then arrest her father and prosecute the bastard to the fullest extent of a law. Any law."

"No," said Officer Pepper, who was now looking at me with the same expression traditionally seen on the faces of people who want to beat the daylights out of another person. "How it works is *you* get a hold of the roster, see who number fourteen is, then call me with the information and then I'll go deal with her father, okay?" before handing me his card, which I quickly glanced at to see and happened to notice his rank.

"You're a sergeant?" I asked.

"Yes."

"You're Sgt. Pepper?"

"Don't start, okay?"

"You must get a lot of teasing."

"I said don't start, okay?"

"Fine."

So while the good folks at Children's Hospital taped my chest in deference to two cracked ribs and fitted my left ankle with a soft walking cast, Hyo went online and found the Princess Daffodils roster on the AYSO website. The player who wore number 14 was Taylor Peckerman. Her parents were Donna and Jeffrey Peckerman, and because the listed address was only about a half mile away from ours, I felt compelled to drive past their house on my way home.

CHAPTER 6

Jeffrey

There is an old legal principle, which I forget the technical Latin name of, but it comes from English common law, and the gist of it is: If you go to a man's home, he can, legally, kill you.

And when we say a man's home, we can legally interpret that to include the man's property, meaning his yard, his sidewalk, and—you will see later why this is important—his swale. A man's swale is his castle, especially if he mows it *and* fertilizes it, which I do. My swale would not be out of place at Augusta National.

So here is what happened:

I was upstairs, lying on my bed watching *SportsCenter*. (This is off topic, but: Has there been an NBA highlight in the past seventeen years where a player scored a basket and he *didn't* travel? I mean, since these are professional basketball players getting paid millions of dollars, shouldn't they have to *dribble the fucking basketball* once in a while? Whereas in your modern NBA, a guy can be nowhere near the basket, he's basically still in the locker room, and suddenly he runs to the basket carrying the ball like it's a ham sandwich, and after three hundred steps he dunks it, and instead of getting whistled for traveling, he gets on *SportsCenter*. And before you think what I think you're going to think, I'm saying they *all* do this, including the white guys.)

Suddenly I heard this shout from Taylor's room: "Buddy! No!!"

Taylor named the lemur Buddy. She thinks it's a male, even though there's no way to tell by looking at it. I did not give her permission to keep Buddy because Donna would kill us both (I mean me and Buddy). But I did say Taylor could have Buddy in her room until the next day, when I would figure out how to get rid of him. Donna, after Category 5 whining from Taylor, had agreed that okay, Buddy could stay one night in Taylor's room, but Taylor was to keep him up there and not let him get anywhere near the Oprah book-and-wine group.

So I jumped off the bed and hustled down to Taylor's room, where she was freaking out in the direction of her canopy. Back when Taylor was in her princess phase, what she really really wanted, more than anything in the whole wide world, was for her bed to have a canopy. It cost $450, and ten minutes after we got it, Taylor was done with the princess phase and on to the next phase, which I think was Hannah Montana. But she still has the canopy, and Buddy had climbed up on it for the purpose of taking a dump. It turns out that lemurs, in their native environment, are tree dwellers; they like to have some altitude when they relieve themselves. So Buddy was perched up there, dropping long, droopy squirts of lemur shit onto Taylor's bedspread, which is currently a Justin Bieber model.

"Why did you let it out of the cage?" I asked Taylor.

"Because he wanted out!" she said.

"He wanted out so he could go to the bathroom!"

"Well, *I* didn't know that!" She said this with that voice that women develop at a very early age, the one where whatever happens—the cable goes out, they have a headache, a lemur is shitting on the bed— it's your fault.

I went to grab Buddy, but here's the thing: A lemur is basically a monkey. It has, like, ten million years of experience with not being captured. So I'm lunging around Taylor's room, trying to grab this thing, but it's skittering around like a big hairy mosquito, up on the light fixture, down on the floor, up on the bureau, back up on the canopy, and every time I go to grab it, it's gone.

One mistake I made, and this is something you should bear in mind if you ever find yourself in this situation: You should close the door. I realized this when Buddy skittered into the hall and headed for the stairs. I was right behind him, but I don't care who you are. I don't care if you're Randy Moss. (Or some equally fast white guy.) You're not going to catch a fucking lemur.

Here was the situation downstairs, as it was later explained to me by Donna after she had calmed down a little and stopped talking about removing my balls with a corkscrew:

The women were no longer discussing *Freedom*, by Jonathan Franzen. It turned out that, of the seventeen of them, exactly one, Jeanette Keebler, actually read the entire book, and she wasn't sure what it was about. So after several minutes, the ladies had dropped literature and switched over to the topic of breast enhancement. At some point, this became a general discussion of the human body, and at some further point diabetes came up, and Denise Rodecker, who had had several, maybe four, glasses of wine, decided she would show everybody her insulin pump. This is a little gadget that looks kind of like a beeper, which pumps insulin into a person, in this case Denise Rodecker. She unhooked it from herself and, as it happened, was showing it to the *Freedom* discussion group at the exact moment when Buddy skittered down the stairs.

Here's another fact about lemurs: They are very curious. When they see something interesting, they want to check it out. Don't ask me why, but of all the things in the living room at that particular moment, including a wide range of hors d'oeuvres, the thing that was most interesting to Buddy was Denise's insulin pump. It was like a magic trick:

Denise is holding her pump up in front of everybody, and there's this blur, and, bam, Denise is holding nothing, and there's Buddy up on the window fixture with the pump in those little hands he has, studying it like it's a Crown Jewel.

At that point, a lot of things were happening at once. Denise was screaming, and some of the other women were screaming, and Taylor was crying, and Donna was yelling at me to—easy for her to say—get the insulin pump back from Buddy. I knew I couldn't catch him bare-handed, so I was looking for something to trap him with, and I grabbed the first thing I saw, which was this carved wood mask Donna got when our cruise ship stopped in Jamaica that depicts the face of an African-American male with the words "YA MON" on his forehead. So I'm holding this mask, moving toward Buddy on the window fixture, and I would have had him except that at that exact moment, Jeanette Keebler, who has never been a rocket scientist, decides to escape, and opens the front door.

Buddy sees the opening and leaps off the window like a little furry batman, still holding the pump, and skitters out the door. Denise is now screaming so loud, my teeth ache. I'm after Buddy, holding the mask, pushing through the women. By the time I get outside, Buddy is standing in the middle of the lawn, looking at me. He still has the pump. I slow down and start creeping forward, saying "Good boy, Buddy, good boy, there's a good boy," in a calm tone. He's watching me getting closer, not moving, like he's sincerely considering what I am saying, and I'm thinking another two steps I will have the little shitter.

Just then, out of the corner of my eye, I see this Prius come gliding up the street. I take another step forward, and I'm slowly raising the YA MON mask into attack position, when suddenly this Prius swerves up onto my swale, and the window goes down, and this voice, which I immediately recognize, yells, "GET AWAY FROM THAT LEMUR!"

An asshole like that, you *know* he drives a Prius.

"GET THE *FUCK* OFF MY SWALE!" I yelled.

"THAT LEMUR IS MY PROPERTY AND YOU STOLE IT," he yelled.

I was going to point out that it was self-defense, but suddenly Buddy took off running toward the Prius, still holding Denise's insulin pump. I took off after him, but before I got there, he jumped through the window into the car. The asshole threw the Prius into gear, and I was yelling at him to stop, but he stomped on the accelerator. The car swerved sideways, and I felt this pain in my hip, and the next thing I knew I was lying on my back with dirt landing on me as this lunatic Prius asshole wrecked my swale peeling out of there. I rolled over and got up on my knees, and I have to say in all modesty that for a guy who had just been legally assaulted by a vehicle and was not in a proper throwing stance, I got a *lot* of mustard onto the YA MON mask. It went through the window clean, and I know I heard a yelp.

By now the Prius was back on the street, tires squealing. Donna and Taylor were out of the house now, running toward me. I was still on my knees, watching the Prius. Just as it turned the corner, under the streetlight, a shape jumped out the driver's-side window.

"Buddy!" yelled Taylor.

The little shitter ran straight to her.

He wasn't holding the pump.

CHAPTER 7

Philip

When I arrived home, Daisy was waiting in the driveway with something less than the greeting I needed, considering all that had happened. There wasn't a "Hi, honey. How was your day?" Or an "Oh my God, why are your ribs taped and your foot in a cast?" And nothing that even resembled the much preferred "I just read that the American Medical Association says the best cure for cracked ribs and a sprained left ankle is a sympathetic wife who cooks her husband his favorite meal (SpaghettiOs!) and afterward dims the lights in his den while he leans back in his favorite chair, closes his eyes, and listens to *The Very Best of Michael Bolton*." Instead, what I got was a growl about how we were going to be late for the recital if we didn't hurry.

Both of our children were supposed to dance that night. Heidi, sixteen, was a star. Lithe. Heavenly graced. Poetry in fluid motion. Every season, Miss Grambs, the owner of Dancing For Fun, the studio where the kids took lessons, featured Heidi in as many numbers as possible. But our eight-year-old, despite boundless enthusiasm, had a slight weight problem, was a dreadful dancer, and the target of ruthless snickering. As a result, these recitals were always an odd duality for us because, on one hand, we were there to accept praise and congratulations for Heidi, while on the other hand, we were there to support and very possibly defend our son, Trace, the only boy ballerina in the twenty-six-year history of Dancing For Fun.

And though I was still furious that the lemur had somehow wriggled free and jumped from my car, I found some comfort in knowing exactly where it was. And that all it would take was a simple call to Sgt. Pepper in the morning, and justice would be served. So I opened the door to the Prius (forty-three miles per gallon!), Daisy got in, and we drove to the recital.

"What's the theme this year?" I asked her. These programs usually had a motif that loosely connected all the individual numbers.

"Music from the movies," Daisy answered.

"That could be good."

"Heidi has a big solo during 'The Way We Were.'"

"That's wonderful!" I said.

We drove in silence for a minute or so, knowing that there was another question to be asked, but we both needed a little time to brace ourselves. Finally, I took the plunge.

"And Trace?"

"Trace also has a solo," she told me.

"Uh-oh . . ."

"During the theme to *The Godfather*."

"Hey, that's great!" I shouted, figuring *The Godfather* was one of the most masculine movies ever made and that, well, maybe it would sort of, you know, change a thing or two.

"Well, yes and no," Daisy answered.

"Which means what?"

"He's going to play Sonny Corleone tap dancing through the tollbooth and getting mowed down by Barzini's gunmen."

"And that would be the 'yes' part?" I surmised.

"That's right."

"And the 'no' part?"

"The gunmen will be doing pirouettes while lobbing pink carnation bullets at him."

Those were the last sounds uttered by either of us for the rest of that drive.

Perhaps now would be a good time to say a few words about a woman in our community who'll soon play a part in this story. An alcoholic named Denise Rodecker. When her husband was still alive, she was a thin, very attractive, very sensual-looking blonde (think Kathleen Turner in *Body Heat*) for whom most of the men harbored a secret crush. But, generally speaking, the wives in Fort Lee were not jealous of this object of their husbands' nocturnal secretions, as they knew about Denise's unwavering devotion to Jerry and the solidity of their marriage.

But then things took an unforeseen turn during what became known in the tri-state area as the Blizzard of '06, when Jerry, a do-it-yourself type with a tendency to overexert himself, suffered a heart attack while buying a snow shovel, and died two days later. After that, Denise started to drink, packed on about sixty pounds (think Shelley Winters in *The Poseidon Adventure*), contracted diabetes attributable to that weight gain, and began hitting on those same husbands who were no longer attracted to her. She became a conversation piece around town whom I hadn't seen until the night of that recital.

Daisy and I found seats in the third row of the Martin Luther King Jr. Junior High School auditorium. We liked sitting close to the stage to provide visual support should our kids glance in our direction during their performances. These evenings always ran in age order—starting with the youngest kids and ending with the oldest. This was bad news for me and Daisy. Whereas most parents could discreetly leave after watching their child dance, this year we did not have that luxury and would have to sit through the six performances before Trace's and then fifteen more until it was Heidi's turn.

"You know, if Trace played Little League like most boys his age, we could be at a movie right now, then grab a bite to eat, return some calls, take a nap, and still get here in time to see Heidi," I whispered to Daisy.

Then the lights went down, the recital began, and we sat through everything ranging from triumphant four-year-olds dancing up steps to *Rocky*, to drenched six-year-olds dancing in water to *Titanic*, to frightened seven-year-olds dancing away from Nazis in *Schindler's List*, and now it was Trace's turn. A slightly overweight Sonny Corleone in a silver suit, tapping his way through the cardboard tollbooth, the emergence of at least a dozen twirling mobsters pelting him with a fusillade of colorful petals, and him crying out as he staggers against its force.

Enter Denise Rodecker. Probably through a backstage door and then onto the set to the astonishment of everyone.

"I've watched this film maybe fifty times," said the guy on the other side of me, "and I've never noticed a fat blond lady in this scene before."

She, too, was staggering. Reeling, in fact. As I found out later, from the bottle of red wine she polished off at a book club meeting at that idiot Peckerman's house. But she knew that the glucose from that merlot would eventually metabolize and she'd need another infusion. So while my slightly overweight son had finally succumbed to the torrent of flowers and was now writhing on the stage in spastic memories of movement, Denise Rodecker pointed directly at me in the third row, reached inside her coat, pulled out the lemur by its endangered tail, and began swinging it overhead as she shouted at the top of her lungs, "Hey, dickweed, if you want to see this monkey alive again, give me back my fucking insulin pump!" before throwing the now dazed lemur straight up into the air, catching it over her shoulder like Willie Mays did in the 1954 World Series against the Cleveland Indians, stepping over my slightly overweight son, and exiting into the New Jersey night through the backstage door.

CHAPTER 8

Jeffrey

I hate dance. Ballet, tap, that modern shit where they all look like crack addicts—I hate it all. I'm not saying dance is gay. It *is* gay, but that's not what I'm saying. What I'm saying is it's boring. I had to watch a live ballet once, when Donna dragged me because her cousin's daughter was in it, and it was the most boring thing I ever sat through, except the time I went to a NASCAR race and there was not one fucking crash.

So it was definitely not my plan to drive to a dance recital. When the lunatic asshole Horkman drove away from my house, I had no plan to follow him anywhere. I was planning to go back into my house, pour myself a drink, and get on the phone. Because that lunatic asshole had just nearly run me over in front of witnesses, *on my own swale*. This kind of situation is exactly why the good Lord created Jewish litigation attorneys named Cohn, of whom I personally know four.

I also know, from experience as an expert forensic plumbing witness in courts of law, that pain and suffering can be very difficult to disprove. Even without *visible* injuries, I could very well be suffering from chronic Prius-related neck and back ailments that could cost me potentially millions of dollars in missed income, not to mention loss of consortium with my wife. It crossed my mind, as I watched the asshole's taillights disappear, that I could be on the road to boat ownership.

So that was one point for me. Point two, I still had Buddy. I didn't *want* Buddy, but the lunatic obviously did, a lot, so that was in my favor, as leverage. Plus I was pretty sure I nailed the lunatic with the YA MON mask. Three points for me, versus bupkus for the asshole, unless you count that he got the YA MON mask, which I hated any-way. (But not because it was African-American.)

So I was feeling pretty good, as I got back onto my feet. That feel-ing lasted maybe eleven seconds, which is how long it took for Denise Rodecker, who is the size of a fire rescue truck but louder, to wobble across the lawn to me, screaming about her insulin pump.

"Denise," I said, "calm down."

This was a mistake. Telling a batshit crazy woman to calm down only makes her more batshit crazy.

"DON'T TELL ME TO CALM DOWN!" she said.

"Fine," I said, "*don't* calm down."

This also was a mistake. Fortunately, Donna had arrived and was attempting to hug Denise, and even though she could only get her arms about halfway around, Denise finally stopped screaming, though she was still blubbering about her pump. She'd had a lot of wine.

"Jeffrey will get your pump back, *won't* you, Jeffrey?" Donna said, giving me a look that said unless I got the pump back, the only con-sortium I was ever going to have again would be with my right hand.

"Okay," I said. "I know where the guy works. I'll call the police and tomorrow they can . . ."

"NO!" said Denise, back in Batshit Mode. "I need it right now!"

"But I don't know where the guy lives."

"Well, *I* do," said Denise.

"You do?" Donna and I both said.

"I saw him," said Denise. "It's Philip Horkman. He owns a pet store. I thought he was a nice man! Why did he take my insulin pump?"

"I think he was actually after the lemur," I said, nodding toward Buddy, who was sitting on Taylor's head.

"That thing is his?" said Denise.

I said it was, which, looking back, was another mistake. For a drunk woman the size of a tool shed, Denise showed excellent quickness. She snatched Buddy off Taylor's head and started toward her car. Donna yelled at me to stop her, and I tried, but Denise threw a stiff arm that caught me right in the throat, and I went down again. I heard Oprah ladies screaming and Taylor crying. Then I heard tires squealing. Then Donna was in my face, grabbing my shirt, pulling me up.

"Jeffrey!" she shouted. "You have to stop her!"

She yanked me to my feet and started shoving me toward my car. "Hurry! She's going to kill herself!"

"She might hurt Buddy!" said Taylor.

I stumbled to my car, started the engine, put it in gear. Then a thought occurred to me. I put it back in park and lowered the window.

"What?" says Donna.

"Where the fuck am I going?"

"Don't use that language in front of Taylor!"

You ever notice this? You make a valid, logical point, and women try to change the subject.

"Well, where *am* I going?" I said.

"After Denise!"

"And where is Denise going?" I said.

That stopped her. She held a quick conference with the other book club women, and they agreed Denise was probably going to find this Philip Horkman. One of the women said he lived in Fox Hollow Estates, which figures because it is a development completely filled with Prius-driving assholes. Somebody pulled out an iPhone and Googled his address. I put the car in gear and took off.

Ten minutes later, I turned into the asshole's street and slammed on my brakes hard just in time to avoid getting hit by Denise Rodecker's Range Rover going the other way at about 280 miles an hour. Just ahead, I saw a lady in a driveway shouting at Denise to slow down. I pulled over and lowered my window, and this lady, who turned out to be Horkman's neighbor, told me Denise had made a big scene, honking her horn, yelling for Horkman to come out.

"So I went out there," the lady told me, "and I told her the Horkmans aren't home. She was *very* rude. I think she's been drinking. She has a monkey."

"It's actually a lemur," I said. "Do you know where she's going?"

"Well, the Horkmans are at a dance recital at Martin Luther King Jr."

"You told her that?"

"I did. Was that a mistake? Should I call the police?"

"I'll take care of it," I said, putting the car in gear. At that point, if there was one thing I was sure of, it was this: If the police arrested Denise Rodecker for driving drunk with a stolen lemur, in the eyes of my wife—for that matter, in the eyes of the entire Oprah book club vagina brigade—it would be my fault.

Five minutes later, I'm pulling into the Martin Luther King Jr. Junior High parking lot. I see Denise's Range Rover parked at a bad angle halfway up on the curb. The door's open, the engine's running. Denise is not inside.

I pull up behind the Range Rover and get out. I'm standing there, trying to decide what to do. What I *should* have done, looking back, is take the key out of Denise's car. But I didn't.

Suddenly, *BANG*, a door on the side of the school slams open. Here's who comes out, in order:

1. Denise, holding Buddy by his tail, like he's a fur handbag.
2. The asshole, who I'm happy to see is limping, yelling at Denise.
3. A woman, who has to be the asshole's wife, because she is yelling at him.
4. A fat kid wearing some kind of douchebaggy silver suit, who's crying, and right away I know this is the asshole's kid, because (a) he looks like him, and (b) he's a douchebag.

The asshole sees me, and he stops short.

"What are you doing here?" he says.

"What are *you* doing here?" I say, which I admit was not a good comeback, but I didn't have anything prepared.

He says, "I'm here to watch my son's dance recital."

I look at his son and say, "What's he supposed to be, Elton John as a refrigerator?"

"What's *that* supposed to mean?" says the wife.

"He's Sonny Corleone," says the asshole.

"He's WHO?"

"It's interpretive," says the asshole.

"Oh yeah," I say. "I can definitely see the Corleone family following Sonny here into battle. 'Come on, fellows! We have to go to the mattresses.'" Only I'm lisping, so it comes out "fellowth" and "mattretheth."

This really pisses off the asshole's wife. She's in my face, yelling, "Just who the hell do you think you . . ."

Then we hear a slamming sound, which is Denise shutting the door of her Range Rover. The asshole hustles over and pounds on the window. She lowers it, but only a half inch.

"Denise," he says, trying to sound calm, which he is not. "Give me the lemur."

"GIVE ME MY INSULIN PUMP!" she says.

"I don't *have* your insulin pump."

It occurs to me that the asshole doesn't know that Buddy left it in his Prius. I'm about to point this out, but before I can say anything, Denise holds Buddy up by his tail and screams, "THEN YOUR FUCKING LEMUR IS GOING OFF THE GEORGE FUCK-ING WASHINGTON BRIDGE." She stomps the gas and fishtails out of the parking lot.

"STOP!" the asshole is screaming. "THAT IS AN ENDAN-GERED ANIMAL!" He's gimping as fast as he can toward his Prius. I head for my car and get in just as the Prius leaves the parking lot. I put the pedal to the floor and am right behind, the asshole and me weaving through traffic, trying to catch up with Denise, who is driv-ing like a maniac.

My cell rings. It's Donna.

"What," I say.

"Did you find Denise?" she says.

"Yes." Up ahead Denise is getting on I-95.

"So she's okay? She got her pump?"

"Um, not yet." Denise is weaving across four lanes. The asshole is staying as close as he can, but he's having trouble keeping up in the Prius, which has basically the same motor as a food processor.

"What do you mean not yet?" says Donna. "Is there a problem?"

"Listen, this is a bad time, okay? I'll call you right back."

In the background, I hear Taylor saying something to Donna. Up ahead I see Denise's arm, which is the size of my leg, sticking out the Range Rover window. She has something in her hand. She's waving it around so the asshole can see it.

It's Buddy.

Donna says, "Taylor wants to know if Buddy is okay."

"Tell her Buddy's fine," I say, and hang up.

CHAPTER 9

Philip

I have absolutely no complaints about my penis. While neither exceptionally long nor formidable in girth, it has performed all duties admirably. It's sired two children, has sexually satisfied a wife on those special occasions when we enjoy a romp in the hay for purposes other than procreation, and has regularly expelled liquid waste from my system without even once waking me up from a night's sleep to do so.

Consequently, I have never been one of those guys with a need to compensate by driving either a souped-up or pimped-out car. Hence, my Prius. It gets me where I want to go, has an AM radio, and the fact that it's eco-friendly (fifty-five miles per gallon!) is in the plus column as well. Is it built for a car chase? Probably not. However, that was never really a consideration, given it hadn't crossed my mind that one day I might be chasing a drunken diabetic motorist swinging an endangered primate out her window while driving at breakneck speed toward the toll booths of the George Washington Bridge.

But that was exactly the situation I now found myself in, although I figured I'd caught a break when her Range Rover didn't go into the

E-ZPass lane. As a result, my plan was a simple one—that is, when Denise Rodecker stopped to pay the toll, I would jump out of my car, run up to *her* car, reach inside, grab the lemur, run back to *my* car, get back into my car, make a huge sweeping U-turn into a westbound lane, then leisurely drive back to the peace and quiet of my home in Fox Hollow Estates. Even with my taped ribs and soft walking cast, I was confident I could easily pull this off. Innate quickness played a major role in my winning four varsity letters in fencing at Haverford College ("Go Black Squirrels!") and I had no doubt it would trump any of my current liabilities, given the short distance between our cars.

So when her Range Rover slowed to a halt to become the second car before the booth, I reached down to shift the Prius into neutral and felt something lying on the console that I hadn't seen in the darkness—a rubber tube. I grasped it, pulled it toward me and could feel that there was something weighted at the other end. From the glow of the lights above the toll booths, I then saw that the tube was attached to a contraption that could very well have been the insulin pump Denise Rodecker kept yammering about. How it had gotten into my car was beyond me. And I had no idea how the weird-looking wooden thing lying next to it got in there as well. I picked up the wooden thing and saw what looked like, well, it looked like some kind of mask of a native of a tropical environment with the words "YA MAN" painted on his forehead. Out of sheer curiosity, I put the mask on my face and checked what I looked like in the rearview mirror when suddenly I noticed that Denise Rodecker's car had moved up and she was now, in fact, being handed her change by the toll collector. So I grabbed the pump, opened the door to my Prius, and hobbled toward the Range Rover, yelling, "Hey, look what I have!" at the top of my lungs, but I wasn't fast enough to get her attention as she pulled away from the toll plaza and onto the bridge.

So I immediately turned, paid no attention whatsoever to the toll collector, who screamed when she saw someone wearing a YA

MAN mask holding a strange-looking device with wires and tubes attached to it, hobbled back to my car, got in, and purposely screeched through the toll without paying as I didn't want to risk losing sight of the vehicle that was now carrying my precious lemur toward Manhattan.

Did my Prius let me down? Not really. Look, it wasn't the car's fault that it ran out of gas about a third of the way across that bridge. Because the Prius was so incredibly fuel-efficient (sixty-eight miles per gallon!) I had a tendency to be lax when it came to refilling—knowing that even if it did run out of gas, since it was a hybrid, the battery could still power it. No problem, except that the battery could only power it up to thirty-four mph before the gas kicked in—which meant that if the car *was* out of gas, that was the fastest it could go. Thirty-four mph. Good news if you're driving on local streets trying to get to an Exxon station. Absolutely dreadful news if you're trying to get away from a veritable armada of police cars, fire engines and EMS trucks that think you have a homemade bomb.

But that's what happened—although at first I had no idea the roadblock at the other end of the GW Bridge was intended for me. All I knew was that as I saw the taillights of Denise Rodecker's speeding car exit onto Manhattan's Henry Hudson Parkway, I was so hellbent on not losing her that I didn't even think that when the cops moved two of their cars to allow me passage to the off-ramp, it was because they were afraid we'd explode on impact.

Yet, once I'd gotten onto the highway, I did become curious when I saw in my rearview mirror that the entire roadblock was now following me. And that when they got about a hundred yards behind my Prius, they maintained that margin. When I slowed down a bit, they did the same. And when my acceleration topped out at a blazing thirty-four mph, they sped up as well. Thus began the slowest low-speed chase in NYPD history, although at the time I was still unaware that it was actually me they were low-speed chasing. It was only when that helicopter came overhead and shined that huge spot-light on my Prius did it occur that I may have been of *specific* interest to them—although I must say, I was dumbfounded as to why they would waste all of this manpower on a motorist just because he didn't pay a measly twelve-dollar toll.

So I signaled and pulled over onto the right shoulder, figuring that we could clear this thing up quickly so these heroic men in blue who risk their lives on a daily basis protecting and defending could turn their sights back to real criminals. I stopped, opened the car door, stepped out, waved at them, smiled, and shouted, "Okay, fellas, I'm guilty as charged. Do with me what you will." Whereupon they forced me to the ground and made sure I lay there facedown by dint of a boot on the small of my back before men in heavy bomb squad apparel went into my car, found what they were looking for, and had a special robot gingerly place it inside a special tub, where they blew up Denise Rodecker's insulin pump.

CHAPTER 10

Jeffrey

I don't know what this Horkman asshole did to piss off the cops, but he definitely got their attention. There was a whole cop army chasing him, including a helicopter, which was pretty funny, because he was going, like, six miles an hour. They could have caught him on skateboards. But they were keeping their distance, like he was America's Most Wanted Terrorist Mastermind, instead of an asshole from Jersey in a Prius.

I passed him when he slowed down on the GW Bridge, so I was between him and Denise when she got onto the Henry Hudson Parkway. My plan was to stay with her, because Donna would kill me if I lost her, in her condition. Plus she had Buddy, who thank God she did not throw off the bridge.

I was right behind Denise when I looked in my rearview and saw the asshole stopping and getting out with his hands up. Right away there were cops all over him, pushing him down on the ground and pointing guns at his head. I admit, I smiled.

I was still smiling when I ran into Denise's Range Rover. She stopped right in the middle of the Henry Hudson Parkway, and *wham*, there's an airbag in my face. After a few seconds of just sitting there and going *"fuuuuccccckkkk,"* I got out of the car, and I saw the whole front end was totally wrecked, steam coming out, green glop dripping down on the road. I knew I wasn't driving home. I went to yell at Denise for stopping in the road, but when I opened her door, I saw her eyes were closed and her skin was the color of oatmeal. Buddy was sitting on her head, looking at me with an expression of "NOW what?"

My first thought was that Denise was dead, which meant I was in a world of shit with Donna. But then she made a sound like *unh*, and her eyes flickered a little bit. So she was alive, but she definitely needed a doctor.

I started running back toward the cops. All of a sudden, I felt something, which turned out to be Buddy, jumping up on my shoulder. So I thought, Okay, at least I got Buddy. Then I heard this explosion—*Bang!*—up ahead, and I thought, Whoa, they shot the asshole. But when I got a little closer, I could see he was fine—still facedown on the ground, but not shot.

Looking back, I realize how it must have looked to the cops when they saw me. They're all tense, they have a guy on the ground they think is Osama bin Whatever, and all of a sudden *another* guy, who they also don't know, comes running toward them in the middle of the Henry Hudson Parkway, shouting and waving his arms, and he has what looks like a monkey on his shoulder. It could arouse suspicions, I can see that now.

But at the time I didn't see it. When a bunch of cops started running toward me, holding guns and shouting, I couldn't hear them, because of the helicopter. But I assumed they were planning to render aid to me as a law-abiding civilian in a bind.

Now, right here is where a lot of shit happened really fast, including some things that I did not realize at the time but found out later.

First, the cops reached me. They were still waving guns and yelling, but I still couldn't hear them. I saw one of them unclipping something shiny from his belt, which it turns out was a Taser. That's right: This hero was planning to Taser a man armed with a fucking lemur.

Speaking of whom: Buddy, despite having just gone through a traumatic experience in the form of being waved out of the window like a pennant by Denise, had retained his natural curiosity, not to mention quickness. So when the hero cop reached out toward me with his Taser, Buddy snatched it. The hero went to snatch it back, but Buddy jumped off me, and onto another cop. The hero tried to grab Buddy, and somehow—I don't know if Buddy did this on purpose, or what—the Taser went off, right into the second cop's neck. He made a kind of whimpering sound, then fell sideways. While he was falling, his gun went off.

This next part, I still don't like to think about. What happened was, the bullet went straight up, right through the metal floor of the helicopter. The good news was, the metal slowed the bullet down enough so that it was no longer traveling at a lethal velocity. The bad news was, it was still traveling fast enough to lodge itself in the scrotum of the helicopter pilot.

I know that most helicopter pilots, and especially police helicopter pilots, are experienced professionals who spend many hours training for emergencies. But I don't care how much training you have: You can never really be prepared for having to fly a helicopter when you have just taken a bullet to the balls.

Next thing I knew, the chopper was coming down, fast, right where I was standing with the cops. We all took off running. I thought I was going to die. The wind from the chopper nearly knocked me over. I jumped over a guardrail and kept running toward some trees on the side of the highway. I heard this really loud *whump* behind me, which was the helicopter making a rough landing. I stopped and turned around. It looked like a war zone: the chopper on the ground, rotors still turning; ambulances coming from somewhere, sirens going; more cop cars coming with *their* sirens screaming; cops running all over the place, shouting.

Then I saw Buddy. He was skittering cross the highway, a little blob of fur, heading directly toward me.

Next I saw Horkman. I guess when the chopper went down, the cops forgot about him, because he was back on his feet, looking kind of dazed. While I was looking at him, he spotted Buddy. He yelled something, which I couldn't hear, and then he started running after Buddy, which meant he was running directly toward me. Cops were yelling at him, but I don't think he could hear them.

Then, over all the racket, I heard popping sounds, like firecrackers. I felt some splinters fly off a tree near where I was standing. More popping.

Suddenly I realized what was happening.

The fucking cops were shooting at me.

Or maybe they were shooting at Horkman. Or both of us. Or even all three of us, if you count Buddy. I wasn't going to wait around to find out. I turned, sprinted up the embankment, jumped over the wall, and started looking for somewhere to hide in Manhattan.

CHAPTER 11

Philip

Here was the sequence as I remember it: a cop stomped on my back, I farted, a helicopter dropped out of the sky. Causes and effects? Possibly. But while I'm certain the downward force of that heavy boot induced the sounding of the rectal trumpet from my unsuspecting sphincter, I honestly can't say whether the resultant wind breakage was strong enough to prompt the airborne whirlybird to spin like a broken dreidel that came this close to crash-landing in the Hudson River.

No matter what, the ensuing commotion made it possible for me to stagger to my feet and take off toward an embankment—first because I saw the lemur running in that direction. And then because the cops started shooting real bullets at me, which, for all intents and purposes, reclassified me to be as endangered as the lemur. Perhaps even more so, because, and I would bet money on this, a lemur can run a lot faster than a middle-class family man with a soft cast on his left ankle.

So it quickly became apparent that I would have to implement Plan B as soon as I could figure out what it was. In fact, if you want to parse things, since *none* of this was considered beforehand, technically there was never a Plan A. So what I did was call out to that idiot Peckerman, who at this point was only a few steps ahead. I thought I'd appeal to whatever modicum of decency he might possess in that ill-fated soul of his, thinking that he'd momentarily put aside our squabble and lend me a hand. Literally. All I needed was for him to stop running, reach back with an outstretched hand that I could grab on to and help me with my last few steps up the embankment. The whole effort would've taken maybe five seconds and, when we reached the top, if we still hated each other, we'd go our separate ways. But he didn't stop. Maybe he didn't hear my cries of "Help me, Peckerman! Please help me!" over the sounds of all that gunfire, or maybe he did hear my cries of "Help me, Peckerman! Please help me!" and just ignored them because he's, you should pardon my language, a scoundrel.

Either way, he just kept going, so I now had to figure out Plan C (or maybe *this* was actually Plan B) because the cops were getting closer, but I never had a chance to give the plan much thought because after hobbling two more steps, my left ankle gave out, so I lost my balance, fell to the ground, and rolled back down the embankment.

To this day, I truly believe it was because it was a moonless night and I was wearing a black shirt that the cops didn't see me and kept advancing up the embankment as I rolled past them, about forty feet away, down the embankment, over the curb, and back onto the Henry Hudson Parkway until I finally came to a stop against the front tire of Denise Rodecker's Range Rover that was just sitting there in the middle of the road. With her inside. Semi-conscious. Slumped over the steering wheel with what looked like strawberry Turkish Taffy issuing from the corners of her mouth.

So once again I found myself staggering to my feet, got inside Denise's black Range Rover, pushed her immense body over onto the passenger seat and slowly drove away, before exiting at 79th Street, where I easily blended into the crosstown traffic.

Where to go? Daunting question, as I knew it was just a matter of time until the cops caught up with me. Surely they'd run the plate number on my Prius, and then distribute my name and picture. Maybe they'd done that already? So I dashed any thoughts of leaving the city because I'd watched enough episodes of *Law & Order* to know that when the police are on the lookout for people they believe brought down a police helicopter, the first thing they do is set up checkpoints at all tunnels and bridges.

What to do? What to do? I became paranoid of every squad car I saw. And then of all cars in general, as I thought they might be undercover cops. I was getting more and more nervous. I needed a Plan D (I think) but couldn't think of anything. I was sweating. I needed help. But from where? I'm not a religious man, but divine intervention would've been nice.

And then I heard it. The voice of God? Not exactly. It was more like the grinding of gears on a tractor-trailer when it's slowing to a halt. It was the sound of Denise Rodecker stirring back into consciousness.

I once read somewhere (*Reader's Digest*, I think) that great men overcome dire situations by making the cards they were dealt work for them. Well, on the seat next to me was a huge card. Denise was sick and in need of a doctor. Badly. If one of the pets at The Wine Shop was in her condition, I would have it put down. So I got excited by the thought that Denise Rodecker could be my ticket out of this mess. All I had to do is get her the medical attention she so obviously needed and then, once she was healthy, she could tell the cops what had actually happened.

"Everything's going to be okay, Denise," I told her. "I'm going to take you over to Lenox Hill Hospital and they're going to make you feel better."

And then I gave her a reassuring smile.

And then she said, "I love you."

And then I said, "Do you know if Lenox Hill is on Third Avenue or Lexington?"

By the time we got to the emergency room at Lenox Hill (it's on Lexington, by the way), Denise Rodecker said she loved me four times. I didn't take it seriously, figuring that these were merely the incoherent murmurings of an obese insulin-depleted nymphomaniac who just happened to be looking in my direction as I drove at my new preferred speed of thirty-four mph so as not to call attention to the car.

And I also didn't take it seriously when she insisted I hold her hand as the bald male nurse with a mole on the top of his head wheeled her into the treatment room. I obliged, figuring it was innocuous. A mere comforting gesture to a nervous patient. Done all the time. Like writing "love" at the end of a letter to someone you couldn't care less about.

"She your wife?" asked the bald male nurse with a mole on the top of his head.

"No."

"Girlfriend?"

"She's just a neighbor," I told him.

"Interesting."

"Why do you say that?"

"Because you two seem rather close for just being neighbors," he said.

"Why? Because I'm holding her hand?"

"No, because she's flashing her left breast at you with her other hand," he said.

"Excuse me?" I asked, before looking down and seeing that Denise had opened her hospital gown and was now exposing what I could only presume was a breast given its location on her massive chest—although any positive ID that a nipple would provide wasn't visible as it was hanging over the other side of the gurney. Still, the bald male nurse with a mole on the top of his head saw my face redden with horror, which he, unfortunately, mistook for embarrassment.

"See what I'm saying?" he asked with a sneer that was just begging to be mauled by a Doberman from The Wine Shop. "She's hot for you."

"Oh, that's just the diabetes talking," I told him.

"Diabetes doesn't talk," he insisted, his sneer getting more sneerish. "High fevers talk. Alzheimer's talks. Certain infectious diseases don't shut up for a second. But diabetes? No. Diabetes comes stag and pretty much sucks the air out of the party."

"Okay, then it's the insulin that's talking!" I shot back. "I'm telling you, she has no idea what she's saying."

"Insulin doesn't talk, either," he countered. "Serotonin talks. Dopamine talks. Ultracet. A lot of your ADD and ADHD medications can be quite chatty. As can certain kinds of marijuana, cocaine and other street drugs. But insulin? Hell no. As boring as diabetes is, it's a veritable one-man band compared to insulin."

"Well, something other than this woman is talking!" I shouted. "Can't you see she's sick? Just look at her! At her skin color and at that stuff that looks like strawberry Turkish Taffy dripping out of the sides of her mouth."

"That *is* strawberry Turkish Taffy," he answered. "Her coat pockets were stuffed with wrappers when she came in. I'm telling you, she knows exactly what she's saying."

Great, I thought to myself before taking another glance at Denise Rodecker who, once she saw I was looking her way, furtively opened the front of her gown, revealing the entire festival that was going on underneath. Needless to say, I was mortified and, for the sake of not having nightmares for the rest of my life, turned my head, and when I did, I caught a glimpse of the television in a patient's room across the hall.

I guess it stands to reason that it's newsworthy when a police heli-copter lands on the Henry Hudson Parkway after its pilot is shot in his scrotum. So there it was, with the newscaster saying that the cops suspect that this was the handiwork of armed terrorists. And then they showed a picture of that idiot Peckerman, and then they showed a picture of me, and I knew right then and there that I should come up with a Plan E or whatever the hell letter I was up to because I, Philip Horkman, was now officially on the lam.

CHAPTER 12

Jeffrey

I couldn't believe the asshole Horkman actually wanted me to help him. A day earlier, I was a successful man with a comfortable lifestyle as one of the top three or four forensic plumbers in northeastern New Jersey. Now, thanks to this lunatic, I'm running from cops who are shooting at me with actual fucking bullets. *Help* him? I wouldn't piss on him if he was on fire.

So I left Horkman behind and kept running. I lost track of Buddy, but at that point my feeling was that Buddy was on his own.

It was dark, and I had no idea where I was, except somewhere in Manhattan. I heard a lot of shouting behind me, ducked into an alley, crossed to another street, then into another alley. I stopped to catch my breath, sweating like a pig. I could hear shouting, sirens, more helicopters, but no more shooting, thank God. I kept moving, walking now, alley to alley.

While I was walking, I was trying to come up with a plan. I decided step one was call Donna, tell her to get hold of a lawyer. I felt for my phone.

Fuck. No phone. It was back in my car.

So I thought, Okay, find a pay phone. But here's the thing: There're no pay phones left in Manhattan, at least that I could find. I swear I walked two miles, and I kept seeing places where there *used* to be pay phones, but all there is now is the smell of piss. There're times when New York City seems like one giant urinal, and this was one of those times.

I was trying to avoid people, but I decided I had to go into some business that might have a pay phone. I was mid-block on a quiet street, and I saw this little sign that said THE CAMEL'S NOSE, next to some steps leading down to a door. I went in. It looked like a typical shithole bar with three guys—a bartender and two customers—clumped together under a TV. They all turned and looked at me, not friendly. I would describe them—and I'm not being racist, I'm just describing—as swarthy.

"You got a pay phone?" I said.

Nobody answered, but while they weren't answering, I noticed a pay phone at the end of the bar.

"Found it, thanks," I said, walking past them. They were still staring at me. To be honest, I was wishing I picked another place to go into, but at that point I couldn't pussy out. So I went to the phone and of course it wasn't a real pay phone belonging to the phone company; it was some phone company I never heard of operated by some raghead in Bangladesh who wanted my credit card number and probably charged me eighty dollars to call Jersey. But what choice did I have?

While the call was going through, I looked back toward the bar. The good news was, the Three Swarthy Stooges weren't still looking at me. The bad news was, they were looking at the TV.

Which was showing my car.

It was an aerial shot of the Henry Hudson Parkway, and there had to be three hundred cops running around. I could see my smashed car, Horkman's Prius, and the police helicopter, which had some smoke coming out. The bottom of the screen said: Terrorist Attack on GW Bridge.

Jesus Christ.

"Hello?" said Donna.

"It's me."

"Where the hell are you?"

"I'm in . . ."

"What the hell did you do?"

"Listen, Donna, just calm down."

"DO NOT TELL ME TO CALM DOWN."

I think I mentioned this before, but: Never tell a woman to calm down.

"Donna, just listen, okay?"

"No! YOU listen! Do you know what they're showing on the TV RIGHT NOW?"

"My car."

"They're showing your car."

"I know that. Listen, what . . ."

"Jeffrey, they're saying you're a terrorist!"

"Donna, if you'll just . . ."

"Shut up a minute. What, Taylor? Oh my God! They're saying you tried to bomb the George Washington Bridge!"

"Donna, I didn't . . ."

"Quiet! What, Taylor? Oh my God! No!"

"What'd she say?"

"Oh my GOD!"

"What did she say?"

"You shot a police officer!"

"What? I don't even have a . . ."

"Quiet! What, Taylor? OH. MY. GOD."

"What?"

"You shot a police officer *in the scrotum!*"

"Donna, I SWEAR to you, I don't . . ."

"Be quiet! Yes, Taylor, it's a body part. On a man. I'll explain it later. What? Oh my God. OHMIGOD."

"What?"

"They're showing your picture! On TV!"

I looked at the TV over the bar. It was showing my New Jersey driver's license photo. Next to it was a photo of the Horkman asshole. The screen said Terrorist Suspects.

Now the three swarthy guys were looking at me.

"Donna," I said. "Listen. You need to . . ."

"Somebody's here! The police are here!"

"Donna . . ."

"Jeffrey, they're at the door! I have to go. I'll call you right back."

"But I don't have my phone!"

Too late. She was gone.

I started trying to get ahold of Bangladesh again so I could call back, when a swarthy hand grabbed the phone from me and hung it up. I turned and saw the bartender, with the other two guys right behind him.

"What the fuck," I said.

The bartender pointed back in the general direction of the TV.

"You did this?" he said, except he had some kind of swarthy accent, so "did" sounded like "deed."

"Listen," I said. "I didn't do anything."

He arched an eyebrow. "But that is you," he said. "On television."

"Yes, that's me, but it's a misunderstanding."

He arched his eyebrow again. He had huge eyebrows. Like he was raising miniature porcupines on his forehead.

"Misunderstanding," he said.

"Yes, misunderstanding. I'm not a terrorist. I live in New Jersey. I was following a lady who lost her insulin pump, so she took this guy's lemur."

"His what?"

"Lemur. It's like a monkey."

"There is no monkey on the television."

"It ran away. The point is, it was all a big mistake. I'm not a terrorist."

The bartender nodded. "Of course," he said, "if you are terrorist, you will say you are *not* terrorist. Terrorists do not say, 'Hello, I am terrorist.'"

"I know, but I'm telling you, I'm really not one. So if you'll just let me make a call here, I'm going to get this all straightened out." I reached for the phone, but he put his hand in the way.

"You are not using phone," he said

"All right," I said. "I'll find another phone." I tried to head for the door, but they blocked me.

"You can't keep me here," I said.

"We are not keeping you here," said the bartender. "We are taking you somewhere."

"What the fuck are you talking about."

The bartender said something foreign. The other two swarthies grabbed me.

"Hey!" I said. "You can't do this!"

But it turned out they could.

CHAPTER 13

Philip

Did the cardiac patient whose television I was watching have that fatal heart attack because he saw my picture on the news and then looked over to see the same man being identified as an armed terrorist standing next to his bed sipping a Diet Fresca? Hard to say. But the moment I saw him grab his chest, followed by those gurgling sounds, followed by that flatlined beep from the monitor on his night table, followed by a veritable stampede of doctors and nurses shouting "Code Blue!" I thought it wise to slip out of the room and give those dedicated professionals all the space they needed to revive that now very dead man.

Now in the hallway, my phone rang. But it drew no attention to me as it was, thank God, still on vibrate from when I set it just before the dance recital (hard to believe this was still the same night) started. The caller ID displayed my home number and I wanted to answer it. It had been several hours since I'd bolted from that auditorium in pursuit of Denise Rodecker and the lemur, and my guess was that Daisy, in the very least, was worried. And, at the very most, homicidal. Turns out she was neither.

"I'll call you right back from a landline," I whispered into the phone.

"Why?"

"Because the cops and probably the FBI are looking for me, and they can trace my whereabouts from my cell phone."

"Okie dokie."

I hung up and walked a few steps down the hall, where I tried the knob on a door labeled "Doctors' Lounge." It was unlocked. I entered and was relieved to see it was devoid of lounging doctors. So I picked up the wall phone, dialed "9" for an outside line and called home.

"Too bad you missed the finale," she answered the phone saying. "All the kids got onstage, in costume, and danced to the Scott Joplin music from *The Sting*."

"Daisy . . ."

"Sort of a ragtime number. It was wonderful."

"Daisy, I'm in big trouble."

"What's wrong?" she asked, with only a slight hint of concern.

"Haven't you heard? Everyone thinks I tried to blow up the George Washington Bridge."

"No, I hadn't heard," she responded, that slight hint of concern now nowhere to be found.

That she didn't know what was going on was not totally surprising. Daisy is not what you'd call a news junkie. Don't get me wrong, she's not uninformed. She knows what's going on in the world and can hold her own in any conversation. But she's prone to seeking out current events on her own terms. As an option. When she's in the mood to be updated about what's happening in the world, as opposed to an addiction to the "all the news all the time" credo of certain media sources.

So it was very possible that after the recital, she drove home listening to a CD instead of the radio, then put the kids to bed, and then drifted off while watching an old movie on cable or a TiVoed episode of *Oprah* instead of CNN, MSNBC or any other commercial station that featured me and that moron Peckerman in bulletins that were now interrupting regular programming.

What *was* surprising, though, was how casually she was taking this whole thing as I was explaining it to her. As if she was merely humoring me when I told her about these absurd charges being levied against me.

"Okay, so the bullet hit him in the scrotum, and then what? Was it a particularly large scrotum or is your aim really that good?"

"Daisy . . . ?"

"You've been drinking again, haven't you?"

"Drinking? Again?" I don't drink.

"Don't pretend you don't remember," she snapped.

"Remember what, Daisy?"

"Then again, if you *really* don't remember, that proves you have been drinking, because that was an episode a sober person would never forget."

I racked my brain.

"Oh my God, Daisy. You've got to be kidding."

"Do I sound like I'm kidding?"

Okay, here goes. Many years before, I was the best man at my brother's wedding. Outdoors. An incredibly hot August night. To cool off, I had four gin and tonics during the cocktail hour that preceded the ceremony. Funny how I didn't feel its effects walking down the aisle. Or when I took my place of honor under the canopy. Or even during the rabbi's sermon about the sanctity of matrimony when I peered outward and noticed a gorgeous teenage cousin from the bride's family sitting in the audience with her legs spread a little too far apart. Wearing mesh underwear. So my best guess is that this was about the time the alcohol kicked in because never, under sober circumstances, when I was supposed to hand the groom the wedding ring, would I have shouted at the top of my lungs, "Beaver! Third row! First seat!"

My brother hasn't spoken to me since. That was also the last time I had a drink.

"Daisy, that was nineteen years ago!"

"And you sound just as idiotic right now as you did that night. So my suggestion to you, Philip, is to have a few cups of coffee and don't get back into the car until you're in control of yourself, because the last thing you need is for a cop to pull you over and have a DUI on your driving record. It will send our auto insurance rates soaring."

And then she hung up. And then I heard voices in the hallway on the other side of the door. And though I couldn't tell if they came from doctors or nurses or even the police at this point, one thing was now certain. Thanks to the media, I was now recognizable and needed to become incognito.

So I opened one of the lockers in the Doctors' Lounge and found a lab coat. It was full-length and covered the clothes I was wearing when I put it on. It also had an ID badge pinned to its breast pocket that could possibly help me pass for a physician as long as I was in this hospital. That was the good news. The not-so-good news was that the badge had the name Jahangir Shahrestaani, M.D. printed on it, with the picture of a man who looked a lot more like a Jahangir Shahrestaani than I do. So I scanned the lounge and saw a scalpel lying on a counter next to an apple that a surgeon apparently cored it with. I picked it up and carefully cut Jahangir Shahrestaani's headshot out of his ID and then replaced it with the picture of me that I removed from my New Jersey driver's license, making it adhere with cellophane tape I found on an unattended reception desk outside the lounge.

I picked up a clipboard, pretending they were my patients' charts, and started smiling and nodding to my "colleagues" as I passed them in the halls, and worked my way to the nearest exit door.

Jeffrey

The swarthy dudes had my arms and were pulling me toward the door.

"Where are we going?" I said.

"To see Fook," said the bartender.

At least it sounded like he said Fook.

"Fook?" I said.

"No, Fook."

"That's what I said, Fook."

"No, is *Fook*."

"Okay, whatever," I said. "Is Fook in charge? Because I need to talk to somebody who . . ."

"You will not talk to Fook. You will *listen* to Fook, and then you will tell him answers about this." He waved toward the TV set, which was showing pictures of me and Horkman over a headline that said BRIDGE TO TERROR. There was also a logo, like a silhouette of the GW Bridge with a bomb in front of it. Say what you want about TV news, they move fast. A gas explosion wipes out a preschool, five minutes later they have a logo for it.

"Listen," I said, "I don't know anything about that. That's what I'm trying to tell you. This is a big misunderstanding."

"Do not be misunderstanding this." He reached into his jacket and pulled out a gun. "If you try to run away, I will shoot you in balls, like you did to police," he said.

"I didn't shoot the police in the balls!"

"Well, somebody shooted police in balls, and this is how I am shooting you if you run away."

If you think about it, there's no way he could hit me in the balls if I was running away, but I didn't point this out. I was getting the feeling these guys were not criminal geniuses. Another clue was, before they took me outside, they put a bag over my head. I guess the idea was to keep me from seeing where we were going, but they used a cheapo plastic bag from a Duane Reade drugstore, and I could pretty much see through it. Plus, even in Manhattan you're going to attract more attention with a guy who has a bag over his head than a guy who *doesn't* have a bag over his head, right?

Morons.

They took me outside and put me in the back of a van. The bartender told me to lie on the floor.

"If you try to get up," he said, "I shoot your balls."

He must have heard that in a movie.

The van started moving. I could hear the bartender talking to somebody in some weird language on his cell phone. I admit I was worried. I was thinking, whoever the fuck Fook is, I hope he has more brains than these cretins.

We drove for maybe fifteen minutes, then parked. They pulled me out of the van, and right away the Duane Reade bag blew off. So much for *that.* We were on a busy street, next to some kind of restaurant, but I didn't get a good look, because they hustled me into an alley, where they opened a door and pushed me inside. We were in a back office—computer, phone, crappy little TV in the corner showing the Bridge to Terror logo, Dilbert cartoon on the wall next to a sign showing how to give the Heimlich maneuver. The bartender pushed me into a chair and told me to stay there and don't move. He said something to the other two dudes, handed one of them his gun, then left. When he opened the door, I heard beeping sounds, like from video games, coming from down the hall.

He was gone awhile. On the TV they showed my picture again, and Horkman's; underneath it said TERROR SUSPECTS.

Finally the door opened. The bartender walked in first. He turned and looked back at the doorway. We were all looking at the doorway, waiting for Fook.

And then Fook walked in.

Fook was Chuck E. Cheese.

I swear to God. He was wearing a furry costume with a big plastic smiling rat head. Or mouse head. Whatever the fuck kind of rodent Chuck E. Cheese is. The bartender pointed to me and said something. Fook E. Cheese came over and stood in front of me, looking down.

"Mempheeoooroofuh," he said. Or something like that. Between his accent and the rodent head, I couldn't make it out.

"What?" I said.

The bartender said, "He asks who are you working for."

"I'm not working for anybody," I said. "I'm self-employed. I'm a forensic plumber."

Fook smacked me across the face. It didn't really hurt, because he had these big soft paws. But I wasn't expecting it.

"Hey!" I said.

"Buhuiniodod!" said Fook.

The bartender said, "He wants to know, do you think he is idiot."

"No!"

"Henheemoinooinfh," said Fook.

"Then why do you telling him lies?" said the bartender.

"I'm not lying!"

"Gighihnggmghfiioongh? Mhhoongnhhon?"

"If you are plumber, why are you blowing up bridge? Do you think bridge is broken toilet that you are fixing?"

"Okay, first, I don't fix toilets. I'm a *forensic* plumber. I know a lot *about* toilets, from an engineering standpoint, but my work is . . ."

"Giinoommaagh!" said Fook, raising his paw again. I admit I flinched.

"He says you are wasting time," said the bartender.

Fook said something to one of the lieutenant swarthies, who left the room. I was getting a bad feeling about this.

"Listen," I said. "If you give me a minute here, I can explain this whole thing."

"This explanation," the bartender said. "Is it the one you tell me before, about the monkey?"

"It's a lemur."

A snorting sound came from inside the Chuck E. Cheese head.

"I would not tell this explanation to Fook," said the bartender.

"But I swear, the . . ."

I was interrupted by the door opening. The lieutenant came in holding two things. One was a foot-long stick of pepperoni.

The other was a pizza slicer. It was one of those wheel things, with a wood handle. The blade looked sharp.

The lieutenant handed the pepperoni and the slicer to Fook. He took them in his paws and set the pepperoni on the desk next to me. He held the slicer in front of my face.

"Magnnhhnnn," he said.

"He says look," said the bartender.

Fook put the edge of the slicer blade on the desk and ran it across the middle of the pepperoni. It sliced it clean in two.

I thought, Oh shit, he's going to cut off my dick.

"Fghnnnghghgm," said Fook.

"Tell him who you are working for," said the bartender.

"I don't work for anybody!" I said. "I had nothing to do with any of this! I swear to God!"

Fook said something, and the two lieutenant swarthies grabbed me, pinned my right arm on the desktop and pressed my hand flat, fingers out. So the good news was, he wasn't going to cut off my dick.

Fook put the blade on the desk, right next to my hand. He rolled it right up to my pinkie, so I could feel the edge. That's when I pissed my pants. If you think you wouldn't, you're a fucking liar.

"Please," I said.

"Ghmminnggh," said Fook.

"Tell him who you are working for," said the bartender.

Before you judge me for what I did next, put yourself in my shoes, which at the moment were filling up with urine.

I pointed to the TV screen. It was showing a close-up of Horkman, the prick who got me into all of this in the first place.

"Him," I said. "I work for him."

Fook pointed his rodent snout at the screen for a few seconds, then turned back to me.

"Ghammeagghnr," he said.

I looked at the bartender.

"Fook says you will take us to this man," he said. "Now."

CHAPTER 15

Philip

I eventually walked through the emergency room and had one foot out the sliding doors when I felt a hand on my shoulder and heard a commanding voice say, "Gnoofnggh!" I spun around and saw that the hand was actually a big furry paw worn by a person dressed in a costume with the head of a grinning, big-eared character that was the spitting image, I'm sorry to say, of my son Trace—who, for reasons that still baffle every dentist we've ever taken him to, has only one front tooth, which is very wide and has a line down its middle making it look like he has two front teeth. Like Chuck E. Cheese.

So whether it was because this character resembled my son or because I reminded myself that I was posing as a doctor and there were sickly children in the emergency room who I was sure needed a good laugh, I grabbed this creature's paws and started dancing with him around the emergency room. And though the children did indeed laugh (I do this funny high kick that always makes my own children giggle and never fails to delight adults as well), I sensed resistance on the part of my partner. As if a jaunty cha-cha-cha was not what he had in mind despite his jolly getup. And my hunch that he may have had a different agenda was confirmed when I spun the two of us around and saw two mean-looking men nonchalantly opening their sport jackets, revealing guns tucked in their waistbands, standing next to that idiot Peckerman, who was pointing at me, saying, "That's him! That's him! That's my boss!"

And though I was curious what this was all about, I had a sneaky feeling that a post-dance Q&A session was probably not in the offing. So when I completed our revolution around the emergency room and was once again about a step away from the automatic sliding doors, I released Chuck E.'s grip (his faux paws absolutely no match for my mightier pet shop owner thumbs), dashed out of the hospital shouting "Help me!" opened the back doors to an EMS vehicle as it was slowly pulling away, and rode in it for a half block while a paramedic asked, "Is something wrong, Doctor?" to which I cried, "Yes, something is horribly wrong!" prompting the driver (who believed I was talking about "medically" wrong as opposed to "in danger of being killed by a foreign man dressed like a restaurant logo" wrong) turned on the siren, shifted into reverse, and sped backward to the emergency room entrance and into the awaiting arms of my captors.

*   *   *

"Why weren't we told about this attack?"

I was now sitting on a rock. A real big rock in the middle of a fenced-in area of the Central Park Zoo. I knew it was the Central Park Zoo because after the EMS guys were gone, the two mean-looking men put a bag over my head, threw me into the back of a van, drove crosstown, and removed the bag just in time for me to see the sign that said WELCOME TO THE CENTRAL PARK ZOO. Then after the goons forced me onto the top of the rock, one of them kept his gun trained on me while the other acted as interpreter for the Chuck E. Cheese guy, who was grunting words devoid of both vowels and consonants.

"I don't know anything about any attacks," I said.

"He's lying! He's the one who told *me* about it!" shouted Pecker-man, who was now tied to a tree. "Now, let me go! Come on, I did what you asked! I took you to him! So let me go!"

"How did he know where I was?" I asked.

"You wife told him," said the gun-toting goon.

"My wife?"

"He borrowed my phone and you wife said you just called from the hospital and that we should also go there because we sounded as drunk as you."

"That's my boss's wife," said Peckerman, shaking his head, laughing. "Always with the jokes!"

"I am not his boss," I pleaded. "And I am also not a terrorist."

"Of course he is!" yelled Peckerman. "Just look at his fucking ID! If that isn't a ragheaded jihad name, I don't know what is!"

The interpreter goon looked at my doctor's badge and read the name on it.

"Jahangir Shahrestaani," he pronounced with frightening ease.

"That's not my name," I told him.

"Sure it is," Peckerman shouted. "That's what *I* always call him!"

"He doesn't call me anything! I didn't even know this guy existed until a few regrettable days ago!"

"Are you related to the Shahrestaanis in Habbaniya?" the goon asked in a whisper.

"I'm not related to any Shahrestaanis anywhere! That's not my name!"

"This picture is you," said the goon.

I said, "Look, my name is Philip Horkman, but I stole this guy's ID and put my picture on it so people wouldn't know who I really am."

"And why don't you want them to know this?"

"Because they think I tried to blow up the George Washington Bridge and that I shot a helicopter pilot in the scrotum."

"We think that also."

"But I didn't. Look in my wallet. Look at the pictures. You'll see I'm just a simple family man who owns a pet shop in Fort Lee, New Jersey."

"Ask him the name of his pet shop!" shouted Peckerman.

"What does that have to do with anything?" I shouted back.

"It's important!" yelled Peckerman, though I wasn't sure if he was answering me or simply saying this to the goon.

"And why is it important?" the goon asked Peckerman.

"It's *not* important," I insisted.

"We have a lot of our terrorism meetings there," said Peckerman.

"We what?!"

This tidbit was of obvious interest to these guys.

"And what is the name of this pet shop?" asked the goon.

"It's not important," I answered.

"I'm going to ask you again," he said, suddenly angry. "What is the name of this pet shop?"

"The Wine Shop."

"I'm going to ask you again," he said, suddenly angrier. "What is the name of this pet shop?"

"The Wine Shop."

This time he turned toward Peckerman and asked the same question.

"What is the name of his pet shop?"

"Jahangir Shahrestaani from Habbaniya's Pet World."

At this point, the goon turned to Fook and brought him up to speed about this conversation. And though they were speaking in a language I couldn't understand, you didn't have to be a linguist to tell that Fook was less than pleased. His Chuck E. Cheese head now spinning atop his gray velvet shoulders. The interpreter goon then shouted something to the gun goon, who then approached Peckerman and started untying the rope that bound him to that tree.

"It's about time," said Peckerman, massaging his wrists where the skin was red from rope burn.

Then Peckerman looked at those guys and said, "Take care, fellas," then looked at me and said, "So long, asshole," then took about two steps toward the exit before the goon stepped in front of him blocking his path, told him to turn around, then marched him at gunpoint to the top of the big rock that I'd been sitting on. They then made us lie down on top of each other, and tied us together.

"Whether or not you are terrorists is no longer of our concern," said the interpreter, who I suspect was translating what Fook was saying. "We have our own mission, and so do these big black bears," whereupon the goon with the gun inserted a big key into the locks on two iron doors at the lower end of the fenced-in area we were in and swung them both open. The three of them then exited through a gate and disappeared into the night about the same time the first black bear emerged from the lair.

CHAPTER 16

Jeffrey

This was my plan:

1. Untie myself from Horkman.
2. Keep Horkman between me and the bear, so that if it started chewing on anybody, it would be Horkman.
3. Get the fuck out of there.

You think I'm a coward? Let me ask you something: Have you ever been in a situation where a bear was about to eat you? No? Okay, then I don't give a shit what you think.

The problem was, I couldn't get free from the rope. Fook's crew did a really good job of tying us up, so Horkman and I were pressed together tight. My arms were pinned to my sides, and my hands were tied in front of me, but I couldn't move anything enough to get at the knots. The worst part was, Horkman was on top of me, his front facing my back, doggy-style. My face was pressed into the rock. His mouth was breathing in my left ear. It was disgusting.

"Get *off* me!" I said.

"I'm trying!" he said.

"Stop pushing on my butt, homo," I said.

"That is offensive," he said.

"Tell that to your boner," I said.

"Shh!" he whispered. "Don't move!"

The bear had reached the rock. It was down on all fours, sniffing the air. Then it stood up. The thing was the size of a UPS truck. It was leaning over us, still sniffing.

"Hold perfectly still," Horkman whispered. "You must not move."

"Fuck that," I said, and rolled hard away from the bear.

We fell off the rock. The good news was, we fell Horkman-side down, so he broke my fall; his head hit the ground with a sound like *THWOCK*. The bad news was, now that I was on top, I was the one closest to the bear. And it was coming around the rock.

"Get up!" I said, trying to get my feet under me.

Underneath me, Horkman was moaning.

"Come on!" I said. "GET UP!"

Nothing from Horkman. Asshole.

I don't know how I did it—adrenaline, I guess—but somehow I got the two of us onto our feet, Horkman still moaning, hanging off me like some kind of giant douchebag backpack. The bear was still coming toward me. It was maybe five feet away.

"Stay!" I said.

Believe it or not, the bear stopped. It was looking at me with this expression of *What the fuck?* Very slowly, I turned around, presenting my Horkman side to the bear. Ahead of me I could see the gate where Fook and the other bastards went out. I started moving that way. I had to do it by making little hops, because my knees and Horkman's were tied together.

I turned my head around to see how close the bear was.

Jesus. Now there were *two* bears. One to the left, one to the right. There was no way I could point Horkman at both of them.

By hopping like a bastard, I made it to the gate. Thank God Fook left it unlocked. I pushed it open and hopped through, dragging Horkman. I was sweating and breathing hard. I could hear the bears right behind me. Up ahead, through the trees, I could see lights and hear cars on Fifth Avenue.

I heard scuffling and growling off to the right. The bears had found a garbage can and were rooting around in it. This was my chance. I started hopping into the woods, toward the traffic.

Suddenly there were people in front of me. The light wasn't good, and for a second I thought it was Fook and his crew. But then I saw it was some young punks, four of them, with those pants they wear so low, you can see the entire ass of their boxer shorts.

"Hey," I said. "I need some help here."

One of them stepped close.

"Why you got that man tied to you?" he said.

"It's a long story," I said. "How about you untie us, and I'll tell you, okay?"

"You got any money?" he said.

"I'll give you some money if you untie us, okay?"

The lead punk turned to the others and said, "Man gonna pay us to untie him." They all thought that was pretty funny. The lead punk started going through my pockets.

"Hey," I said, which I admit was stupid, but that's what I came up with.

The punk found my wallet. Then he searched Horkman and came up with his wallet and phone.

"Okay," I said. "Now you got our money. So if you could just . . ."

"What else you got?" he said.

"Nothing," I said.

He frowned.

"Where you got your phone?" he said.

"I don't have it with me," I said.

He reached down to his pants pocket, which was down around his knees, and pulled out a gun. He showed it to me. This was my night for having assholes show me their guns.

"Everybody got a phone," he said.

"I swear I don't have it with me."

He jammed the gun barrel between my hands, into my gut. I would have pissed my pants, except I already had. The punk was about to say something—I'm guessing it involved my phone—but I never found out, because that was when the bears showed up. They must have finished the garbage.

You always hear that if you see a bear, you shouldn't try to run away. I'm here to tell you that this is good advice. Because all four punks took off, and both bears took off after them. Which left me standing there with Horkman still on my back.

I started hopping again. I reached Fifth Avenue and somehow, I still don't know how, I heaved Horkman and me over the wall, onto the sidewalk. I did it so we landed Horkman-side down again, my feeling being that I did all the work getting us there, and he needed to pull his weight.

We were lying on the sidewalk, me on top. People were walking past, and I was like, "Hey! Can you give us a hand here?" In Des Moines, if people saw two guys tied up on the sidewalk, they'd stop and help out, but this was New York, so nobody slowed down. Most of them didn't even look up from texting.

After a few minutes, I managed to get us back up onto all four of our feet, and hopped over to the curb. There was a cab right there, stopped at a light. I hopped to it and managed to get a pinky on the latch and open the door. I turned around and pushed hard, shoving Horkman in, me falling backward on top of him.

It turned out the cab was occupied, so now both of us were on top of the occupant, a guy in a suit.

"What the *hell*?" he said.

"Sorry," I said. "If you could just . . ."

"Get the hell out!" he said. "This is my cab!"

The driver was also shouting at me, but he was a New York City taxi driver, so I had no idea what language he was speaking.

I shifted Horkman around so I could sort of sit up and face them.

"Listen," I said. But before I could say anything else, the suit opened the door on his side and bailed out. While I was trying to figure that out, the driver, who suddenly could speak English, said, "Please. No trouble. Please."

He was staring at my stomach. I looked down, and all of a sudden I understood what was happening.

I was holding the punk's gun.

"Please," said the driver again. He was scared shitless.

"Take me to New Jersey," I said, "or I'll shoot you in the balls."

Philip

"**Did you ever see** a movie called *The Defiant Ones*?"

Those were the first words I said upon regaining consciousness in the back of that cab.

"You talking to me, dickhead?"

Those were the first words I heard upon regaining consciousness in the back of that cab.

My entire body hurt. A lot. Like I imagine it would hurt if I somehow happened to roll off of a huge rock and onto the ground while tethered to an obnoxious forensic plumber who I was now trying to have a conversation with.

"It's a movie where two escaped prisoners, who hate each other, are shackled together but have to cooperate in order to survive."

"And did *you* ever see a movie called *Tom Thumb*?" asked Peckerman. "I suggest you take yours and shove it up your ass."

That there was something out of whack with that retort (my Tom Thumb?) wasn't a discussion I felt like having at that exact moment. But, for the record, let me just say that it was far beyond idiotic.

The sun was up. A new day for everyone else, but for me a continuation of the nightmare that was yesterday. We were still tied together. My stomach pressed against his back. So we were sitting there sideways, each with our right butt cheek on the seat, looking out the same window. At first I couldn't get my bearings, but when I saw Lincoln Center, I knew we were on Ninth Avenue heading downtown.

"May I ask where we're going?"

"Home," said Peckerman, with an inflection implying that I'd asked a question with an obvious answer.

"Are you sure that's a good idea?" I asked.

"You have a better one, assplunge?"

"Well, let me put it this way," I said. "Do you live in a brick ranch house with a crab apple tree on your front lawn and a mailbox the shape of a locomotive at the curb?"

"You know I do. You came to the house last night and kicked the shit out of my swale with your bullshit Prius, remember?"

"Yes, but it was dark, so this is actually the first time I'm seeing it during the daytime. Nice place."

"What the hell are you talking about?"

"Take a look to your left," I told him. He did. And now saw what I was seeing on the TV screen embedded into the back of the driver's seat. A newscaster was standing in front of Peckerman's house, interviewing his neighbors.

"I never liked him," said a heavyset woman walking a Saint Bernard. "He's a foulmouthed blowhard and he never returned our rake. So when I know he's not home, I let Winston here squeeze out a brown beauty onto his front lawn. Everyone does. The kids call this place Doodyville."

The news then switched to the front of my house, where a similar media circus was taking place. Cameramen running alongside the cars taking my kids to school, pictures of me and Daisy as volunteers at a local soup kitchen last Thanksgiving—and then they cut to a reporter standing in front of The Wine Shop asking some of the other storeowners questions about me.

"Did I ever think Horkman was capable of doing this?" said Marty Jaffe, who owned the Bagel Chateau two doors down. "Yes. I knew it the minute I saw that his lower lip drooped slightly on the left side. If I'm not mistaken, Lee Harvey Oswald had that same droop."

And then that reporter turned back to the camera and said something about a reward for our capture or knowledge of our whereabouts.

"Still think we should go home?" I asked Peckerman.

"I did so return that fat fuck's rake," he said, with daggers in his eyes. "How much you want to bet three-quarters of the shit on my lawn is hers?"

It would've been extremely difficult to get back to Jersey anyway, because the news mentioned checkpoints at every outbound river crossing. In fact, up ahead I could see that the Ninth Avenue entrance to the Lincoln Tunnel was already backed up.

"Change of plans," I shouted to the driver. "Make the next right turn."

"Okay. I will. I promise," said the cabbie, on the verge of tears.

"What's with him?" I asked Peckerman.

"He's scared. He thinks I have a gun."

"And why would he think that?" I asked.

"Because of this," said Peckerman, as I followed his gaze downward and saw he was holding a gun.

Then he filled me in on what had occurred after my head crashed against the cement sidewalk. About the thugs taking our wallets, about the thugs being chased away by big black bears, about him hopping away from the big black bears up to a cab on Fifth Avenue, and about discovering that he had the thugs' gun and it all made perfect sense. Now the question was what to do next.

"I'd love to get out of these ropes," said Peckerman.

I felt the same way. Peckerman had a small mole, the kind that has a little black hair sticking out of it, on the back of his neck, and I truly felt I'd used up more than my allotted time to stare into that thing and it was only fair to let someone else enjoy the view.

"Pull over here," I told the sobbing cab driver on what appeared to be a deserted West Side street with dilapidated buildings and unused loading docks. It bothered me that the poor guy was so upset, so I tried to calm him down with a little small talk to show that we were human and, despite Peckerman's gun, meant no harm.

"That's a nice picture of your children," I said about the photo that was taped to the dashboard.

But my good intentions were misinterpreted, as he apparently perceived that to be some kind of threat to his family. Whereupon he stopped the car, got out, came around to the back, opened the door for us, reached in and untied us.

Then, once Peckerman and I got out and stepped onto the street, the still-sobbing cabbie ran back to the driver's side, opened his door, reached inside, grabbed something, ran around the cab, handed me a cigar box, then ran back to his side of the cab, got in, closed the door and drove away.

I opened the cigar box and looked inside. It was cash. $74.38. Probably all the money the cabbie made that day. I felt horrible. Peckerman?

"You know, I don't think this counts as robbing the guy, because we didn't ask him for any money," he said. "The putz gave it to us voluntarily."

I looked at Peckerman and felt the distinct urge to smack him. But we had bigger fish to fry. Plus he was holding the gun.

Then, as if on cue, the sound of approaching sirens was followed by three NYPD cars roaring around the corner. My stomach dropped. Like back in school when a teacher's voice saying my name startled me out of an effective daydream. We both turned around, our backs to the street. The wailing of the sirens becoming slightly less insistent.

The speed of the cars seemingly slower than just a few seconds before. My head down, I wondered if it was possible that Peckerman was actually peeing into his shoes.

And then, as if they'd gotten a second wind, the cars sped up again and headed toward some other place. After the few seconds it took to settle nerves, I garnered the strength to speak again.

"It's obvious we can't just stand out here like this. Any thoughts?"

"Well," said Peckerman, "I'm wondering if there's a way we can leave Manhattan other than by a bridge or a tunnel."

"Huh? I'd like to remind you, Mr. Peckerman, that Manhattan is an island, which, by definition, means that it is surrounded by water. So they need things like bridges and tunnels to attach them to other places. That said, how else do you suggest we get out of here?"

"How about . . . ?"

Peckerman didn't bother finishing his sentence. He merely pointed across the highway, to the piers that jutted out into the Hudson River, where the SS *Windsong*, a cruise ship to vacation spots in the Caribbean, was boarding passengers.

CHAPTER 18

Jeffrey

"Come on," I said, starting toward the ship.

"Wait a minute," said Horkman.

I turned around, ready to shoot the asshole. "What?"

"Maybe we should turn ourselves in."

"What?"

"Look, we didn't actually do anything, right?"

"They think we tried to bomb the GW Bridge."

"But we *didn't.*"

"They also think we shot a cop."

"We didn't do that, either."

"Right. But the fucking helicopter came down, and they think we did it."

"Yes, but we know we didn't, and if we got good lawyers, given time, we could get this all sorted out. Otherwise, if we just keep running, where do we stop?"

I hated to admit it, but the asshole had a point.

"So what are you suggesting?" I said.

"We make a call," he said. "I know a good defense attorney. We contact him and he helps us turn ourselves in. That way we don't look guilty."

We were a few yards from a coffee shop. I stuck the gun in my pocket and we went in. Two guys behind the counter were waiting on a half-dozen customers, but nobody looked our way. A TV behind the counter was showing the news, but at the moment we weren't on it.

We spotted a pay phone back by the restrooms and headed that way, keeping our heads down. Horkman picked up the phone, keeping his face toward the wall. I grabbed a newspaper off a table and held it in front of my face, pretending to read it while I peeked over the top and scanned the room. My eyes fell on the TV screen.

"Oh shit," I said.

"What?" said Horkman.

"Look."

The TV screen said TERRORISTS IN PERVERT SEX ZOO MAS-SACRE.

"Oh shit," said Horkman.

Everybody in the coffee shop was staring at the TV. A counter guy turned up the volume.

". . . just getting details on this horrific crime," the announcer was saying. "Police have released this video from surveillance cameras at the Central Park Zoo. We warn you that some of what you are about to see is graphic, and quite frankly disgusting."

And there we were on the screen, me and him in grainy black and white, tied together, with me hopping and Horkman's head jerking up and down.

"Police have identified these two men as Peckerman and Hork-man, the same two suspected members of a New Jersey terrorist cell being sought in connection with the attack on the George Washington Bridge and the gruesome shooting of a courageous NYPD helicopter pilot. It is not yet known exactly what the two men were doing at the zoo, but one police source speculated that they were engaging in some kind of sick, twisted sexual bondage victory dance."

Now they replayed the video and slowed it down, so Horkman and I were bouncing in slow motion. You couldn't really see Horkman's eyes, but his mouth was opening and closing with every hop. I was gasping for air, but on the video it almost looked like I was smiling.

"That's disgusting," said one of the coffee-shop customers.

"But what is truly disturbing," said the TV announcer, "is what happened next. Apparently there were some youths at the zoo, and they had the misfortune to stumble upon this sordid scene."

"Youths?" I said. *"Youths?"*

I said it a little too loud. One of the customers, a guy in a Yankees cap, glanced my way.

"According to police," the announcer said, "the bodies of two youths were found near the scene, disemboweled and being eaten by bears. Sources have identified these as Central Park Zoo bears Hansel and Gretel, which were brought to New York by Mayor Bloomberg as part of an animal exchange program with the Berlin Zoo, which for its part received porcupines. It is not clear at this point whether the terrorists deliberately set the bears loose to kill the youths, or if they disemboweled the youths themselves and then set the bears on them in an attempt to cover their tracks."

Yankee cap glanced back at me again, for a second longer this time.

"What is clear," continued the announcer, "is that this new, sickeningly horrendous act on the part of these alleged terrorist perverts, who are still at large, has the entire city—and yes, the entire nation—on edge. That is especially true of the police department, which very nearly lost one of its own in a savage attack by these same alleged depraved killers. For more on that, we go to reporter Warren Pristine, who's on the West Side with members of the police special antiterrorism unit. Warren, what's the mood like out there?"

The screen showed a guy in a trenchcoat in front of a bunch of pissed-off-looking cops wearing helmets and body armor and carrying guns the size of piano legs.

"Steve," said the reporter, "the mood among these officers is tense and, quite frankly, angry about the brutal and, as you say, savage attack on one of their own. As one officer said to me, and here I quote, cleaning up his language just slightly, 'If you shoot one of us in the testicles, it's like you shot all of us in the testicles. Even the women.' So there's a lot of anger, Steve—anger and rage. I'm speaking only for myself here, and I am certainly not suggesting that any of these brave and highly professional men and women would deliberately violate departmental regulations, but if they do encounter these alleged terrorists—and we all fervently hope they do, and soon—it would not surprise me if their tactical philosophy could best be summarized as 'shoot first, and ask questions later.' Back to you, Steve."

"Thanks for that report, Warren," said Steve. "And be careful out there. To summarize: As the terror campaign against the people and zoo animals of New York City escalates and takes a twisted, disturbing turn, police as well as federal agents are intensifying their search for two suspected terrorist leaders, Jeffrey Peckerman and Philip Horkman."

And there we were, on the screen, this time sharp and clear, in living color.

Now Yankees cap was staring at me.

"Hey!" he shouted. "HEY!"

I had the gun out.

"Don't move, asshole," I said.

"You better listen to him," said Horkman. "Because he *will* shoot you in the balls."

Five seconds later, we were out the door, running toward the ship.

CHAPTER 19

Philip

So the hope was that the twelve hundred or so passengers now boarding the SS *Windsong* had been up most of the night packing, grabbed maybe a couple of hours sleep, and then groggily left their homes at dawn to get to Pier 92 by seven a.m., making it feasible they hadn't the time to see the morning news with our pictures plastered all over the place.

The ship's personnel were going to be a different story.

"Do you have a valid passport on you?" asked Peckerman while we were running toward the cruise ship. "They're going to want to see one before we board."

"No, Peckerman. Call me nearsighted, but when I left my house to drive the two miles to my pet shop I didn't consider the possibility that I'd be sailing upon international waters before I got home."

"I have mine."

"You have your passport on you?" I asked.

"In here," he said, pointing to a zipper on the leg of his Dockers. "Those guys in Central Park never bothered looking in this pocket. I just realized it was still in there."

"Why's it in there to begin with?"

"Last summer my wife and I went to Spain for our anniversary. These were the pants I wore on the flight home. I guess I never took the passport out of there."

"Well, there's a bit of good luck. That today's the first day you've worn those pants since last summer."

"You kidding? I wear these pants all the time. They're real comfortable. Good thing I didn't wash them, though. Would've ruined the passport."

"So you haven't *cleaned* those pants since last summer?"

"Oh, way before that. I wore them almost every day in Spain."

"Lovely."

I knew from the few times Daisy and I went on cruise ships that they just want to see that you have a passport so there won't be a problem with customs once you get to your destination. They don't run checks on them. So if Peckerman simply flashed his to the captain or the admiral or the chef or whoever the hell that guy dressed in the white uniform at the top of the ramp leading to the ship's deck was, he would be fine.

But what about me? Since our wallets were stolen, I didn't even have the two alternate pieces of identification that they also accepted. The only ID I had was that bogus doctor badge pinned to the lab coat I was still wearing. Plus there was one other minor problem.

"We also don't have tickets," I whispered to Peckerman.

We were now standing on a line of excited vacationers awaiting their turns to board.

"But we *do* have a gun," said Peckerman, discreetly lifting his sweater revealing the handle sticking out the top of what I can only imagine was the worst-smelling pair of Dockers in the tri-state area. Any tri-state area.

"And exactly what are you planning on doing with it, Peckerman? Boatjack the SS *Windsong*?"

Something about his expression alarmed me.

"Just for the record, Peckerman, that was intended to be a rhe-torical question," I told him. "Besides, you see that metal detector at the top of this ramp? Well, from everything I've read, guns are made of metal."

His expression still alarmed me.

"Will you be talking soon, Peckerman? Because this line is moving quickly and I'd like to know if you're about to do something incred-ibly stupid so I can get off it and pretend I never met you, which has been my profound regret since I met you."

"Look" is all he said before nodding at an angle that sent my gaze downward toward the open beach bag of the couple in front of us. An elderly man and woman whose tickets for this very cruise were sitting on top of a towel and next to a few pairs of sunglasses and tubes of Coppertone.

I looked at Peckerman again and, yes, his expression still alarmed me when he held his finger up to his lips. Everyone moved forward and we were now third in line from having to show our travel docu-ments. It alarmed me even more so when he furtively placed his hand on the gun and started whistling "Camptown Races" in a way I can only describe as the way a person would whistle "Camptown Races" when he doesn't want anyone to think he has his hand on a gun.

But his hand wasn't there much longer because just around the time that his whistling reached the second "Oh, de doo-da day," the line was moving forward again and Peckerman, in one fluid motion, bent over, dropped the gun into the older woman's beach bag and rose to a standing position with their tickets in hand just as she and her husband went through the metal detector. And while it isn't worth describing every detail of the ensuing commotion involving about six security guards descending out of nowhere on two flailing elderly people crying out "We have no idea how it got in there!" as they were carted off and packed into a special bus that took them to someplace

that I'm sure was unpleasant, Peckerman (sighing as if he was growing impatient by this delay) pushed me through the metal detector
and waved the tickets along with his and the old man's passport to an
apologetic captain or admiral or chef or whoever the hell he was who
perfunctorily waved us onto the SS *Windsong*.

"How the hell did you pull that off?" I asked as we walked through
a sliding door and entered a large reception area where flutes of cham-
pagne and a carnival of hors d'oeuvres greeted the passengers, who
helped themselves before drifting down carpeted hallways in search
of their accommodations.

"Come on, let's find our room and then we can come back for
food," he said, as if that was an answer to my question.

We took an elevator up to the "H" level, which was the most upper
deck on the ship. It was also the most exclusive.

"My God," we said in unison when we opened the door to
Room H22 and stepped into the stateroom. That had a living room.
Bedroom. A marbled master bathroom with a steam shower. Two
flat-screen TVs. Doors that stepped out onto a private balcony over-
looking the water.

"Sue and Arnie really know how to live," said Peckerman.

"Who?"

"Sue and Arnie Kogen. That incarcerated old couple who were
kind enough to let us use this place for the next ten days. Hungry?"

"Yes," I answered. "But I'm also exhausted."

"Me too."

So we took naps. Peckerman won the coin toss, so he took the
king-size bed and I was just fine sacking out on the foldout from the
couch in the sitting room.

And when we woke up, we were at sea. Cruising the Atlantic. Away
from the police. And from the news reports with our pictures and
"800" phone numbers to call if we were spotted.

I took a steam shower and shaved, using the razor and shaving cream that was in the complimentary toiletry bag on the counter next to the sink. Peckerman didn't shower or shave or even wash his hands after he used the bathroom for a real long time. The guy was a walking sump pump.

"Let's explore the ship," I suggested.

"Sure."

So we left the stateroom and went down the elevator to the main deck. Through the casino, where dozens of people were playing black-jack and roulette and pulling down the arms on slot machines, now that we were beyond the three-mile limit where it was legal to gam-ble. Past the stores, where dozens of people were shopping for jewelry and books and sunscreen. And then into the dining room, where dozens of people were seated or on line helping themselves to an un-believable assortment of the foods from many nations being offered as a buffet lunch.

It was then, because I couldn't take it any longer, that I turned to Peckerman and asked, "Have you noticed something out of the ordi-nary about every single person we've seen so far?"

"You mean that they're all naked?"

"You noticed it, too, huh?"

Yep, Peckerman and I were now stowaways on a "clothing op-tional" cruise on its way to the Caribbean Islands.

CHAPTER 20

Jeffrey

Horkman pulled me over next to a salad bar the size of a war canoe.

"We have to get naked," he said.

"No," I said.

"Yes."

"We'd look like a pair of homos."

"Okay, first of all, that's very offensive."

"Why? Are you a homo?"

"No, I am not a gay American."

"Me neither. That's why I don't want to look like a fucking homo."

His face got red, and he raised his voice. "Listen," he said. "There is nothing wrong with two men having an intimate physical relationship. It's perfectly . . ."

He stopped there, because a woman who'd been grazing her way down the salad bar had stopped and was looking at us. She was in I'm guessing her late fifties or early sixties, a large woman with hair the color of a traffic cone and large tits. I'm usually a fan of bazooms, but not when they're resting on a tray that's also supporting what looked like four pounds of potato salad.

"He's right," she said to me.

"What?" I said.

"Your friend is right. On this ship, we don't judge others. If you want to explore your sexual identity, this is the place for it."

"Lady," I said. "Number one, I'm not a faggot. Number two, butt out."

Now her face was the color of her hair.

"*What* did you say?" she said.

A guy came up behind her, skinny wrinkled dude who weighed maybe as much as one of her thighs. He was holding a banana.

"Something wrong, honey?" he said.

"This man," she said, nodding her head toward me, "is being very offensive."

The guy stepped between us, giving me the eyeball. "Is there a problem?" he said. He was trying to look badass, but that's a look a guy can't pull off when he's built like Olive Oyl and he's naked except for a banana, which for the record—not that I made a point of looking; it's just the way the angles lined up—was a good five inches longer than his dick.

"I wasn't talking to you," I told him, nodding at his wife. "I was talking to the manatee here."

His hand tightened on the banana. "*What* did you call her?" he said.

"Christ," I said, "is *everybody* on this boat deaf?"

"We were just leaving," said Horkman. He grabbed my arm and pulled me toward the dining-room exit. I looked back; Banana and Saggy Tits were talking to a crew member and pointing our way. We ducked out the door, hustled to the elevator, and went back to the cabin.

"Listen," said Horkman. "You can't draw attention to us like that."

I didn't say anything. The asshole was right.

"We have to fit in," he said. He was taking off his pants.

"That's our plan?" I said. "Get naked? That's it?"

"For now," he said, still undressing. "We lay low on the ship, let things cool down in New York. We get to the Caribbean, get off on an island down there, call our families. We get lawyers, get this whole mess straightened out."

He was naked now. He went to the door.

"I don't know about you," he said, "but since we're stuck on this ship for now, I'm going to try to get something positive out of the experience. I believe there's a lecture on Japanese flower arranging in the Sea Urchin Salon in twenty minutes."

He opened the door, stepped out into the hallway, and closed the door behind him.

"Homo," I said, and began undressing.

CHAPTER 21

Philip

There are precious few activities that grown men should do while naked. Showering. Swimming when no one else is around. Sex, whether someone else is around or not. And anything that takes place in front of blind people. Beyond that, all unclothed activities performed in the presence of those who're sighted should be filed under the heading of "Dear Lord, If He Bends Over One More Time I'm Going to Hang Myself."

So, as much as I thought it was a good idea that Peckerman and I blend in with everyone else onboard this floating genital convention, I opted to spend the next hour taking a Japanese flower-arranging lesson because it stood to reason that even if there were other men in this class, they would be seated.

I was right. There were twelve other nude flower-lovers in the room where the class was taking place—all women. Even the instructor, who stood in the open area in the middle of the desks arranged in a circle, was a woman. I don't mind telling you I found it fascinating that if someone had asked me what my reaction would be if I'd ever found myself in an enclosed space with thirteen stark naked women,

I would've said something along the lines of "I should only be so lucky." But as I sat there I found that the novelty wore off shortly after checking out the bodies that surrounded me and I was surprisingly unexcited—with the exception of the extremely attractive woman who was sitting to my right, although I didn't realize I was staring at her until she looked at me and smiled.

"First time?" she asked.

"Yes," I said, in an attempt to subtly deny what I was obviously doing. "I've never taken a Japanese flower-arranging class before."

She smiled some more. The kind of smile that told me that I was not off the hook.

"I mean, is this your first clothing optional cruise?"

"Yes," I answered, totally embarrassed upon getting busted like this. "I'm sorry if I made you feel uncomfortable."

Again she laughed. Like someone who understood.

"It will take you a little while," she explained. "But you'll get used to it."

I figured she was in her mid-thirties. With a slight accent. Boston? Portugal?

"So you've done this sort of thing before?" I asked.

"I'm very much a naturalist," she said, nodding. "It's a great equalizer. No clothes or uniforms, no telltale signs of wealth or social standing. On this ship you've got doctors, schoolteachers, bank presidents, gas station attendants, and you can't tell who's who until you get to know them as people. It's nicer that way."

I liked this naked woman. A lot. And not just because she was naked. I liked her because she was one of those people who, by the way she looked at you when she spoke, made *you* want to speak. Made you feel safe to say what you wanted to. What you *had* to. And that's what I had to do. Until that very moment, I hadn't had a conversation, I mean an honest heart-to-heart dialogue, with another human being (Peckerman was of another species) about what had happened and how I felt about it since this entire ordeal started the night be-fore, and I was ready. Ready to talk about all the running and shoot-ing and hospitals and big black bears and policemen's punctured scrotums that were pent up inside me and, now that I was finally in an idled state, was ready to express.

So as the naked instructor passed out ayakas, azamis, sakuras and other Japanese flowers for us to work with, I had a feeling it wouldn't take much prompting from the naked woman to my right for me to start spilling my guts.

"Aren't these flowers colorful?"

That's all the prompting I needed.

"Yes, they're quite colorful, and you wouldn't believe what's going on in my life right now . . ."

I didn't stop talking for the next hour. The floodgates had opened and the outpouring could have buried a medium-size village. Careful to keep my voice below a whisper, I started with the soccer game and took her straight through to how Peckerman still hadn't bathed, how much I missed Daisy and the kids, and how I was silently praying that Hyo (the sixteen-year-old Korean American who worked for me after school and on weekends, to mind the register and assist customers) would have the good sense to feed the animals at The Wine Shop when he sees that I hadn't been there.

She listened and I could tell she heard every word. What a refresh-ing phenomenon that was after so many years of marriage—to say words that were actually heard.

Neither of us even attempted to make a flower arrangement, and when the class was over, we took a walk along the outside deck, where naked people were taking in the last few rays of a setting sun, playing shuffleboard, swimming and sipping pre-dinner cocktails. And while the conversations we overheard were very much about the beautiful weather, they also mentioned a forecast of rain and high winds that were supposedly ahead of us.

We had no destination. But we stayed with each other because it seemed like the most natural thing to do. As if this was merely the silent walking portion of the same conversation we were having in the flower-arranging class, and for either of us to say "Good-bye, it was nice talking to you" would have been out of the moment and rude.

I then followed her through an opening that took us back into the ship, then down a carpeted hallway, until she slowed down and came to a stop in front of the door to a room on the "G" level. She turned to me, but we remained silent. Furtive side glances up and down the corridor revealed no one else around. We were alone. I looked at her again. She really was beautiful.

"Do you feel better after telling me what you did?"

"I do."

"I know it doesn't change the situation," she said, nodding, "but something always happens when our words hit the air. The emotions are shed and what's left are the bare facts that we have to deal with in a logical manner. It's a big step."

She exuded an air of calm radiance. She made me feel calm. And, okay, radiant.

"And please know that your secret is safe with me," she added.

"Thank you."

I suddenly felt a stirring. The kind of stirring that a red-blooded naked man tends to feel when he's standing maybe one foot away from a beautiful naked woman in an empty carpeted corridor on an ocean liner.

"And I'd like you to feel free to speak to me if and when the need hits you again."

"Okay."

"And, for what it's worth, I believe you. I believe in your innocence."

"It's worth a lot," I said, while wondering if she noticed my stirring.

"Listen," I then heard myself saying. "You were so nice to listen to me, but I never gave you a chance to tell me about yourself."

She smiled in a way that told me that it was okay.

"My name is Maria."

"I'm Philip Horkman."

"Nice to meet you, Philip Horkman."

I was now wondering if she was having a stirring of her own. I couldn't tell. I could never tell. To this very day, I never met any man who can tell.

"You're so easy to talk to, Maria."

"It comes with the territory—make people feel comfortable so they tell me what's troubling them."

"Are you a therapist?"

"No, I'm a nun."

CHAPTER 22

Jeffrey

I didn't want to be recognized, and I wasn't comfortable being completely buck-ass naked, so the first thing I did, after I got undressed, was head for the shopping deck. I got a ship-logo ball cap and a pair of sunglasses, which cost a total of $238.50, which was a complete rip-off, and which I charged to the room of Sue and Arnie Kogen.

After that I spent an hour walking around the ship, pretending it was no big deal to be walking naked around a ship full of naked people. In a situation like that, you can't be every ten seconds pointing at some woman and yelling, "Hey! I can see your vagina!" Even though that's pretty much all you're thinking. I'm not saying all the women were hot. Some of them, if they fell overboard, they'd be harpooned by Japs. But there's something about a naked woman, any naked woman: Your brain always wants you to take a look. Your brain never says, "Nah, I've seen enough naked women for now."

After a while, I got thirsty from all that looking, so I found a seat at a bar on the sundeck called the Anemone Lounge, where I had a Heineken, which cost twelve dollars, which was picked up by my good friends Sue and Arnie Kogen.

I'd been sitting at the bar for maybe five minutes when this couple came up to me. She was a blond middle-aged woman, but you could see she worked out, with a nice fake rack. He was a big guy, some muscle, some fat, very hairy, like he was wearing a full-body sweater. He had on one of those fanny packs, which is a douchebag look even if you're not naked.

I had this weird feeling that I knew them, but I couldn't figure out from where.

The Rack said, "Mind if we join you?"

I shrugged. They sat down.

"I'm Sharisse," said the rack. "This is Mike."

Mike stuck out his hand and we shook, him holding it a little too long, letting me know he had a grip.

He said, "Are you enjoying the cruise so far, Jeffrey?"

I pulled my hand away. "Do I know you?" I said.

"Not yet," he said.

"Then how do you know my name?"

Sharisse smiled and said, "Everybody knows you, Jeffrey."

"I don't know what you're talking about."

"I have to say," said Mike, "going on a nude cruise, that's a very creative way to hide out."

"I'm not hiding out," I said.

"No," said Sharisse, looking straight at my dick. "You're not."

"Listen," I said, "I don't know who you think I am, but . . ."

"You're Jeffrey Peckerman," said Mike. "We recognized you when you got on board." He unzipped his waist pack, and for a second there, the way things had been going lately, I thought he was going to pull out a gun. But what he pulled out was an iPhone. He tapped on it for a few seconds, then handed it to me. On the screen was the *New York Post* website. The headline said ZOO SEX PERVERT BRIDGE TERRORISTS LINKED TO AL-QAEDA CELL. There were the usual pictures of me and Horkman, but now there were four new pictures, crappy black-and-white head shots taken from video. Three were of the ass-holes from the bar who kidnapped me, with raghead names under their pictures. The fourth was Fook. At least I figured it was; the ac-tual photo showed the head of Chuck E. Cheese, underneath which it said *Mystery Cell Leader*.

I read the first few paragraphs of the story. The cops had checked surveillance videos from Central Park the night Horkman and I had been at the zoo. They'd identified the three assholes, who it turned out were serious al-Qaeda, wanted by the FBI. So now the story, accord-ing to "federal sources," was that Horkman and I were working with al-Qaeda, taking orders from the highest levels, and we were planning major new terror attacks. There was a nationwide manhunt on for us; the president had declared a state of emergency; the public was com-pletely freaking out; and Fox News was spearheading a boycott of Chuck E. Cheese.

"Jesus," I said.

"Yes," said Sharisse. She rested her hand on my thigh. "You're a popular man, Jeffrey."

"Listen," I said. "This is a huge mistake. I have nothing to do with al-Qaeda."

"Then why'd you go to the zoo with them?" said Mike.

"I didn't. I mean, I *did*, but they forced me."

"I see," said Mike. "And did they force you to bomb the GW Bridge and shoot down the police chopper?"

"No."

"So you did that on your own?"

"No! I didn't do any of that!"

"I see. And after not doing any of that, you suddenly decided to take a nude cruise, get out of town for a while."

"With your friend Philip Horkman," said Sharisse. "Traveling under the names Sue and Arnie Kogen."

"I'm curious," said Mike. "Which one of you is Arnie, and which one is Sue?"

I took a swig of beer, put the bottle back down. "Okay," I said. "I know it looks bad."

"Yes, it does," said Mike.

"Very bad," said Sharisse. Who, by the way, still had her hand on my thigh.

"But," I said, "I swear to you, I can explain, if you'll just give me a minute, okay? A couple of days ago, I was at my daughter's soccer game, and I don't know if you're familiar with the offside rule, but . . ."

I stopped there, because of how they were looking at me.

"You're not gonna buy this, are you?" I said.

"No," said Mike.

"I'm blond," said Sharisse. "But I'm not stupid."

"So," I said. "Are you going to turn me in?"

"No," said Mike.

"You're not?"

"Jeffrey," said Sharisse, breathing right in my ear. "Whatever happened, it's not your fault."

Then it hit me, where I knew them from. "You're the lawyers!" I said. "In that ad. On cable. Somebody and somebody."

"Fricker and Fricker," said Mike. "Whatever happened, it's not your fault. That's more than just a motto for us, Jeffrey. That's how we live our lives."

"We help people who need help," said Sharisse. "Even if they don't know it."

"And you, my friend, need help," said Mike.

"Okay," I said. "But why would you help me? What's in it for you?"

Mike leaned in. "Let's say we're able to help you out," he said. "Maybe you know some people who would appreciate that. Maybe these are people with resources. And maybe they'll be inclined to feel a certain degree of gratitude toward the law firm of Fricker and Fricker."

"What people? Who are you talking about?"

"You know," said Sharisse. "Important people you might happen to know. With resources."

I stared at her. "You mean *terrorists*?" I said.

A big smile from Sharisse, and another squeeze.

"Such an ugly word, 'terrorists,'" said Mike. "Why can't we stop the name-calling and the labeling? Why can't we just get along?"

"Listen to me," I said. *"I don't know those people."*

Mike smiled. "Of course you don't," he said. "As your lawyers, we wouldn't want to hear you say anything else."

"Wait. You're my lawyers?"

"I would hope so, for your sake," said Mike. "Because if we weren't your lawyers, this wouldn't be a privileged conversation. And if that were the case, we'd have no choice, as citizens, but to turn you in."

"We'd hate to do that," said Sharisse.

I stared at them. They were smiling at me, big smiles. Like moray eels, but without the warmth.

"You know what?" said Mike. "It's getting windy out here, and we have a lot to talk about. Let's go find your friend Philip."

He stood. Sharisse pulled me to my feet. It really was getting windy; the ocean looked rough, and the deck was moving. I stumbled a little, and Mike and Sharisse grabbed me, holding me up between them. My legal team.

CHAPTER 23

Philip

With the possible exception of the semi-erection that involuntarily sprouted when I thought I saw Diane Sawyer in an airport, I had never cheated on my wife Daisy. We'd exchanged sacred vows some eighteen years earlier and I was proud that even my fantasy life, at its wildest, was of the PG-13 nature. That's to say that my most lurid wanderings permitted a woman to peel (or be peeled) down to her underwear. Hey, I'm a guy! But the moment any move was made to undo the hooks on her bra, I was quick to pull the plug on the proceedings by smacking the back of my head and switching to another daydream. Yes, that's how faithful I'd been and planned to remain. So it stood to reason that if I were to step out on Daisy, the perfect situation would be to do so with someone who was celibate.

Maria, the twelfth of seventeen children born to extremely Catholic parents, had wanted to enter the clergy since grade school. But now, at the age of thirty-four, was questioning whether she still had the same passion and was taking time off to reassess.

"So you're sort of like the Maria in *The Sound of Music*," I said.

It was about a half hour later and we were now walking on the ship's outer deck again. Because the winds were blowing a little stronger and the temperature was a little lower, we'd both taken the time to exercise the 'optional' part of this clothing optional cruise and got dressed—me in the only pants and shirt I had with me, she in a pair of jeans and bathing suit top.

"Remember that movie?" I continued. "Julie Andrews played a nun who temporarily left the convent because she had the same questions you do and ended up marrying Captain von Trapp and helping him lead his seven children over the Alps and into Switzerland because the Nazis were bearing down on them."

She thought for a moment, and then shook her head.

"There's a big difference between that Maria and me."

"How so?"

She looked at me and smiled.

"I'm a better yodeler."

And then I smiled.

"Oh, is that a fact?"

And then she started singing.

High on a hill stood a lonely goatherd,

And then she started yodeling.

Lay-ee-odl, lay-ee-odl, lay-hee-hoo . . .

And then I started laughing as she continued.

Loud was the voice of the lonely goatherd,

Lay-ee-odl, lay-ee-odl-oo.

I was falling for her. In the purest of ways. We were both clothed. And the earlier stirrings that had made Lieut. Longfellow stand and salute were now at ease. Still, I was more enchanted than ever.

"Can Daisy yodel?" she asked.

"Who's Daisy?"

She laughed again because she thought I was joking. What she didn't know was at that particular moment, I literally had no idea who she was talking about.

I looked at her. She looked back. We held those gazes and I wondered if I was going to kiss her. As if I was a spectator to this couple standing alone on this ship's outer deck with no control of my own actions, I seriously wondered if I was going to surrender to the magnetic pull I was feeling, lean in, and kiss this beautiful nun. So it didn't surprise me when I allowed my face to drift toward hers. Or when I closed my eyes. Or when my lips lightly touched her lips. What did surprise me, however, was the sound of a voice, the last voice I'd ever want to hear at this tender moment.

"Hey, Horkman! We gotta talk!"

As if suddenly jerked into another reality, I turned to see that idiot Peckerman, naked except for a hat and sunglasses, flanked by a man and woman whom I'd immediately recognized as the ambulance-chasing couple from those tacky television commercials, coming toward us.

"Who's that?" Maria whispered.

"Don't worry, I'll get rid of him," I whispered back.

Because I had no desire whatsoever to expose Maria to the hideous behavior of this lummox and his new friends, I walked away so I could put as much distance between her and this unsightly trio as possible.

"What's up?" I asked.

"Philip Horkman, say hello to our attorneys, Fricker and Fricker. This is Fricker," he said, pointing to the woman. "And this is Fricker," he said, pointing to the man. "Or is it the other way around?" he asked, and then started snickering as if he'd just said something funny. And the fact that both Frickers started laughing as if this was the first time they'd heard anyone make a joke about their names made me despise them before we even exchanged a syllable.

"Our attorneys?" I asked.

"We need them," he said, leaning toward me as if they couldn't hear him even though he somehow forgot to lower his voice. "They know everything."

The wind kicked up a little more, rocking the boat. The four of us instinctively shifted the weight on our feet and grabbed the railing to keep our balance. I took a quick peek back at Maria to make sure she was okay. She was.

"If you can take your mind off of pussy for a second," he now said under his breath, "I think we should go inside and talk to them."

"With all due respect," I said to the Frickers, "if you do know everything, then you know we're innocent and really don't need legal representation." I opted to leave out the rest of that sentence, which would have been, "by shysters such as you."

"It's because we know everything that makes us perfect to fight for justice on your behalf," said the male Fricker.

"And we'll prevail," said his female counterpart, who I'd just noticed had her hand on Peckerman's thigh. "That is, if you allow our team to represent your team."

They were obviously able to read my hesitance.

"Give it some thought, Mr. Horkman."

"Okay," I responded, with every hope that this conversation was over and I could return to Maria.

"Hey, we're on an ocean liner in the middle of the ocean," he unfortunately continued, with a smirk that would make a used car salesman look as honest as our nation's sixteenth president. "So I know you're not running away."

"And it's like we told your partner here," said Mrs. Fricker, tapping her index finger on Peckerman's stunted thigh for emphasis, "these conversations are privileged, so there should be no fears about any of this coming back to haunt you."

"I appreciate . . ."

"But what we can't control," interrupted her husband, "is if someone onboard this ship should make an anonymous call to the proper authorities, who'll be there to greet you when we dock tomorrow."

A threat? Absolutely. There was no other way to take it. I looked over at Peckerman, who was silently urging me to take these Frickers seriously. But I couldn't. I wouldn't. And I was going to tell them this had I the time. But I didn't have the time, because just then a particularly large wave caused the boat to rock. As if it were a huge seaborne cradle with the side we were standing on dipping into the Caribbean, before rocking back to where we were high off its surface and then slamming back down again with a thud which sent Maria over the railing and into the water.

I saw it out of the corner of my eye. One second she was there, the next she'd lost her balance, and her attempt to grab the railing failed. In an instant, the ship righted itself and I looked overboard and caught a glimpse of her when she surfaced.

"Maria!" I yelled at the top of my lungs, but had no idea whether she yelled back or even heard me over the sound of the mounting wind. All I then saw was her getting smaller as she receded into the distance.

"Let's get back inside!" shouted Peckerman.

"Yes! Let's discuss our legal strategy!" shouted Fricker.

"Yes! There's so much we have to do!" shouted Fricker.

And then I jumped into the Caribbean. So I could save Maria.

Jeffrey

Even for Horkman, that had to be some kind of record for assholery. We're in the middle of the ocean, in the middle of a storm, and he *jumps off the fucking ship*?

Dipshit.

I looked over the railing, but it was dark down there, and I didn't see anything except waves. I yelled "Horkman!" but looking back on it, that was pretty useless.

Meanwhile, Sharisse was screaming like she had fire ants in her woowoo. To be honest, the only person who did anything practical was Mike, who ran to a life preserver, grabbed it, ran back to the rail, and gave it a mighty heave. It would have been impressive, except at the exact moment he heaved, the ship lurched again, and Mike went over the side after the life preserver. The last thing I heard him say was, quote, "FUUUUUUuuuuuuuuu . . ."

Sharisse stopped screaming, ran to the rail, looked over, then looked back at me.

"Ohmigod," she said. "Mike fell overboard!"

"I know!" I said.

She was pointing at the deck. "Look at that!" she said. "Do you know what that is?"

"A deck?" I said.

"Moisture," she said.

I looked. "Well, yeah," I said. "I mean we're in a storm, so it's . . ."

"It's negligence!" she said. "This deck is extremely slippery."

I have to admit I felt a stab of admiration for this woman, who had just seen her husband fall off a ship, probably to his death, and yet somehow had the presence of mind to start planning the lawsuit, possibly before he hit the water.

I looked over the side again, keeping a good grip on the railing. "We should find a crew person," I said.

"Good idea," she said. "Start documenting our case."

That wasn't what I meant, but I let it go. "Maybe we should put on some clothes first," I said. I was cold, and somehow it didn't seem right to go report three deaths with my schlong waving around.

"Right," agreed Sharisse. "We want to look businesslike. My cabin's right near here. You can wear some of Mike's clothes." Apparently she was completely done with grieving over Mike.

We went to her cabin. She found me a pair of shorts, a shirt and some sandals. It was all a little too big, and the shirt had that giant Ralph Lauren horse on it that basically says, when you wear it, "Hi! I'm a douchebag!" But it was okay for an emergency. I kept the hat and shades on, to maintain my disguise.

While Sharisse was dressing, I found the remote control and turned on the TV to check out CNN. The two big headline stories were NEW YORK TERROR ATTACK and SUDDEN HURRICANE GROWS IN ATLANTIC. So basically there were two big shitstorms in the news, and I was in the middle of both of them.

"Come on," said Sharisse, all dressed now. She grabbed my hand and pulled me out the door and down the corridor. I realized I still had the TV remote in my hand so I stuck it into a pocket.

"Where, exactly, are we going?" I asked.

"We're going to see the captain," she said.

"Um, not to piss on your parade, but maybe you noticed we're in a hurricane here."

"So?"

"So the captain might be a little busy to be talking to passengers."

Sharisse looked at me like I was a retard and said, "We'll see about that."

And we did. Never again will I underestimate the persuasive power of a woman with legal training and big tits. She went through the ship's chain of command like a chainsaw through a fruitcake. Fifteen minutes later, we were escorted onto the bridge to meet with the captain. His name was Sven Lutefisk, and he was one of those tall blue-eyed Norwegian-looking dudes who probably shits icicles. He and several other officers were standing in front of a console with a dozen screens showing radar, GPS, and other nautical things. He did not look happy to see us, but he was polite.

"My first officer tells me you have an urgent situation you must discuss with me, and only me, Mrs., ah . . ."

"Fricker," said Sharisse. "Sharisse Fricker. You may have seen my TV ad." She stuck out her boobs.

"I cannot say that I have," said Captain Lutefisk. He looked at me. "And is this Mr. Fricker?"

"No," said Sharisse and I together.

Lutefisk studied me for a second, frowning, then looked back at Sharisse. "As you can see," he said, gesturing at the nautical screens, "we are quite busy at the moment, with the weather. So perhaps you can tell me what this urgent matter is."

"I'll get right to the point," said Sharisse. "You have a problem."

"What kind of problem?"

"A serious problem. With your ship."

"What are you talking about?"

"People have been hurt," said Sharisse. "And more people could get hurt."

Lutefisk looked at me again, longer this time, then back at Sharisse. "Are you threatening me?" he said.

"It's not a threat if you can back it up," said Sharisse. "And I am fully prepared to back it up."

She was going to keep talking, but just then one of the officers, who'd been staring at me, stepped forward and whispered something to Lutefisk. Now both of them were staring at me. Lutefisk said something Norwegian, and the officer walked briskly to a cabinet against a wall. The other officers formed a circle around Sharisse and me.

"What's going on?" I said, although I was pretty sure I knew. Especially when the guy came back from the cabinet holding a handgun.

"What's going on," said Lutefisk, "is that we are going to take you into custody, Mr. Jeffrey Peckerman. And you as well, Mrs. Fricker, or whatever your real name is."

"You're making a big mistake," said Sharisse. "Do you have any idea what I can do to you?"

"Is that another threat?" said Lutefisk.

"You bet your ass it's a threat," said Sharisse. "You're going to lose your whole fucking ship, sailor boy."

Lutefisk's eyes narrowed. He said something to the officers, and they took a step closer. Lutefisk pointed to me. "Empty your pockets," he said.

I reached into the right front pocket of Mike Fricker's shorts. My hand closed around the TV remote control.

"Slowly," said Lutefisk.

Slowly, I pulled my hand out of the pocket.

The sailors froze, staring at my hand. The only part of the remote showing was about an inch of the black casing, and the red power button.

Lutefisk said something to the officers, and they took a step back. Their eyes—all, for the record, blue—were locked on the remote.

"Is that what I think it is?" said Lutefisk.

"Well, what the fuck else would it be?" I said. I was wondering what kind of cheap-ass cruise line would make such a big deal about taking a TV remote. You can get those things for ten bucks at Best Buy.

Lutefisk was staring at me. "Where is it?" he said.

"Where is what?"

"The bomb," he said.

My mouth fell open. I was about to show him that it was a TV remote, but Sharisse put her hand on my arm.

"You think we're going to just *tell* you?" she said.

Lutefisk shifted his attention to her.

"Mrs. . . ."

"Fricker," she said.

"Mrs. Fricker, there are over two thousand innocent people on this ship."

"Right," said Sharisse. "And they're all going to be fine, as long as you do exactly as I say. First, I want that gun."

Lutefisk hesitated, then said something Norwegian. Reluctantly, the officer handed the gun to Sharisse. She took it, then smiled her moray smile.

"Now," she said, "let's talk money."

CHAPTER 25

Philip

The first thought I had after I jumped off that ship was, I can't believe I jumped off that ship. The next thought I had, upon hitting the water was, I wonder if I'll survive the jump off that ship or will the impact turn me into a floating Rorschach blot? And the third thought I had, upon surfacing intact was, Now what?

I immediately focused on swimming toward where I thought Maria was. I'm a very strong swimmer. In a pool. Or a lake. But until that very moment, I never had the occasion to test that prowess in a choppy sea during a raging storm on a moonless night. Truth be told, it was never even on my "to do" list.

But I'm sure you know that adage about necessity being the mother of invention. Well, as I was feverishly trying to work my way across the Caribbean, it occurred to me that now would be an excellent time for someone to invent a car that rode on top of the water so it could stop, give me a lift to wherever Maria was, and then drive the two of us to the nearest place where a person could actually stand without drowning.

Presuming the possibility of that happening was, at best, a long shot, I continued onward, not even sure at this point that I was heading in the right direction. So I stopped and looked back at the SS *Windsong*, whose lights were still on. I tried my best to gauge where Maria was standing when she went overboard, then turned around and resumed swimming into the darkness. Exactly two strokes. I swam exactly two strokes before becoming entangled in something that felt like a body. A human body whose arms were flailing about in a losing battle to stay afloat! Was it possible? Dear Lord, I have no idea how I reached her so quickly, but then again, the Lord works in mysterious ways, does he not? And it stood to reason, given that she was a nun, that the Lord would mysteriously work overtime on her behalf.

"Maria!" I shouted. "Hold on to me, honey! I'll save you!"

I'd always wanted to say the words "I'll save you" to a woman. Even as a kid, the fantasy of saving the damsel in distress, whether it be Sir Lancelot swooping down from a white horse and saving Guinevere from a flame-breathing dragon or The Man of Steel himself swooping down from the sky to untie a bound and gagged Lois Lane from the rails seconds before she's crushed by an oncoming train. That's what I wanted to do. I wanted to swoop. And now was my chance.

"I'm swooping, Maria! I'm swooping!"

And swoop I did, as I dove under the water, grabbed her around the waist and, employing a Red Cross method I once saw a lifeguard use on my son Trace after he fell into the deep end of our country club's pool when he tripped while practicing demi-pliés on the high diving board, I scissors-kicked the two of us upward until we broke surface. Her back to me, I reached around and positioned my right arm across her chest and started treading water.

The question now was, where were we going? Obviously the shorter distance was the ocean liner, which was about a hundred yards behind us, still aglow. I could swim toward its lights and then yell for help. Surely someone would hear me. Although it did cross my mind that it was potentially risky for me—that by drawing attention to myself, I increased the chances of being recognized should any of the passengers or crew had been online since we left New York and had seen mine and Peckerman's pictures on CNN.com or any other news source, which was now a very distinct probability.

Still, it was a visible, nearby destination that was safest for Maria. And wasn't that an integral part of the swooping procedure? To put the needs of the swoopee before that of the swooper? Of course it was.

"Don't worry, we'll be back at the ship in no time at all," I said, as I started my one-armed swim back toward the SS *Windsong*.

"Thank you," she answered in a gurgling voice that sounded nothing like her. Even allowing for fatigue, the prevailing elements and the trauma of this entire situation, it was deeper than I'd remembered it being. Almost masculine. I was now concerned this was due to water in the lungs, similarly to the way my slightly overweight son Trace, after that lifeguard rescued him, had water in his lungs and his voice sounded deeper and almost masculine. In which case it was advisable, if not necessary, to expel the water.

So I stopped swimming again and, with her back to me, put my arms around her, placed my hands on top of each other in two fists, and pulled them toward me—like in a Heimlich maneuver—and couldn't help but notice, when I moved my hands up and down the front of her body to get a better grip, I didn't feel any breasts but did feel, from what I knew from personal experience, a penis. So after I yelled real loud, I spun her around and found myself looking straight into the face of the lawyer Fricker. The *male* lawyer Fricker.

He said, "At Fricker and Fricker, we may bend the law but we don't break it," which I recognized as his firm's motto from those hideous television commercials. A shyster to the very end, those were his last words as his eyes rolled back into his head, his entire body went limp and, despite the darkness, I was able to tell that his face was turning bluer than the testicles of a pet shop dachshund when denied access to its mate in the cage next to him.

Now I was scared. Really scared. Whether Fricker died from exposure or from whatever fall he took off that ship, I didn't care. All I knew was I was holding a dead lawyer in the middle of the Caribbean, the SS *Windsong* was now cruising into the distance, making it no longer a real option as a destination. And, unless those fins I saw approaching belonged to a convention of upside-down surfboards, sharks were on their way.

So, hoping like hell that aquatic sharks were attracted to legal ones, I let go of the erstwhile Fricker and started swimming as fast as my arms could propel me. With long overhead strokes that reached as far ahead of me as possible, and legs kicking like two Rockettes on Dexedrine, I moved forward. Fueled by fear-induced adrenaline, I kept going. Non-stop. For how long? One hour? Two hours? Hard to say. All I knew was that I was determined to keep going as long as I humanly could.

God knows how much later, I noticed that once the sea became less choppy and calmer waters were under me, the current was running in the direction I was going. Did that mean I was getting closer to land? That these ripples would eventually build into waves that would crash onto some beach? I had no idea. So I kept my arms churning, as I took nothing for granted. And when I was lifted up by the rising force of water, was that indeed the wave that would carry me ashore? I had no idea. So I kept my arms churning, as I took nothing for granted. And when the wave sent me flying through the air and deposited me on what was definitely land, I kept my arms churning, as I took nothing for granted.

And then after my arms started to really hurt from me just lying there and churning them into the ground, I stopped. And lay there exhausted. And then I fell asleep. For how long? All I knew when I finally awakened, before I even opened my eyes, I was able to tell it was daytime. Still exhausted and aching like I'd never felt before, I lay there with my eyes closed until I heard a voice.

"Philip?"

I opened my eyes and saw Maria.

CHAPTER 26

Jeffrey

For a few seconds there, I thought about coming clean to Captain Lutefisk and his crew, showing them that all I had in my hand was a TV remote.

What stopped me was Sharisse, who was giving me a look that said *Do not fuck with me.* Remember that this woman (a) was not particularly upset to see her husband go over the side, and (b) had a gun. So I kept the remote in my pocket.

"What do you want?" said Lutefisk.

"What we want," said Sharisse, "and thank you for asking, is one hundred million dollars."

"That's absurd," said Lutefisk.

"You're absolutely right," said Sharisse. "We want *two* hundred million dollars."

"We don't carry anything like that amount of money on the ship," said Lutefisk.

"Of course not, Sven. That's why you're going to arrange to have it delivered to the ship by helicopter."

"This is impossible! We are in a hurricane!"

"Sven, Sven, Sven," said Sharisse. "I'm sure a great big strong ship captain like you can handle a little wind."

"I'm sorry, but I cannot—what are you doing?"

"I'm aiming the gun at your face, so you'll pay close attention," said Sharisse. "I want you to get on the radio or the satellite or the sonar or whatever the hell you get on, and I want you to tell your company that we want two hundred million dollars in unmarked bills, and we want it in twelve hours. And if we don't get it"—she gestured with her non-gun hand toward my pocket—"my associate Jeffrey here is going to press the button, and what happens then will make the *Titanic* look like the SS *Minnow*."

Lutefisk looked puzzled.

"What," said Sharisse, "you never heard of *Gilligan's Island*?" She started singing, off-tune: "Just sit right back and you'll hear a tale, da da da da da da dum . . ." She looked at me. "How's it go?"

I shrugged. She shifted the gun slightly in my direction.

"Something something something," I sang. "A three-hour tour."

"Right!" she said. "A three-hour tour!" She aimed the gun back at Lutefisk and his men. "Everybody!" she said.

"A three-hour tour," they sang, hesitantly.

"That sucked," said Sharisse. She looked at Lutefisk. "Get to work on the money, Sven. The clock is ticking. And have somebody bring me a satellite phone. I need to make some calls."

I spent the next two hours standing on the bridge with my hand in my pocket while Sharisse yakked on the phone a few feet away. I didn't know who she was talking to, and she didn't tell me. There was a TV monitor on the bridge tuned to international CNN. Horkman and I were on the screen basically all the time; they had worked our pictures into a logo that said AMERICA UNDER ATTACK. There was also a picture of the cruise ship, with a headline that said TERROR AT SEA; the passengers had found out that they'd been hijacked and were sending texts and e-mails to relatives back on land.

I watched a CNN anchorwoman, frowning so hard she cracked her makeup, interview a man labeled "Terror Expert." She asked him whether he expected the international terror gang, meaning me and Horkman, to strike again.

"I hate to add to the climate of fear," said the Terror Expert, "but yes, I believe they will strike again, probably soon. And they could strike anywhere. These are not bumbling amateurs; this is a highly organized, well-trained organization, led by a pair of very smart cold-blooded killers who have obviously been planning this operation for a long time while posing as ordinary suburban family men. These people managed to paralyze New York City and somehow escape from one of the most intense manhunts in NYPD history. Now, despite heightened security, they've taken over a cruise ship, which means they have more than two thousand hostages. God help those poor, innocent people if that bomb is detonated."

"One question about that," said the frowning anchorwoman. "Why can't the ship's crew find the bomb and just toss it overboard?"

"I'm sure they would if they could," answered the Terror Expert. "But a cruise ship is a huge, complex vessel. And remember that this man Peckerman is a highly trained forensic plumber. He would have detailed knowledge of the ship's plumbing infrastructure, and he could have hidden the device anywhere."

"Diabolical," said the anchor, frowning even deeper to show she meant it. "Thank you, Dr. Smeltwater, for those insights. Meanwhile, the entire nation remains on edge, wondering where the terror gang will strike next. Nowhere is the mood more tense than in New York City, which is still reeling from the recent wave of attacks. City wildlife authorities were finally able to recapture Hansel and Gretel, the two bears let loose from the Central Park Zoo by the terrorists during what experts believe was some kind of sexually deviant celebration ritual. In a highly dramatic scene this morning, the bears were felled by tranquilizer darts when they burst from a cluster of trees in

Central Park and attempted to attack Donald Trump, who was doing a remote appearance on *Good Morning America* in the park to discuss the terror attacks and promote his upcoming special all-transgender edition of *The Apprentice*. The bears are now safely back at the zoo, along with a third animal, a rare endangered lemur, which was also inexplicably in the area."

"Buddy," I said, to the screen.

"What?" said Sharisse, who had just finished a call.

"Nothing," I said. "Listen, how far are you planning to take this?"

"What do you mean?"

"I mean, you don't really think they're going to give us two hundred million dollars, do you?"

"Absolutely."

"Okay, say they do. How do we get away? Every cop in the United States will be looking for us."

"They were already looking for you, and you got away, right? You and your terrorist friend."

"I told you, *we're not terrorists*. I'm a fucking *plumber*."

Sharisse looked at the TV, still showing me and Horkman, international terrorist kingpins. "Right," she said. "You're a plumber. And I'm Hillary Clinton."

"I'm *serious*."

"Fine. Stick to that story. I don't give a shit. The point is, the money's coming."

"Great. So we'll be rich until the ship gets to port. Then we'll be in jail."

"No, we won't. We'll be welcomed with open arms."

"What the fuck are you talking about?"

"I'm talking about where we're going," she said, holding up the phone. "It's all arranged. They're very excited to meet you."

"Who is? Where the hell are we going?"

Sharisse only smiled.

CHAPTER 27

Philip

I was standing now. My legs were incredibly wobbly, but I'd somehow staggered to my feet, and Maria and I were looking at each other but not saying a word. For about a minute. Overwhelmed by the fact, by the impossible odds, by the miracle that must've occurred to have the both of us survive a night in the raging waters of the Caribbean and then deliver us onto this beach.

"How is it that you're here?" she asked.

I'd forgotten how beautiful she was. Especially when compared to the faux Maria I had tried to save from drowning. The Maria with the hairy back, the breastless chest, and the penis-toting crotch.

"I jumped off the ship to try to save you."

She smiled. Then we hugged. Then I collapsed to the ground because my wobbly legs gave out on me.

"You okay?" she asked, laughing.

"By any chance, would you happen to have a long string on you?"

"String?"

"To tie around me and a big stake in the ground so I won't topple over. Like you do when you're growing tomato plants."

Laughing again, she extended her hand and helped me back onto my feet. Still holding hands, we started walking.

"Any idea where we are?" I asked.

"None whatsoever," she said. "There are a lot of islands in the Caribbean that you never hear about. Some are privately owned. And some of them are uninhabited."

Uninhabited appealed to me. For the time being, anyway, as it would offer a much-needed respite from the uneasiness you feel when inhabited places are filled with people who think you're a hunted terrorist. Besides, how often does the fantasy of being stranded on a deserted island with a beautiful woman actually materialize in real life? A beautiful woman that if you ended up sleeping with her it wouldn't affect your marriage, as your wife would just roll her eyes when you told her, "Hey, guess what? I had sex with a nun on a deserted island," and then change the subject to her mother's new titanium hip.

Unfortunately, that break from other humans was short-lived. Because as we walked a little farther, hearing no sounds other than the ones the sea was making and the words of our own sparse conversation, we suddenly heard voices. Faint at first. But with each step we took toward a small bluff that rose beyond the water's edge, they got louder. A small group of people. A small group of people in what sounded like a chorus of plaintive murmurings. Responsive incantations, as if in prayer. With one voice in particular wailing above those of the others.

I looked at Maria, who seemed to have a better sense of the urgency we were overhearing. She said nothing, but started walking faster. Up the slight incline and through some brush, before coming upon five women on their knees, rocking back and forth with their focus alternating between the heavens and a young boy lying on the ground in front of them.

From the looks of him, I gathered that he was about fourteen years old. I also gathered that something was terribly wrong, as he was hardly breathing, his eyes were dilated, his skin had large black blotches on it, and there was foam frothing at his mouth. I also immediately recognized that these women were speaking Spanish, which was fortunate as I'd taken Spanish II my sophomore, junior and senior years in high school, so communication would not be a problem. When they saw Maria and me emerge from the forest, they fell silent.

"Lo siento, pero la biblioteca está á la izquerida," I said to them.

Maria looked at me and smiled.

"Philip, may I ask you what you're doing?"

"Trying to instill some confidence in these women, who are obviously upset about that young boy," I whispered.

"By telling them you're sorry that the library is on the left?"

Right there was still another reason I was so attracted to Maria. She had just called me an idiot without using the word "idiot." That had never happened before.

"Do you speak Spanish?" I asked.

"Yes," she answered. "Fluently."

"Hablamos Inglés," said one of the wailing women.

"But I don't think I'm going to have to speak Spanish," said Maria.

"Why?" I asked.

"Because that woman just said that they speak English."

"She said in Spanish that they speak English?"

"Yes," said Maria.

"Why would she do that?" I asked. "Why wouldn't she say in English that they speak English?"

"Maybe because she didn't know that *we* speak English."

"Then how did she know to even tell us that they spoke English?"

"Maybe she just assumed we did after she heard how you spoke Spanish."

Again I was an idiot without being called one, and I think I would've kissed her right then had our attention not been drawn back to the women, who resumed their wailing over the fallen boy, who was now making the same sounds an old car makes when it has post-ignition syndrome.

"What happened?" Maria asked the woman who was wailing louder than the others.

She told Maria that her son had been bitten by a spider and that their village's doctor was on his way with medicine. She also told her that the village was about an hour away.

"This kid won't last an hour," I told Maria. "I've seen this before."

"Where?" she asked.

I looked around. Back at the woods we'd just walked through to get here from the beach.

"I'll tell you later," I said. "Right now, have these women make a fire. I don't care how they do it. Aim the sun's reflection on a mirror toward a piece of paper, or try to create friction between a flint and a rock, or rub two sticks together . . ."

"How about these?" asked one of the wailing women, showing a book of matches she'd just taken from her pocket.

"Matches would also work," I said, before telling Maria to have them boil water once they got the fire going.

"What for?" she asked

"I'll tell you later," I said, before asking Maria to then put the boiling water in a cup or some vessel from which a person can drink.

"Let me guess," she said. "You'll tell me later."

"No, I'll tell you now. I want to make tea," I said, and then ran back into the forest and found an old oak tree whose protruding bark made it easy for me to remove small sections of it with my hands. I grabbed a few pieces, placed them on a flat stone that was embedded in the ground, found a rock with a sharp edge and started pounding the white oak bark until it was crushed into tiny pieces. Not a fine powder, which would've been preferable, but still small enough that when I sprinted back to the wailing women and mixed it with the hot water, I was confident it would be effective when I lifted the young boy's head and carefully had him sip the brew.

"The active ingredients of oak bark, especially tannin, make it an herbal cure for a lot of medical conditions, including the effects of insect bites," I told Maria. "I'm just hoping it's not too late for it to handle that spider's toxins."

Maria was looking at me with a combination of awe and disbelief. "What other ailments does it cure?"

"Internal bleeding, bladder infections, hemorrhoids . . ."

Big mistake. Because upon hearing the word "hemorrhoids," all five of the wailing women raised their hands and asked that I make tea for them as well.

"You said you've seen this before," said Maria. "May I ask where?"

"In my pet shop. I once ordered two tropical parrots, and a brown recluse spider had somehow gotten into the crate, and that's when I learned about Dengue Shock Syndrome, which is what I believe this young man has."

"Were you able to save the parrots?"

"Oh yeah. The spider didn't bother the birds at all. But he bit my assistant, Hyo, who started looking like this kid until the owner of the GNC in my strip mall came in and gave him some of this stuff until the ambulance arrived."

And that's what happened here. After the second cup, the young boy's high fever apparently dropped, and he slowly started to show signs of awareness by the time a jeep pulled up with two men in it. The passenger was obviously the doctor, as he jumped from his seat before it came to a full stop and raced to the boy's side, while the driver was met by the mother of the ailing boy, who spoke to him and then pointed to me.

After checking on the boy and getting the doctor's assurance that he was going to be all right, the kid's father approached and hugged me while crying his thanks. I introduced him to Maria and he invited the two of us to his home for dinner as a way of showing his appreciation. We accepted.

"By the way, where are we?" asked Maria.

He smiled and said, "Cuba."

CHAPTER 28

Jeffrey

I'll say this: When you hijack a cruise ship, you eat well.

Of course, you eat well even if you're a regular passenger. They feed you, like, eight times a day, which is why cruise people always look like hairless water buffalo wearing sneakers.

But when you take over a ship with a bomb threat, you really go first-class. Whatever Sharisse and I asked for, it got delivered to us right away—steak, lobster, shrimp, chocolate mousse, you name it. We washed it down with a couple of bottles of Dom, and then—this was Sharisse's idea—we both steered the ship for a while. Lutefisk didn't like that, but fuck him, he didn't have the remote control.

Another thing we did to pass the time while we were waiting for the money helicopter was make announcements over the ship's PA system. I'd get on there and say, "Emergency! We're about to tip over! Everybody run to the left side of the ship!" And then a little while later, Sharisse would get on there and say, "We are now going to have a mandatory penis inspection. We want all the men to line up on the poop deck according to length." And the thing was, those morons actually *did* it.

But the funniest thing we did—this was also Sharisse's idea—was to make the officers strip down to their underwear, then march down to the ship's theater and put on costumes. The main show was *South Pacific*, so we had Lutefisk and his men wear grass skirts and coconut brassieres. They looked like total douchebags. For me, that really lightened the tension of being a wanted international terrorist.

While we were at the theater, we saw that the headline entertainer on the ship was Charo, so we told the crew to go get her. She didn't want to be there, and at first she refused to perform for us, but she changed her mind when Sharisse fired a warning shot through her guitar. That got her up on stage pretty quick, and she sang a song, which was in Spanish, so I don't know what it was about, except she seemed to be singing it mainly to Sharisse and it had a word that sounded like "poota" in it a lot. When she finished, Sharisse gave her a five-dollar tip, which I thought was hilarious, but Charo was definitely pissed. She's getting old, and when you look at her up close, her eyes are a little too close together, but I'll give her this: she still has a nice rack.

The point being, Sharisse and I actually had a pretty good time that night, considering the situation. I was starting to really like Sharisse as I got to know her as a human being instead of just a lawyer/hijacker; she definitely showed her fun side. I'll be honest: I was starting to think maybe she and I might have a future together, seeing as how Donna would probably never take me back after all this, and Sharisse's husband was shark chow.

We stayed up all night, thanks to some pills we got from the ship's doctor. The next morning, just like Sharisse predicted, the helicopter came. We went up to the helipad deck with Lutefisk, just the three of us, Sharisse making sure the chopper guys could see she had a gun pointed at Lutefisk. She had the whole thing figured out. When the chopper touched down, she told the crew to stay inside and toss the money out. They heaved a couple of duffel bags out.

"Open them," Sharisse told me.

I unzipped the duffels and looked inside. They were both jammed with packets of hundred-dollar bills.

"Is it all there?" Sharisse asked.

"How the fuck would I know?" I said.

She laughed so hard, she banged the gun barrel into Lutefisk's head. We were definitely developing a rapport. "Good point," she said.

"I'll tell you this," I said. "There's definitely a shitload of money."

Sharisse signaled the chopper to take off.

"All right," said Lutefisk. "You got your money. Now you will give me my ship back."

"Sven," said Sharisse. "You don't give the orders. You're a schmo wearing a coconut bra. *We* give the orders on this ship."

I liked that, the way she said "we."

"This is unacceptable!" said Lutefisk. "We have done everything you asked!"

"And you're going to *keep* doing everything we ask," said Sharisse, "or Jeffrey and I are going to get into a lifeboat and blow up this crate, and you'll be famous forever as the captain who lost his ship while dressed like a hostess at Trader Vic's."

That shut Sven up. I really had to admire Sharisse: The woman had balls. She was so convincing, I had to remind myself that we didn't actually have a bomb.

"All right," said Sharisse. "Let's get this money downstairs, and Sven here can get this ship pointed toward Havana."

"*What?*" said Sven and I, pretty much simultaneously.

"We're going to Havana," said Sharisse.

"We are?" I said.

"But we cannot go to Havana!" said Lutefisk. "The Cuban government—"

"The Cuban government is expecting us," said Sharisse, giving me a look that said *No more questions.*

And so we went to Cuba. It took us six hours, with CNN, Fox, and the rest of the news networks covering every second. They were showing aerial shots of our ship, and you could see that there were big U.S. navy vessels surrounding us, just out of sight over the horizon. Also there reportedly were submarines in the area, including some from China and Russia. There were all kinds of Terrorism Experts on TV, and they were going nuts, throwing out theories about what was happening, what our plan was, what the U.S. should do, what would happen next. Everybody agreed that tensions in the Caribbean had not been this high since the Cuban Missile Crisis. Sharisse and I had a couple more bottles of Dom.

When we got close to Havana, it seemed like the entire Cuban navy came out to meet us, plus a bunch of fighter jets. We went into the harbor and dropped anchor. A bunch of Cuban navy boats came alongside, and in a few minutes the ship was swarming with soldiers carrying machine guns. Sharisse and I waited on the bridge, with our money and the officers. A group of soldiers came in and looked over the situation, and when they decided it was safe, they gave a signal, and a tall officer came in.

"I am Major Nunez, of the Cuban Revolutionary Armed Forces," he said, speaking English with a very slight Spanish accent. "Who is the captain of this ship?"

"I am," said Lutefisk. He stepped forward, and as he did the left side of his coconut brassiere slipped down, revealing his left nipple. He shoved the coconut back into place. He didn't want to look unprofessional.

Lutefisk pointed at Sharisse and me. "These people are criminals," he said. "They have placed a bomb aboard this ship. That man has a detonator."

Major Nunez looked at me and said, "Is this true?"

"Give it to him," said Sharisse.

I reached into my pocket, pulled out the remote control and

tossed it to him. He caught it, looked at it, and tossed it to Lutefisk. Lutefisk caught it and looked at it for a few seconds. Then he said something I didn't understand, which I'm guessing was Norwegian for "motherfucker."

Nunez smiled a little.

"Mr. Peckerman, I presume?" he said.

I nodded.

"And this is Mrs. Fricker?"

Sharisse smiled and made a little curtsy.

"Welcome to Cuba," said Nunez. "The comandante is expecting you."

CHAPTER 29

Philip

The man's name was Ramon. His spider-bitten son was Ramon Jr. His wailing wife was Ramona.

"I wonder if they ever get confused," I yelled to Maria.

We were sitting next to each other in the backseat of the jeep that was taking us to their home. But even by yelling we could barely hear each other over the grunting of its engines and the noises the tires made as it sped along the top of a primitive road.

"Why would they get confused?" she yelled back. "To them, they are Mom, Dad, and Junior. I don't see a problem."

I had never been in the backseat of a jeep before. Or in the front seat. So I guess you could say this was my first time in a jeep.

"What about mail?" I asked. "What happens when a letter comes to the house and it's addressed to Ramon, but the sender meant for it to go to Ramon Jr.?"

My arm was around her. And when I pulled her closer so she could hear me, her head stayed on my shoulder.

"In that case, when Ramon realizes the mistake, he hands the letter to his son and simply says, 'This is for you.'" She was smiling. "You okay now, Philip?"

"I think so."

The jeep pulled off the dirt road and onto a potholed paved one that was just as bumpy. We looked out, and on either side what we saw could only be described as squalor. Run-down stores, abandoned gas stations with bone-dry pumps, white curtains in the windows of decrepit buildings attempting to make things look homey. And when we turned off that road into Ramon, Ramon Jr., and Ramona's neighborhood, we entered what was basically a suburban version of the shabbiness we'd just seen.

"I hope you like *quesadilla de harina de yuca rellena con camarones y queso*," said Ramona as we walked on a gravel path from the driveway to the front door. "That's what I make for dinner every Monday."

I was hungry. Famished, in fact. So hungry I could eat a *quesadilla de harina de yuca rellena con camarones y queso* no matter what that was.

The inside of the house was somewhat more cheerful than the outside, thanks to the good intentions of the colorful rugs and threadbare furniture sitting on them. And to the framed pictures of a smiling Ramon, Ramona, and Ramon Jr. in formation on top of end tables. And to Nacho, a frisky mutt that needed approximately five more pounds on him to be considered scrawny. And to the rumba melodies coming through the single speaker on a triangular shelf nailed into the corner where two walls met.

Yes, it was home sweet home to a happy family protected by the statuettes of a watchful Jesus deployed about the room. And by the arsenal of machine guns that were stacked from floor to ceiling in their kitchen. And bathroom.

"I just flushed the toilet and almost shot my ass off," I whispered to Maria.

"What's this all about?" she whispered in response.

"Don't let this number of weapons throw you," said Ramon, who'd obviously taken notice of our reactions. "There's plenty more in the shed out back. Grenades, too."

"Oh, good," I heard myself saying. "I was worrying there wasn't enough firepower."

"What the hell are you talking about?" Maria whispered to me.

"I'd just humor him," I whispered back. "He may be dangerous. By the way, I can't remember the last time I whispered this much."

"We are a happy family, but it is time for us to become happier," said Ramon as the smell of what I could only assume was *quesadilla de harina de yuca rellena con camarones y queso* came wafting from the huge tray Ramona was carrying into the dining room.

"Now is the time for my family and all the other families who've been under the heels of this man to live the lives our fathers died for," Ramona continued.

"What man are you talking about?" asked Maria.

"The Premier," he answered. "In 1959, his *own* father led the revolution and then became a worse dictator than the one he overthrew."

"The average Cuban today lives on twenty dollars a month and relies on government ration cards," said Ramona, who was now setting the table.

"This will soon change. And we'll discuss this all at dinner," said Ramon. He then added, "Those *quesadilla de harina de yuca rellena con camarones y queso* sure look good," while trying to grab one off of the huge tray.

"You'll spoil your appetite!" said Ramona slapping her husband's hand away. "He really loves my *quesadilla de harina de yuca rellena con camarones y queso*," she told us. "If it were up to him, he'd have *quesadilla de harina de yuca rellena con camarones y queso* every meal. Sometimes I think he married me because of my *quesadilla de harina de yuca rellena con camarones y queso*."

They both laughed as if this was a joke they always shared. Maria and I felt it right to laugh as well. Like idiots. It was about then that I noticed how many place settings Ramona was putting on the table.

"I wonder if other people are joining us for dinner," I said to Maria.

"Well, there's you and me, the two of them makes four, and if Ramon Jr. has recovered enough to join us it makes five."

"Okay, but the table's set for eight," I said.

"Let us celebrate," said Ramon, who then took a bottle of wine out of a cabinet and took the cork out with a knife he pulled from a sheath attached to his belt.

"To our son's good health," said Ramona, with a nod in our direction.

"And to the coming revolution," Ramon said, while pouring.

Maria and I looked at each other, but said nothing, as he handed his wife and the two of us our filled glasses. And as the four of us lifted them, he completed his toast.

"And to the Lord for delivering you to us at this exact time, Señor Horkman."

Before I had a chance to react, the front door opened and the other dinner guests arrived. A tall man we would come to know as Nunez, followed by, of all people, Peckerman and Sharisse Fricker, who were as shocked to see us as we were to see them.

"Our liberators are here!" proclaimed Ramon, pointing to me and Peckerman.

Nunez raised his fist in agreement.

"They will lead us to our victory, Comandante."

CHAPTER 30

Jeffrey

This was definitely not what Sharisse and I had in mind, winding up in some rural Cuban shack in some rural Cuban area with a bunch of rural Cubans. What we had in mind was a whole different scenario, which was this:

We would land in Cuba with the two hundred mil. We would make a deal with the Cuban government, give them a nice commission for their trouble. Let's say 20 percent, which is $40 million. Then Sharisse and I would proceed to live like kings, because $160 million goes a long way in a shithole like Cuba, where the average person makes, like, eighty-seven cents a month. We could pay them way better, say five bucks a month, and they'd be like, "Wow! Let's give them excellent service! *Nacho gusto!*" (I took some Spanish in high school.)

This was actually Sharisse's scenario. When she explained it to me on the ship going to Havana, I had a couple of questions, the main one being: Was she *nuts*? Why would the Cuban government go along? I mean, they have an army, right? Why not just point machine guns at us and say, "Thanks, but we'll take the whole two hundred mil. You two can go to prison and survive by eating each other's toenails."

That's what I would do, if I had machine guns, and a couple of bozos showed up with a ship they hijacked with a remote control.

But Sharisse said, "That's not going to happen."

"Why not?"

"Because you're a dangerous international terrorist."

"But I'm not. I keep telling you that."

"And I'm starting to believe you. But the United States government says you are, and the Cubans believe you are. So they're going to show you some respect."

I still had my doubts, but when we got to Havana, everything seemed to go exactly the way Sharisse said it would. Nunez and his men didn't take the money; they let us keep the duffels as they escorted us off the ship to a convoy of military trucks lined up on the dock. We got into the middle one, us in back, Nunez and a driver in front. Then we took off, like a motorcade, which I assumed was going to the presidential palace. So far, so good. (Or, as the Spanish say, *Mi casa, su casa.*)

We drove through the city for a while, but we didn't see anything that looked like a palace. After about forty-five minutes, it began to dawn on us that we weren't going to the middle of the city: We were heading into the suburbs. The roads were getting shittier and shittier, worse even than the Brooklyn-Queens Expressway. Pretty soon we were bouncing along what that looked like a yak path.

Sharisse tapped Nunez on the shoulder. He turned around and said, "Yes?"

"Where the hell are we going?" she said.

"I assumed you knew," he said.

"You assumed wrong. Where are we going?"

He nodded toward me. "To see his comrade," he said.

"What?" I said. "*What* comrade?"

Nunez smiled. He had those really, really white teeth that some people just naturally have. It pisses me off, because I use whitening strips that cost so much that the drugstore keeps them locked in cabinets, like precious jewels, or nicotine gum. I've used enough of those strips to wallpaper my living room, and my teeth are still more or less the color of the margins of the Declaration of Independence.

What gets me is, I can remember when nobody gave a shit about this. You'd see people on TV, big stars, Johnny Carson for example, or Barbara Eden, and I'm not saying they had ugly teeth, but their teeth were not exceptional. You didn't *notice* their teeth, is my point. Their teeth were *human*. But now, in the entertainment industry, everybody's teeth are the color of a brand-new urinal. There's, like, a miniature men's room in their mouths. When they smile, they're giving skin cancer to people around them from the reflection. But *that's* what we're all supposed to look like now. *That's* why we're paying forty bucks a box for those stupid strips that probably cost eighteen cents to make and sting the hell out of your mouth. And you *still* have yellow teeth. And then you see some guy like Nunez, he lives on this shithole island where they don't even have drugstores, probably brushes his teeth with a sea urchin, and he has teeth like Tom Fucking Cruise. Which is why I was pissed off when he smiled at me the way he did when I said, "*What* comrade?"

"Please," said Nunez. "You do not have to play this game with me."

"*What* game?" I said. "I don't know what the hell you're talking about!"

Nunez nodded. "I understand," he said. "You will trust nobody but Ramon himself."

"Who's Ramon?" said Sharisse.

Nunez flashed his urinals at her. "So the lady is playing the game also. Fine. We will talk when we arrive."

"Arrive *where*?" I said. But Nunez had turned away; he was done talking.

We kept driving, and the road kept getting shittier. After a couple of hours, we came to a village, turned down a side road and stopped in front of a shack.

"We are here," said Nunez.

"*This* is where we're going?" said Sharisse. "An outhouse?"

Nunez only smiled. We got out of the truck, Sharisse and I grabbing the duffel bags. We followed Nunez into the shack. There were some people sitting at a table, including a Cuban guy who I figured was Ramon. He and Nunez said something to each other, but I wasn't paying attention. I was staring, with my mouth open, like a grouper, at another person at the table—the last person I expected to see, here or anywhere else. Horkman. He was with the woman who fell off the ship before he jumped.

"What the fuck?" I said.

"It's nice to see you, too," he said.

"How the hell did you get here?" I said.

"I swam," he said. He put his arm around Maria. "*We* swam."

I couldn't believe it. The asshole fucked up his own *death*.

Sharisse stepped forward, looking very tense. "What about Mike?" she said.

"Mike?" said Horkman.

"My husband."

Without saying a word, Horkman stood up, came over to Sharisse and grabbed her in a big hug. Then he held her at arms' length, gave her a big sad moony-face look, and said, "I'm afraid he didn't make it."

Sharisse relaxed. "Jesus," she said. "You had me worried there."

Ignoring Horkman's surprised look, she shoved him away, turned to Nunez and said, "Now that we're here, can you please tell us *why* we're here?"

Nunez looked at Ramon, who smiled. He also had really nice teeth. The prick.

"I assume you know already," he said, "and you are simply testing me to see how much *we* know. Fine. I will go along with this. I am the comandante of the People's Army of the People, which has been preparing to strike down the regime of the corrupt pig who has sucked the blood out of this nation."

"Waitwaitwait," said Sharisse, turning to Nunez. "Don't you *work* for the corrupt bloodsucking pig?"

"He believes I do," said Nunez. "The old fool trusts me. In fact, he personally ordered me to meet your ship. But by then Ramon had told me the *real* reason you were coming here."

"Which is what?" I said.

"Please," said Ramon. "We are not fools. First your comrade swims ashore, undetected by the authorities, and within hours is able to make contact with me, even though my location is a closely guarded secret."

"Horkman did that?" I said, looking at Horkman, who was looking puzzled.

"He is a highly skilled commando," said Ramon.

"He owns a pet store," I said. "Called The Wine Shop."

"Yes, of course, he has a cover story. But he is an extraordinary soldier."

"He's a putz," I said.

"That is a military rank, I assume," said Ramon. "I am unfamiliar with it. But to continue: Only hours after Señor Horkman swims ashore, you, his comrade, the famous Jeffrey Peckerman, arrive by the brilliant maneuver of hijacking a cruise ship, bringing with you enough American dollars to finance our cause."

"What?" said Sharisse and me, pretty much at the same time.

"For years," said Ramon, "we have been secretly sending out requests for help—hoping that somewhere in the world, we would find allies willing to fight with us. We had almost given up hope. But now you are here, Horkman and Peckerman, famous revolutionary fighters as seen on CNN. With your leadership, and with this great financial gift you have brought us, we can finally begin our fight." Ramon was pounding the table now, shouting, "We have waited long enough! We will not wait a moment longer! The revolution begins now! But first, we will enjoy Ramona's delicious *quesadilla de harina de yuca rellena con camarones y queso!*"

He shouted something in Spanish, and some soldiers came in and took away our duffel bags. Next thing we knew, we were sitting at the table, me across from Horkman, being served heaping plates of some Cuban glop that looked like they scraped it off the bottom of an aquarium while Ramon and Nunez toasted us. Outside, people were singing and firing guns into the air, getting ready for the revolution, which was going to start right after dinner. And which this asshole and I were supposed to lead.

CHAPTER 31

Philip

"I think we should wait till morning."

We were sitting in the dining room eating what I could only assume was dessert, for no reason other than it was an orange solid served alongside a cup of brown liquid that I could only assume was coffee.

I hardly touched my dinner, as I wasn't a fan of Latin cuisine. I'd eaten it for the first time about three years earlier when a restaurant called La Casa del Sol opened in the same strip mall as The Wine Shop. So, as a gesture of strip mall solidarity, I gave the place a few tries until it became evident that if I were going to continue eating there, I'd have to surgically line my large intestine with copper tubing to withstand the corrosive torrents careening through it after every meal.

"What should wait till morning?" asked Ramon, looking up with a mouthful of the orange solid.

"The revolution," I told him.

"But why?" asked Nunez, also with a mouthful of the orange solid in his mouth. Seated next to each other, with their mouths alternately opening and closing, they looked like warning lights at an intersection.

"Because it's been our experience that governments are more apt to fall in the daytime," I said, with every hope that the omnivore to my left (aka Peckerman) would take maybe ten seconds away from making sure there wasn't a morsel left on anyone's plate to hold up his end of the word "our" and chime in.

No such luck. So I ventured onward.

"It adds to the element of surprise," I explained.

"But isn't it more surprising to attack at night when everyone's sleeping?" asked Ramona.

"That's done so often these days that there's really no surprise. It's almost expected at this point," I told her. "But in the late morning, say eleven, maybe even eleven-thirty, when the regime you wish to overthrow is inside the very buildings you're looking to take over, it's so much more effective."

"At night you're just attacking empty offices," said Maria.

"Exactly," I said.

It felt good to hear a voice that wasn't my own. Especially Maria's. And from the nods now coming from the other side of the table, it looked like my stalling tactic, as feeble as it was, had a logic that Ramon and Nunez were willing to consider.

"We will follow your lead," Nunez said.

"We will go outside and tell the rebels to get a good night's sleep," said Ramon, as they left the table and walked toward the front door.

Dealing with Peckerman was another story. While Maria and that silicone-infused bimbette he was traipsing around with helped Ramona clear the table, I was off in a corner trying to knock some sense into him.

"I'm just trying to buy us some time so we can figure out how we can get out of this mess, Peckerman. Don't you get it? They think we know what we're doing and that we actually *want* to do what they think we're doing."

"I know that. But it's you who doesn't get it, Horkman. I want them to think that you've got the brains and that I'm the dumb one—like those guys Lenny and Squiggy in *Of Mice and Men*."

"You mean Lennie and George."

"Lenny and George?"

In the millisecond between the time I heard him say that and when my lips got into position to respond, I was somehow able to mentally scroll down the list of the biggest imbeciles I've ever met and saw Peckerman's name sprout wings and fly to the top.

"Peckerman, Lenny and Squiggy were the goofy sitcom characters who lived upstairs from Laverne and Shirley. Lennie and George were the migrant farmworkers in the novel *Of Mice and Men* by the Pulitzer Prize–winning author John Steinbeck. I pray you can appreciate the difference."

Maria and Sharisse came back to the dining room table and grabbed some more plates. Apparently Peckerman caught my gaze that followed Maria back to the kitchen.

"Fuck her yet?"

"Excuse me?"

"The nun. A word to the wise, Horkman. Nuns consider themselves married to God, so I'd watch my step if I were you," he said, pointing skyward. "That is one jealous husband you don't want to piss off. He's God, for God's sake! Fucking guy can turn your dick into a fried wonton just like that," he said while snapping his stubby little fingers.

"Do you have to talk that way, Peckerman?"

"What way?"

"Your choice of words. Effing this. Effing that. Especially when you're talking about nuns and God . . ."

"I never said 'effing,' Horkman. I said 'fucking' . . ."

"I know what you said."

"So if you're going to quote me, I'd like for you to quote me accurately."

"Fine."

"Fine?"

"Yeah, fine."

"Then say it, Horkman. Say 'fucking.'"

"No."

"No? You just said fine."

"Cut it out, Peckerman."

"Come on, Horkman. You're an adult male who has a mortgage and a pet shop, so there's no reason whatsoever for you to say 'effing' like you're some choirboy who's going to get cornholed by a priest who thinks that if you say 'fuck' it's a request. Now say it, damn you! Say 'fuck'!"

And then, without warning, he lunged and wrestled me to the floor like I was a rodeo steer and proceeded to pummel me while yelling, "Say it! Say it, you weasel!" until Ramon, now with a rifle slung over his shoulder, came back into the house also yelling "Say it!"

"Huh?" Peckerman and I said in unison, as Ramon pulled him off me and helped us both to our feet.

"You heard me!" shouted Ramon. "Go out there and say to them what you said to us. That we should wait till morning before we go to the capital city, because they're ready now, but maybe they'll listen to you because of who you are."

He then motioned us out the front door, where we suddenly found ourselves staring into the face of a mob of maybe a hundred excited rebels who were raising rifles and torches and upon seeing us, much to my horror, began cheering *Vive El Horkman!* and *Vive El Peckerman!*

"Well, I guess they think you're a more important terrorist because they said your name first," whispered Peckerman, with a tone that simply reeked of jealousy. "Either that or they're chanting in alphabetical order."

"Yeah, that must be it," I said, with just enough sarcasm to make him even more jealous.

"For the most part, they speak Spanish," Nunez told us. "So let them hear your voices and I will tell them what you've said."

". . . Okay," I heard myself saying, and then felt the two of them staring at me and Peckerman as we each fell silent with hopes that the other would speak first.

"You first," Peckerman finally said.

"Why me?" I asked.

"Because they're not chanting in alphabetical order," he said, like the whiney turd that he was.

I then looked out at the mob, extended my arms, and patted the air downward as a signal for them to be quiet. They did.

"Big shot," I heard Peckerman say under his breath.

"All people should be free!" I shouted before Nunez shouted its Spanish translation to the crowd, who became vocal again upon hearing it.

"They should be free because they're endowed by their creator with certain unalienable rights, including life, liberty and the pursuit of happiness!" I proclaimed with every hope that very few of the people in this raucous mob had recently taken a look at our Declaration of Independence.

Apparently they hadn't, as Nunez's translation stirred them even more so.

"And toward that end, every government should be dedicated to the proposition that all men are created equal!" I went on to say with every hope that the mob hadn't recently taken a look at Lincoln's Gettysburg Address.

This time Nunez's translation caused them to cheer louder.

"So, give me liberty or give me death!" I shouted with every hope that Cuba's public school system didn't deem it important to spend an inordinate amount of time teaching their barefoot students about Patrick Henry.

And this time Nunez's translation managed to bring the crowd's passions to a glorious crescendo as the very thought of their impending freedom simultaneously ignited a celebration of singing and dancing combined with the mounting cries of *"Cuando? Cuando?"* which even I knew meant *"When?"* and was the actual reason that Ramon had brought us outside to begin with.

"Cuan-do? Cuan-do?" The crowd's single voice kept growing louder.

"Well . . . ?" Ramon asked.

"Cuan-do? Cuan-do?"

"What shall I tell them?" Nunez wanted to know.

"Cuan-do? Cuan-do?"

So I guess now would be a good time to tell you that what happened next still stuns me to this very day. For at the exact moment I was about to answer the mob's rallying cry of *"Cuando"* by shouting *"Mañana,"* that idiot Peckerman, who'd remained mercifully quiet thus far, pointed to a group of rebels who were celebrating by holding hands while dancing in a circle and shouted at the top of his hideous lungs, *"A hora!"* which is an Israeli folk dance—though it was only natural that a Spanish-speaking mob, who'd just asked when they should start the revolution, heard it as *Ahora!* which means "Now!" and then let out loud cries of *"Vive El Horkman!"* and *"Vive El Peckerman!"* as they turned on their heels and headed toward the capital.

CHAPTER 32

Jeffrey

I'll be honest: I didn't know Cubans could be Jewish. But it turns out at least some of them are, because while Horkman was giving his asshole speech they started dancing the hora, and then all of a sudden the whole mob of them was running down the road waving their guns.

I thought, Okay, good, they're going off to get killed. Time for me to find Sharisse and the duffel bags and get the hell out of here. But before I took two steps, a truck roared up, and Ramon and Nunez and their men shoved me and Horkman into a middle seat. There were Cubans with guns all around us, so forget about getting away.

I looked around for Sharisse, and spotted her behind us. She was getting into another truck with some Cubans, who happened to be carrying, guess what, the duffel bags. I'm yelling, "Sharisse! Hey!" But she was talking to the Cubans and didn't hear me, or she pretended she didn't hear me. She was definitely sticking her boobs out.

The truck took off, and we were bouncing down the road, Horkman squashing into me every two seconds like a big sack of duck shit. In front of us, Ramon and Nunez were talking to each other in

Spanish. After a few minutes, they turned around, and yelled something in Spanish to the guys behind us, who yelled something in Spanish back.

Next thing I knew, they were handing me and Horkman guns.

I don't know anything about guns. The only time I ever used one was in fifth grade, when Brian Krepmer and I stole his brother's BB gun and I shot the UPS man in the ass, and he pounded on the door and told Mrs. Krepmer he was never going to deliver anything to their house again, which meant she had to quit her Amway business, which was actually a relief to the rest of the neighborhood, but Brian and I were both grounded for two weeks anyway.

But this thing the Cubans gave me was a whole different level of gun. It was heavy and had a lot of parts and looked like it was maybe for shooting down airplanes. I looked over at Horkman and whispered, "What do they think we're going to do with these?"

"Lead them into battle," he whispered back.

"I'm not leading them anywhere," I said. "I wouldn't lead them into a Chick-fil-A. I don't even know how to *shoot* this fucking thing."

Now, at this point, if you have been paying attention, you already know that Horkman is the biggest douchebag in the history of vaginal hygiene. But you can't really comprehend the true magnitude of how *big* a douchebag he is until I tell you what happened next. What happened was, instead of helping me solve the problem at hand, namely, we're with a bunch of lunatic Cubans trying to get us all killed, this imbecile moron *showed me how to shoot my gun.*

"I think all you do is take off the safety," he said, leaning over and flipping something. "Then it's just a matter of—"

At that exact moment, the truck hit a pothole the size of Long Island Sound, and Horkman went flying sideways onto my lap. I don't know whose finger pulled the trigger. Could have been him; could have been me. Could have been his dick, for that matter. All I know is, while Horkman was on top of me, my gun started shooting. And not just one bullet. A *lot* of bullets.

Then things happened fast:

First of all, Horkman screamed like a girl into my ear. I figured this was him getting shot, but it later turned out he wasn't, unfortunately.

Next, the truck made a sharp left-hand turn into the jungle. This was because the driver had bailed out, along with Nunez, Ramon and the other Cubans, who were interested in not getting shot.

Next, I pushed Horkman off me, and the gun finally stopped shooting, and Horkman fell out of the truck, still screaming.

So I was alone in a driverless truck, smashing through all kinds of trees and branches, and suddenly it burst into a clearing and OH GOD right ahead I saw a canyon. There was no time for me to bail; the truck went right over the edge. I could see down into the canyon. There was a shallow river on the bottom, but mostly big rocks. I knew I was going to die. You know how they say that when you're about to die, your whole life flashes before your eyes? Well, they're full of shit. Because I was in that exact situation, and all I thought was, *This is totally Horkman's fault.*

That's when Spider-Man showed up.

He wasn't the actual Spider-Man, of course. He didn't have the gay spandex costume; he was wearing dark clothes and a dark wool cap, and his face was painted black. But he definitely had Spider-Man skills. He dove off the side of the canyon, grabbed me in mid-fucking-air out of the truck with one hand, and yelled "Hold on!" Then he yanked something on his backpack with his other hand, and suddenly there was a parachute wing over us, and we're swooping down to the river. The truck hit first; it landed on some rocks and exploded, just like in the movies. I could feel the heat from the fire when we went over it. We landed in water that was maybe two feet deep, both of us going under for a second. The guy yanked me to my feet, shoved me and yelled, "MOVE!" I stumbled down the river to a break in the canyon wall. The guy shoved me in there.

"Stay here," he said. "And keep quiet." He had a knife strapped to his leg that looked like it could decapitate a mastodon. I kept quiet.

A few seconds later, the end of a rope slapped the ground next to me. The spider-guy grabbed it and quickly tied it around me in some kind of harness.

"Hang on," he said, and next thing I know, I was being hauled up the canyon wall. When I got to the top, I saw who was hauling me up: more spider-guys. There were five of them, including the guy who rescued me, who climbed the rope after they got me up.

We were now in some bushes on the far side of the canyon from where the truck went off. Peering through the bushes, I could see a bunch of Cubans on the other side, including Ramon and Nunez, looking down at the burning truck. I could also see Horkman with them.

I looked around at the spider-guys and said, "Who are you guys?"

"We'll ask the questions," answered my rescuer. He definitely had an American accent. Suddenly it hit me who these guys had to be.

"Jesus," I said. "Are you Navy SEAL Team 6?"

One of them snorted. "We call Navy SEAL Team 6 the Campfire Girls," he said.

"So who *are* you?" I said.

He took a step closer and said, "Did you ever hear of the U.S. Coast Guard Salamander Unit 9?"

"No," I said.

"Good," he said. "Because we don't exist."

CHAPTER 33

Philip

By now you know I am not a negative man. And that I have never used the misfortunes of others as a salve for my own shortcomings. No, I was brought up to believe happiness can best be attained when a person makes an honest self-evaluation, sets realistic goals, then works his butt off to make them come to pass. So in the end, a man's contentment is his own responsibility, unaffected by the fates of those around him.

That said, I would be less than honest if I didn't say that when I saw that driverless truck go over that cliff with Peckerman inside and then burst into flames after crashing to the bottom of that ravine, my gut reaction was a profound regret that a driverless truck with Peckerman inside didn't crash and burst into flames on his way to that AYSO championship soccer game so I would never have met him after I called his daughter offside (which she was, by the way) and become a wanted international criminal enmeshed in a foreign war. So I confess I was not altogether heartbroken as I stood at the edge of the ravine, staring down at the burning truck.

Next to me, Ramon and Nunez spoke a few hurried words to each other. With my limited Spanish, I was able to gather that they thought that we'd been attacked by enemy snipers; apparently they weren't aware that it was Peckerman's gun that had done the shooting. Concerned about being targets, they turned and trotted back into the safety of the trees.

Alone now, I lingered a moment longer, looking down at the flaming wreckage, thinking about the horrible fate that had fallen Peckerman.

Then I saw something even more horrifying.

Peckerman was still alive.

Somehow, impossibly, he had escaped the crash and was now standing with some other men on the far side of the ravine. I glanced behind me; no sign of Nunez or Ramon. I climbed down into the ravine and, with some effort, made my way up the other side, where Peckerman and I had a joyful reunion. If you think I am being sarcastic, I am, because what he said to me was, "Thanks a lot, asshole."

"For what?" I said.

"Shooting my gun, dickwad. I'd be a dead man if Spider-Man here hadn't saved me." He pointed at one of the half-dozen tough-looking uniformed men standing nearby, observing us.

I was going to point out that it wasn't my finger that had pulled the trigger, but I was more curious about the men. "Who are they?" I asked.

"They're Salamanders," he said.

"They're what?"

"Salamanders."

"No offense"—I nodded politely at the tough-looking men—"but I never heard of them."

"That's because they don't exist," said Peckerman. "At least that's what they tell me. Seems to me they have to exist, because there they are."

"Peckerman, you idiot, it's a figure of speech. They must be such a secret unit that no one knows about them."

"But now we do," he said.

"And if you tell anyone, we'll have to kill you," said one of the Salamanders, apparently the leader. I got the distinct impression that he was dead serious, but Peckerman, imbecile that he is, laughed. A hardy, derisive laugh. With his ridiculous head pitching this way and that—as if he'd somehow left his neck muscles back at Ramon, Ramona, and Ramon Jr.'s house.

"You think that's funny?" asked the lead Salamander.

"Not at all," Peckerman answered. "'If you tell anyone, we'll have to kill you,'" he said, mimicking. "Jesus, you couldn't come up with anything more original than that? You've been watching too many movies."

Another derisive laugh or two later, after the laws of physics were kind enough to make his bobbing head eventually slow to a halt, Peckerman swiveled it in my direction.

"What crawled up your ass and ate your vocabulary?" he asked.

With the Salamanders now surrounding us, I chose each of the following words like they were vials of plutonium. As though they had the incendiary power to explode and launch chunks of me and Peckerman skyward, before they ultimately rained back down and hung like ornaments from the nearby foliage once they returned from their missions high above the Earth's surface.

"First of all, Peckerman, they just saved your life, so I'm thinking something that even resembles a 'thank you' may be in order. Secondly, unless I'm misreading the angles of the guns these gentlemen are pointing at us, the phrase 'we'll have to kill you' is not a figure of speech the way 'we don't exist' was a figure of speech." I then turned to the Salamanders and said, "I'm helping him bone up on his figures of speech."

Apparently the Salamanders couldn't care less what kind of linguistic lesson I was conducting. They stared at me in unified non-acknowledgment for about ten frightening seconds before retreating deeper into the jungle, where they began having an animated conversation.

Peckerman then leaned toward me, cupped his hand to his mouth and began speaking in hushed tones, which made absolutely no sense to me.

"I don't want them to overhear us," he explained.

"But they're thirty yards away and they're not whispering and we don't hear them."

"Point taken," he said, and then lowered his cupped hand but continued to whisper. "Look, I've already figured out that they're Americans."

"Me too."

"From their accents, right?"

"That and the American flag patches on their sleeves," I said, nodding.

Peckerman looked over at the six Salamanders and, apparently for the first time, noticed the patches.

"Fine," he said. "So anyway, if they're really a secret operative, it means our country is helping overthrow the Cuban government, the way we do in a lot of countries."

I agreed with him. It seemed obvious that was the objective. In recent years, democracy had come to so many other suppressed nations around the world and it made sense that it was now Cuba's turn. But I was also affected by Peckerman's referring to the United States as "our country." Was it still? As far as I was concerned it was. I'd always been a devoted American who voted every November and watched football every Sunday and had a flag proudly waving on my lawn every national holiday. But now that I was considered to be a threat to the way of life of the country I loved, I was a man without a home.

From there my thoughts took me to my kids, and I wondered if

they were worried sick about me. Or if they were actually happy
about the absence of a reviled father who'd let them down. And
branded them forever. Like Osama bin Laden Jr. would've been
branded if Osama bin Laden had a son and named him Osama bin
Laden Jr. Or if Lee Harvey Oswald had a son and named him Osama
bin Laden Jr.

As for Daisy. Well, a part of me wondered if she'd find a new man.
We were high school sweethearts. The first and only lovers each of us
had. But now? Like all marriages over the course of a long run, ours
had a fair amount of peaks and valleys—but I couldn't help feel that
this current valley was one we might never emerge from.

Then again, did I even want us to? What about Maria? Where was
she? I wondered. The last time I saw her was the night before. After
the rally outside Ramon's house. After he and Nunez shoved me and
Peckerman into that truck. And after Sharisse and those duffel bags
filled with money and those breasts filled with enough rubber to
erase the Empire State Building entered the back of that other truck
with those Cuban rebels. I saw Maria voluntarily take a seat in a jeep
that was driven by what I could've sworn was a priest, and speed away
in the opposite direction.

"You know," said Peckerman, "I wonder if this revolution can help
you and me in the long run."

"How so?" I asked.

"Well, everyone thinks we're enemies of democracy, right? But
if we help bring freedom here to Cuba, wouldn't it show the world
that we're not terrorists? And that what happened was just one huge
misunderstanding?"

Peckerman had caught me off guard. So much so, all I could do
was stare at him in silence for a few seconds.

"Make sense?" he asked.

"Yes, it makes a lot of sense," I finally uttered. And it did. What
didn't make sense was that this imbecile thought of it.

What occurred next happened rather quickly and without further discussion: Our grabbing clumps of mud and streaking them onto our faces. Our tearing off a sleeve from our shirts and tying them on as headbands. Picking up rifles and raising them aloft. And our running out of the jungle with Peckerman shouting across the ravine to a stunned Ramon and Nunez, "*Venga!* We have a dictator to kick the shit out of!"

CHAPTER 34

Jeffrey

You know those *Rambo* movies? Where Sylvester Stallone runs around some dirtbag communist country with no shirt on and shoots down a helicopter with a slingshot and kills 237 communist soldiers with his bare hands?

Those movies are unrealistic. Here's what reality is like: Horkman and I are on one side of the ravine, holding our guns over our heads. The Cubans are on the other side, going nuts, shouting "YI-YI-YI!" ready to go kick some ass. In a movie, the next scene, we're all charging into battle.

But what actually happened was, first, Horkman and I had to climb down our side of the ravine, which was hard because those guns are a lot heavier than they look, plus it was really steep. We both kept dropping the guns and falling down, so we ended up mostly sliding on our butts, which took a while. The Cubans tried to keep cheering, but after a while they realized they'd better pace themselves. Like every twenty seconds or so, one of them would go, "YI-YI-YI!" But you could tell they were losing the mood.

Plus—I'm just going to come right out and say this—I had to take a shit. I mean, *bad*. Which is something that never happens in the movies. You never see Rambo take a shit. You never see whatshisname, the guy in those Bourne movies, Matt Damon, when he and his co-star hot babe are fleeing through some foreign city and he's killing enemy agents with kung fu, speaking nine languages, hotwiring a car and driving like a stuntman, etc., you never hear him say to the babe, "Geez, I'm sorry, but even though those enemy agents are, like, twenty yards behind us shooting at us, I need to make a pit stop, because if I don't get to a toilet *right now* I'm going to turn this car into a septic tank."

That's the way I felt, when Horkman and I got to the bottom of the ravine. I had a cramp in my gut like I was about to give birth to a walrus. I had no choice but to drop my pants right then and there.

"What are you *doing*?" Horkman said.

"What does it look like I'm doing?" I said.

"You can't at least go *behind* something?" he said.

"Go behind *what*, asshole?" I said, because (a) there was nothing to go behind, and (b) Horkman is an asshole.

"I don't believe this," said Horkman. He walked about ten yards and sat down on a rock, facing away. Thanks a lot, douchenozzle.

So there I was, squatting, and I don't want to get too specific here, but it was a severe firehose situation. I was splattering the gravel bigtime, plus there was a certain amount of gas noise, plus you had the natural echo in the ravine. I don't think this was what the Cubans were expecting in the way of military leadership. I could hear them up there talking about me, and then one of them went "YI-YI-*YI*!" definitely sarcastically, and then they were all laughing. Assholes. Like *they* never had diarrhea in a ravine.

I firehosed for I would say a good three minutes, off and on. When I was finally done, I realized I had nothing to wipe with, and of course Horkman was no help, because he's an asshole. I looked up at the Cubans, but I didn't see Ramon or Nunez, just a bunch of morons who didn't speak English. I yelled, "TENGO TOILET-O PAPER-O?" I don't know the Spanish word for "toilet paper," not that it would have made any difference, because they probably haven't had toilet paper in Cuba since 1964. So of course the idiot Cubans didn't know what the hell I was talking about. I pointed at my ass and made a wiping motion, which they thought was very funny, ha-ha, YI-YI-YI! Jerkoffs. But finally they got the point and threw down some kind of big jungle leaves. I wasn't too happy about that, because I remembered a situation at the 1983 Northeastern New Jersey Boy Scout Council Camporee when this kid in my troop, Lenny Vitali, wiped his ass with leaves that turned out to be poison sumac, and by the time they got him to the hospital, according to his brother Victor, his butt was the size of a truck tire.

But I figured I had no choice. I wiped myself as best I could, and then Horkman and I started up the other side of the ravine. It took us even longer than going down did, but we finally made it to the top. Nunez was waiting for us.

"I must ask you," he said, "how did you survive the attack? I confess that when I saw the truck explode, I feared the worst."

Horkman gave me a nudge. I looked at him and he shook his head, indicating *Don't say anything about the Salamanders*. I gave him the finger, indicating *Fuck you*. Then I looked back at Nunez and said, "You ever hear of Bourne?"

"Who?" he said.

"Bourne," I said. "Like *The Bourne Identity*, *The Bourne Extremity*, etc.?"

"No," he said.

"It's a special kind of agent training," I said. "Bourne Training. We train for this situation."

"You train for going off a cliff in a truck?" he said.

"Exactly," I said.

"Impressive," he said.

"Yes," I agreed.

Ramon came out of the jungle and said, "We must go. We have lost time."

We got into a different truck, Ramon and Nunez in the front seat, Horkman and me behind them. The convoy started up and we were bouncing down the road again, if you can call it a road, going maybe two miles an hour. Horkman leaned over to me and, keeping his voice low, said, "While you were making the River of Poop, I did some thinking."

"Good for you," I said.

"Listen to me, Peckerman. This is important. Why do you think the Salamanders let us go?"

"What do you mean?"

"I mean, we're supposed to be wanted terrorists, right? Wanted by the United States?"

I nodded.

"Well, they're United States military. Why didn't they kill us? Or capture us? Why'd they save you, and give both of us guns, and send us back to the rebels?"

"We already discussed this, Horkman. They're secret whaddycall-its, operators. They're helping the rebels overthrow the government."

"That makes no sense," he said.

"What do you mean?"

"The Salamanders saw us up close. They know we're not military threats. I think they know we're just a couple of schlubs from New Jersey."

I had to nod. He's an asshole, but he had a point. The Salamanders didn't seem impressed with us.

"So," continued Horkman, "why'd they send us back over to lead the rebels?"

I shook my head.

"I think," said Horkman, "they want to make sure that the rebels lose."

"Why?"

"I don't know. But it's pretty obvious they're not on the rebel side; they didn't even let the rebels see them. In fact, it wouldn't surprise me if, once the battle starts, the Salamanders are fighting *against* us."

I thought about that. "So they're gonna let us go in there and get killed."

Horkman nodded and said, "I think they might even help kill us."

If there's one rule that I always try to live my life by, it's this: Don't get killed. I knew I had to do something. In the seat ahead, Nunez and Ramon had their backs to us. I glanced behind. There were three Cubans in the backseat, but they were all dozing. Behind our truck were some more, but they were a ways back, and there were dust clouds on the road. I moved over toward the edge of the seat.

"What are you doing?" whispered Horkman.

"I'm getting the fuck out of here," I said.

"Bad idea," said Horkman. He pointed toward the trees. I looked. There were dark shapes moving in there, keeping pace with the truck. The Salamanders. As I watched, one of them came closer to the road, so I could see his face: It was the guy who saved me, Spider-Man. He pointed at the road, then shook his finger back and forth, indicating *Don't get off the truck*. Then he reached down and pulled something out of his boot. It was a really big knife. He held it up, indicating *I have a really big knife*. With his other hand, he pointed two fingers at his eyes, then one at me, indicating *I'm watching you*.

I slid back into the middle of the truck, leaned over, and put my head in my hands. Indicating *Fuck me*.

CHAPTER 35

Philip

It was so hard to believe.

Even as I sat in the back of that truck with a bandanna around my head and a machine gun across my lap, it still hadn't sunk in that I, Philip Horatio Horkman, a pet shop owner who wore corrective shoes well into my junior year of college, was on my way to Havana to help overthrow the Castro regime.

I had never been in a war. I'm a member of that in-between generation that made me too young for Vietnam and then too old for any of the Gulf Wars—which my father, a decorated WWII veteran, could be counted on to throw up to me whenever the mood hit him.

"Enlist, you coward!" he once shouted, apropos of nothing anyone was talking about at that particular moment.

"Dad . . ."

"Julius, we're in the middle of a seder," I remember my mother saying after this outburst. "Your only son is reciting the Four Questions at a meal celebrating freedom from bondage and you're shouting for him to serve in a war effort?"

"Why not?" he asked.

"Because there's no war right now," Mom said.

"And because I'm only seven years old right now," I reminded him.

But now, so many years later, I was in a war. And looked to for answers before that first shot was even fired.

"What do you suggest we do, El Horko?" asked Ramon. The rebels had taken to calling me El Horko, a nickname I was flattered by until I learned its translation meant "The Vomit."

The truck was slowing down, so it would be just a matter of moments until we began the mission of liberating Cuba from the grip of a ruling class whose greed became even more palpable when I saw their homes and neighborhoods on the outskirts of the city. Sprawling ostentation worthy of Beverly Hills zip codes, as compared to the squalor inhabited by Ramon and millions like him.

"Secure the perimeter," I advised.

It was a phrase I'd heard dozens of times in movies, and it seemed to work in those situations where soldiers wanted to contain the enemy, so I figured I'd give it a whirl.

"Of the entire city?" he asked.

"No reason not to," I answered with the nonchalance of someone who wasn't soiling himself.

"With all due respect, El Horko, I do not believe that would be effective. As well armed as we are, there are but a few hundred of us. And in a city that covers 280 square miles, unless the enemy decided to run toward each of our soldiers, we'd be too far apart to be able to keep them within that perimeter."

I felt stupid. And then Peckerman chimed in.

"So why don't we just secure the radius?"

I no longer felt stupid.

"What are you saying?" asked Ramon.

"Well, if I remember my high school geometry," explained Peckerman, "the radius extends from the edge of the circle to the middle. So if we all lined up that way, at least half of the perimeter will be secure, which is better than nothing."

"But the very concept of guerilla warfare is for a small group of camouflaged rebels to hide, ambush, and then quickly retreat," said Ramon.

"It's based on the element of surprise, which standing in the middle of a circle where the enemy can not only see us but also pick us off one at a time as if we were ducks in a shooting gallery completely compromises that strategy," added Nunez.

"Oh," uttered Peckerman.

At this point, no one anywhere had reason to feel stupid ever again.

A few silent seconds later, we were in Havana where every rebel soldier jumped out before the trucks even came to a complete stop. Because it was still morning, the city square known as Plaza Vieja was relatively empty of shoppers and tourists. This was good as it was Ramon's wish that no innocent bystanders become casualties, as their beef was with the people *inside* the big buildings at the heart of the promenade.

The objective was to stealthily go through the doors and seize control of the government without firing even a shot. Peckerman and I liked that part of the plan very, very much. The not-getting-shot part. But there were no guarantees.

"Any suggestions, asshook?" Peckerman asked, as we were at the front of the pack heading up the steps of what is called El Capitolio.

"Let the others pass us," I told him. "No reason for you and me to be the first ones in that building."

So we slowed down and, needless to say, that proved to be a wise decision, because as soon as the rebels opened those doors, they were greeted by fusillades coming from the guns of fully armed Cuban soldiers awaiting their arrival.

Who'd tipped them off about this "secret" raid was a debate Peckerman and I didn't wish to have at that very moment, as the steady gunfire coming from the inside of the government building was sending rebels flying backward to the point where the marble steps we'd just climbed were becoming littered with their bodies.

So Ramon then ordered the rest of their troops to retreat. To not enter the buildings so no more brave young men would sacrifice their lives for what had suddenly turned into a suicide mission. The rebels were outnumbered, out-armed, and betrayed—so Ramon felt their next move should be to recede back into safety at the perimeter and regroup.

"Now what, shit sniffer?" asked Peckerman.

"Run as fast as you can," I said. "No reason to be the last ones to get away from this building."

And because Peckerman and I now outran all the other rebels back toward the perimeter, we didn't realize it when we veered toward the left side of the esplanade that everyone else would be peeling off to the right, heading toward a small park at the far edge of the promenade that was out of the line of fire. No big deal, I figured, when we stopped running and saw what had happened. We'd just circle around and meet up with everyone else.

So we took a couple of steps in their direction, when suddenly all the doorways filled with Cuban army soldiers emerging from the buildings, their weapons still drawn, looking out at the promenade for any more living rebels they could make an example of.

They saw none. Except for me and Peckerman. And while some of them dropped to a knee and took aim, the greater majority started running toward us. So we broke into a run—not in a straight line, but rather in an arc to where Ramon and Nunez and the rest of the rebel army were still in crouched hiding. But then the entire Cuban army started running in the direction we were heading.

I never ran so fast. Not even as a soccer referee who no longer required corrective shoes. But still, I was used to the exertion, so my

stamina, fueled by the torrents of adrenaline that were now cours-
ing through my system, made it easier for me to sprint toward our
comrades. As opposed to Peckerman, lumbering buffoon that he
was, who looked as if he was going to have the incredibly rare life
experience of actually seeing his heart burst through his chest, given
the seismic breaths he was expelling.

I reached the other side first. Though panting heavily, I rejoined
the other rebels, so now I, too, was out of sight of the Cuban army,
who now started shooting at Peckerman who was only about twenty
feet away from us.

What did I feel when I realized that he would probably not make
it? Nothing. Under these circumstances, there was simply no time to
indulge *any* emotions. What was needed was action.

So, as if I'd shifted into a gear I didn't even know I had, I took a
deep breath and yelled at the top of my lungs.

"Secure the radius!"

Whereupon all the rebels, including Ramon and Numez, stood
up, forming a line from the edge of the perimeter to the midpoint of
the promenade and started firing at the unsuspecting soldiers who
were running right toward them.

As an exhausted Peckerman collapsed onto the safe ground behind
this cordon, the rebels unloaded everything they had and, when the
shooting finally ceased, all of the enemy soldiers were dead.

"El Horko! Señor Peckerman!" said a jubilant Ramon, who somehow figured that this was all done by design. "We would be honored
to have you lead the way."

So me and Peckerman moved to the front of the pack, walked across
the esplanade, up the marble stairs, entered El Capitolio and took
it over.

CHAPTER 36

Jeffrey

I've been to some pretty wild parties.

I was at a wedding once where, at around the three-hour mark in the reception, the best man went up to the bandleader and requested "Horse with No Name," and the bandleader said he was sorry but the band didn't have that particular tune in their repertoire, and the best man—a large individual—picked up the bandleader by his tuxedo jacket and said, "It's two fucking chords." That was all the encouragement that the bandleader needed. The band started playing a half-assed version of "A Horse with No Name," at which point the back door to the reception hall burst open and the rest of the groomsmen came in leading *an actual horse.*

I still don't know where they got it. The reception hall was in Weehawken, New Jersey, which is not exactly the frontier. But wherever they found it, the horse was funny as hell, at least at first. After a while, the groomsmen got tired of holding it and went back to the bar, which meant the horse was just wandering around unsupervised. You almost forgot it was there. You'd be going to take a leak, and you'd see it grazing on the buffet lasagna, and you'd go, "Oh yeah, the horse."

Finally the owner of the hall showed up, and as you can imagine he was pissed. He wanted the horse out of there, and he wanted more money, and the father of the bride, a lawyer, was shouting that there was nothing in the sales contract that said you *couldn't* have a horse. Finally the police came, and they were trying to grab the horse, but the groomsmen lifted the groom onto its back and the horse threw him off, breaking his collarbone, and the horse started freaking out, barging around, knocking over tables, and the bride and her mom were screaming, and it basically turned into a riot. A bunch of people got arrested, and the father of the bride got Tasered. That's when I left. I never did hear what happened to the horse. I do know the marriage lasted less than a year.

My point is, I've seen some parties. But I never saw a party like the ones the Cubans put on the night we won the Battle of Havana. We wound up eating a victory meal in a huge marble-floor room with potted palms around the sides and a big long table in the middle. Every man at the table had a bottle of rum and a glass in front of him. Guys were getting up and giving speeches in Spanish, and at the end they'd hold up a glass and yell, "Secure the radius!" We'd all stand up and gulp down the rum, and then—here's where the party went to the next level—guys would fire their weapons at the ceiling. Of course the bullets ricocheted right back down, which you might think would put a damper on the shooting, but that's because you've never partied with Cuban revolutionaries who have just overthrown a regime. What they did, as soon as they toasted the radius and squeezed off some rounds, was dive under the table, which fortunately was a hardwood, I'm guessing walnut. We'd all be crouched under there, laughing like maniacs, with bullets hitting the table above us and the floor around us. It was probably still risky, but after the seventh or eighth glass of rum nobody gave a shit.

Speaking of which: I still had diarrhea. You'll see in a minute why this was important. I think it was from that *quesadilla de harina de yuca rellena con camarones y queso* crap. All I knew was, all of a sudden I needed to get to a toilet, bad. So I stood up to leave the table. When the Cubans saw this, they thought I was about to make a speech, so *they* all stood up. So I waved my arms like *nonono*, and they all waved *their* arms *nonono*. So I pointed to my ass to indicate that I had a medical condition, and they thought this was hilarious. They all pointed to *their* asses, and then they all started yelling "YI-YI-YI!" And then some idiot yelled "Secure the radius!"

I knew what was coming next, so I started running for the door. I got maybe three steps before somebody tackled me, and if you have been following this story you know by now there is only one asshole who would be asshole enough to be the asshole in question.

"IT'S NOT SAFE OUT HERE!" he's yelling. Like I didn't notice the bullets bouncing all around us.

"I KNOW THAT, FUCKNUT," I informed him. "I HAVE TO GET TO A BATHROOM."

And he goes, "Oh."

Dipshit.

So he gets off me, and now we're both running toward the doors at the end of the hall. There were a few stray bullets still pinging around, and the Cubans were still under the table, so I don't think they'd noticed yet that we were missing. As I ran through the doorway, I thought I saw the potted palms on either side moving, but I was concentrating on getting to the toilet. Suddenly *WHAM!* the doors slammed shut behind us. I looked back and saw why the palms had been moving: the Salamanders.

Two of them were wrapping a chain around the door handles to lock in the Cubans. The others grabbed Horkman and me, picked us up and started running. I tried to explain that I needed a bathroom, but they weren't listening. They hustled us down some stairs and through some hallways, and then all of a sudden we were outside in an alley. There were two cars waiting there, old American ones. The Salamanders threw us into the backseat of one and we took off. It was nighttime; they drove on side streets, with the lights off.

"What's the meaning of this?" said Horkman, because that's the kind of asshole thing he says.

The oldest Salamander—the leader—looked back from the front seat. "The meaning of this is, you fucked up."

"What are you talking about?" said Horkman. "We *won.*"

"Exactly."

Horkman looked at me. "I was right," he said. "These guys *wanted* the rebels to lose."

"I *really* need a toilet," I said.

"What are you going to do with us?" said Horkman.

"We're gonna take you for a little ride," answered the leader. "On the Dildo of Doom."

"The *what?*"

"Technically," said the leader, "it's the DD-2038X, a very small, very fast, very advanced nuclear stealth submarine. Officially it doesn't exist, so don't tell anybody, okay?" He smiled. "Not that you'll have anybody to tell, where you're going."

"I can't hold it much longer," I said.

"Where *are* we going?" demanded Horkman.

The leader smiled again. "Gitmo."

"Is there a bathroom there?" I said.

"Guantánamo?" said Horkman. "You can't do that! We're American citizens!"

"What you are," said the leader, "is wanted international terrorists. Who are about to go missing. Like Osama."

The cars stopped in a deserted waterfront area. It was very dark. They hustled us out and onto a rotting dock. The sub was tied there, low in the water, almost invisible. They opened a hatch and shoved us down a ladder into a cramped area with a little bench. They told us to sit on it and stay there. They cast off the lines and closed the hatch. The helmsman flipped switches and worked the controls. The sub started moving.

"Is there a bathroom on this thing?" I said.

"Just a minute," said the leader. "We're diving."

"I don't have a minute," I said.

I felt the sub going down. And then I felt something else. Something bad.

"I'm sorry," I said.

And then a volcano erupted in my bowels.

Horkman, sitting next to me, smelled it first.

"Ohmigod," he said.

I couldn't answer. I was still erupting. I was the Old Faithful of feces, the Space Shuttle of shit

"Oh. My. God," said Horkman, looking at the floor. I don't even want to tell you what was happening on the floor, other than to say it was not a color usually found in nature.

Almost immediately an unbearable stench filled the sub. It was like being sealed in the business end of a Porta-Potty at a chili cookoff in Phoenix in July. The Salamanders were gagging.

"SURFACE!" shouted the leader, his eyes watering. "NOW!"

"But, sir," responded the helmsman, "we're still in the—"

"TAKE IT UP RIGHT NOW!"

The helmsman yanked on levers. The sub shot up. The Salamanders were already opening the hatch when we reached the surface; some water splashed in as the Salamanders scrambled up the ladder and out. Horkman was right behind them. I was right behind Horkman.

I stuck my head out the hatch and sucked in a breath of air. We had popped up in Havana Harbor near some big ships, freighters. The Salamanders were on the front end of the sub, lying down, retching and puking into the harbor.

"Psst," said Horkman. He actually used that word: "Psst." He was crouching at the back of the sub, waving at me to go that way. "Come on," he whispered, and he slid off the deck into the water.

I wasn't crazy about the idea, but I also wasn't crazy about staying with gung ho maniacs on a diarrhea-filled submarine, even if it was my diarrhea. So as quietly as I could, I slid into the water after him. We swam toward the closest freighter, and spotted an opening almost at water level toward the back. We climbed up the ladder there and found ourselves inside what looked like the ship's garbage-collection area, which smelled almost as bad as I did. We followed a corridor into the ship, found an empty cabin and ducked inside. There were some hanging bunks, and we decided we'd spend the night there and figure out what to do when it was daylight. Horkman made me take off my pants and throw them out the porthole.

We collapsed on the bunks; I fell asleep in maybe a minute.

When I woke up, sunlight was coming through the porthole.

And the ship was moving.

CHAPTER 37

The NBC Nightly News

BRIAN WILLIAMS: Good evening. Our top story tonight again comes from Cuba, where the extraordinary events of the past two days have taken yet another astonishing twist. It now appears that the military masterminds behind the astonishing lightning-strike revolution that overthrew the Cuban regime were, of all people, Philip Horkman and Jeffrey Peckerman, the New Jersey–based international terrorists believed to be responsible for the recent attacks in New York City and the hijacking of the cruise ship *Windsong*, including the traumatic assault on Charo. For more on this remarkable development we go to NBC correspondent Richard Hanft, in Havana. Richard, what, exactly, is the connection between the rebel forces and these wanted terrorists?

HANFT: It's not clear, Brian. The rebel leaders claim they had no prior contact with Horkman or Peckerman. Yet somehow the two men were able to evade capture by the Cuban authorities, locate the secret rebel headquarters, take charge of the insurgent army,

and lead the attack on Havana, achieving an astonishing victory
by means of a highly unorthodox and innovative military tactic
called "the radius."

WILLIAMS: "The radius?"

HANFT: Correct, Brian. The rebels say their victory was totally the
result of this innovative maneuver, led by these two apparently very
charismatic men. And in yet another strange twist, Horkman and
Peckerman apparently vanished only hours after the battle ended.
One minute they were at a victory banquet here in Havana, and the
next minute they were gone—disappearing, in the words of the
Cuban rebels, like *fantasmas de la noche*, or "ghosts of the night."
To add to the mystery, early today the Cubans found a top-secret
American spy submarine floating in Havana harbor, with a team of
commandos clinging to the hull. Apparently the submarine had
been disabled by some kind of powerful biological weapon.

WILLIAMS: Could this also be the work of Horkman and
Peckerman?

HANFT: The Cubans believe so, Brian. The American government
has no official comment on the sub, but sources have told me the
Pentagon is deeply embarrassed that Horkman and Peckerman
were able to neutralize an elite commando unit apparently sent
here to capture them.

WILLIAMS: For more on the U.S. reaction, we go to NBC Washington correspondent Jeffrey Berkowitz. Jeffrey, what is the American
government saying now?

BERKOWITZ: Brian, officially Horkman and Peckerman are still
wanted as terrorist enemies of the United States. But their role
in the Cuban revolt has caused many here in Washington to re-
evaluate these shadowy figures. There's speculation that they may
actually be some kind of super double agents, if you will—*posing*
as terrorists, but actually using their international clout, and their
formidable abilities, to advance a different agenda altogether.

WILLIAMS: What agenda is that?

BERKOWITZ: Nobody knows for sure, Brian, although some are now calling them freedom fighters. The singer Bono is strongly hinting that he has been in contact with them, as are Geraldo Rivera and the Nike Corporation. And in an indication that the public image of these fugitives may be changing, here in Washington we're already seeing young people wearing T-shirts like the one I'm holding here, with the words *"Fantasmas de la Noche"* above the faces of Horkman and Peckerman.

WILLIAMS: That's Horkman and Peckerman?

BERKOWITZ: I'm told these are their Bar Mitzvah photos.

WILLIAMS: Fascinating. And does anyone have any idea where these two are now?

BERKOWITZ: Apparently not, Brian. They have indeed vanished like ghosts in the night. They could be, literally, anywhere on Earth. But wherever they are, it's a good bet, based on their track record, that excitement is not far behind.

WILLIAMS: "Excitement" is definitely the word for these two.

CHAPTER 38

Philip

"Thank me, Horkman!"

"Get off of me, you bloated mammal!"

"Only if you thank me first!"

"Not a chance in hell!"

"Then I'm not budging!"

"Ow!"

I was in great pain. I was on the floor, Peckerman's knee was in my back, and his grubby hands were under my chin, yanking my head upward in the general direction of Saturn, with the promise that he would not stop doing this until I said "thank you."

And there lay the problem.

Call me arbitrary, but I truly felt I had to draw the line somewhere.

Again we were at sea. It was our first morning. After a surprisingly good night's sleep, my eyes opened to the disorientation of not recalling where I was. Lying in what was, for all intents and purposes, a hammock hanging from the ceiling near the bowels of what were, for all intents and purposes, bowels. A corridor filled with waste being swept along by waves of tainted liquid toward a huge opening at the far end.

It was about the time that I saw two rodents lying on their backs on top of a flattened Dixie Cup as if in a water park, when I heard Peckerman approach from behind demanding that I thank him for getting us where we were.

"Why in God's name should I thank you for that?"

"Because otherwise we'd still be inside that submarine."

"So you're asking me to thank you for having diarrhea?"

"Yes."

"No."

"And why not?"

"First of all, it was involuntary. It's not like you had a brilliant strategy that you implemented and it affected our escape. You simply got sick at an opportune time. And secondly, from the looks of things," I said, while I could've sworn that one of those floating rodents had fed the other one some grapes, "I'd say, at best, this was a lateral move."

That's when he knocked me to the floor and started hurting me.

Funny thing, though. While Peckerman was snapping my head backward and forward like I was a giant Pez dispenser with colored candy issuing from my neck, it did cross my mind that we were indeed lucky to be away from those angry Salamanders who were going to take us to Guantánamo. Where, as presumed terrorists whose objective was to destroy America, we'd be thrown into dark cells and waterboarded.

So being here on this freighter, despite not knowing exactly where we were or where we were going, was a reprieve from what I was certain would be my fate. The country that I love hating me so much that when I died, either in prison or at the hands of a death squad that hunted me down, spontaneous parties would break out around the peace-loving world like they did when they finally found Osama bin Laden. So as much as it pained me to offer anything that even resembled positive feedback to this buffoon, I bit my lip and gave him what he so desperately needed.

"Thank you, Peckerman."

"You're very welcome, douchebag."

Then the moron got up. And then I extended an arm the way football players do when they're seeking assistance getting up after they've been tackled. The way virtually every time, even the most barbaric players from the opposing teams help them up.

So, as if I needed further confirmation that the Neanderthal I was traveling with was somewhere to the left of them on the evolutionary scale, I staggered to my feet unaided as he ignored my request and walked away whistling "I Whistle a Happy Tune," still with no pants on.

The freighter we were on is called a container ship. A long flat transport that carries its cargo in rectangular truck-size containers. Stacked on top of each other by cargo cranes. This particular ship had about seventy-five of those huge containers filled with bananas from Ecuador, then stopped in Cuba where it picked up a smaller amount of sugar, and was now continuing on to a place that apparently needed bananas and a little sugar.

"They're probably green, huh?"

"What's probably green, Peckerman?"

"The bananas. Because if they're yellow, by the time they get to where they're going they'll be overripe."

"Okay."

"And mushy."

"Uh-huh."

In general, it was easy for me and Peckerman to anonymously blend in with the crew of thirty merchant marines after we stole work uniforms from the ship's laundry. And the fact that most of the men were from different countries made communicating, in general, a nonfactor. These were veteran tattooed seafarers who knew the jobs they had to perform and simply went about the routine.

So the two of us merely did what they were doing. Whether it be swabbing, chipping paint, or operating forklifts, we insinuated ourselves into the group and worked alongside of everyone else. We also ate with them. And at night, after watching a movie in the ship's theater or sitting in a corner of the game room pretending that we knew how to play chess, we went back to our room and those hanging bunks.

"But here's what I don't understand about bananas."

"Jesus, Peckerman. We're still talking about bananas?"

"I mean, I've been to the supermarket and a lot of times I've seen green bananas there."

"So . . . ?"

"Well, if they're green by the time they get to the store, what color were they when they were on the boat before they got to the store?"

"Go to sleep, Peckerman."

"Maybe it's a darker green."

"Peckerman, can't you find a shiny object that you can stare at for a while?"

With the exception of this idiocy, it was an easy routine to settle into, and all seemed to be under control until our third day out.

Dinner. A bowl of unrecognizable sludge that everyone merely withstood, but Peckerman scarfed down like he was on death row.

"Slow down," I said under my breath. "Peckerman, our fellow mariners affectionately call what you're shoveling into your piehole 'S.W.A.T.,' which, in this particular instance, stands for 'Shit With Alotta Thorns.'"

"Fuck 'em, I'm hungry!" Peckerman declared at the same unfortu-

nate moment that a sneeze with the force of a tsunami sent a mouthful flying across the table and into the face of a Dutch seaman who
was crying because he'd just found out his sister died.

I knew Peckerman was in big trouble when everyone at the table
fell silent in deference to their splattered comrade, before the guy to
Peckerman's right grabbed him from behind. And then I knew I was
in big trouble when the guy to my left (wrongly thinking Peckerman
and I were friends) grabbed me from behind. They pulled us to our
feet and dragged us to the center of the room, where the rest of the
crew formed two lines to take turns punching us in the stomach.

"Him first!" I heard Peckerman yell, at which point the guy at the
front of that line clenched his fist and belted him with power that
caused him to keep bowing at the waist like it was sundown at the
Western Wall.

And then it was my turn. I looked at the guy who was about to
punch me. He was small. Asian. Sort of pudgy. Sort of reminded me
of what I would look like if I was small, Asian and pudgy. What I
mean is, he seemed like he wasn't used to this kind of thing. But that
he was aware that the other seamen, from both lines, were watching,
and this scared me, because from the look on his face I could tell he
felt he had something to prove to them. Especially when fueled by
the cheering that was egging him on in at least four languages that I
was able to discern.

His look seemed to say he was sorry but this was something he just
had to do, so I closed my eyes and braced myself for the ensuing impact when I suddenly heard a word I never imagined I'd hear in
my life.

It came from an officer rushing into the mess hall and shouting in
a voice that cut through the mounting chorus of the others, causing
them all to stop cheering, to break ranks and scatter in all directions.

"Pirates!"

CHAPTER 39

Jeffrey

It didn't register with me right away, the pirates thing. I was focused on the fact that my stomach hurt like a mother, and a whole crew of assholes were waiting their turn to punch me. I knew I had to think of something, fast.

This is going to sound weird, but my mind flashed back to Artie Bermitt. He was this bully in eighth grade who used to take my lunch money, give me wedgies, stuff like that. One day he roughed me up pretty good after school, and when I got home I was crying. My mom asked why, so I told her, and that night she told my dad.

My dad was the kind of guy who never backed down from a fight, even when the other person didn't *want* to fight, if you know what I mean. He got thrown out of a lot of bars in his day, and at least two funerals. One time he punched a cassowary. Google it. It's a giant flightless bird, bigger than an ostrich, with a weird head and huge *Tyrannosaurus rex* feet.

The way it happened was, we were at this wildlife tourist attraction in Florida called Jungle Adventure, and we went to a bird show in an outdoor theater where, for the big climax, a guy chosen from the audience holds up a plum so a parrot can swoop down from the back of the theater and snatch it from his hand. At least that's what the announcer *says* is going to happen. What really happens is, while the guy is looking up at the parrot, a totally unexpected and fugly bird the size of Shaquille O'Neal comes barreling out from backstage and grabs the plum.

Then what's supposed to happen is the victim, totally surprised, lets go of the plum, jumps back, maybe even screams a little. The audience has a big laugh, and the cassowary, swallowing the plum, trots off to his trainer.

That's not what happened with my dad. He jerked the plum away and threw a left hook at the cassowary's noggin that connected pretty good. The cassowary totally freaked out. Things got hairy then—workers trying to restrain this huge, pissed-off bird, people running for the exits, a lot of screaming. When things finally calmed down, the trainer tore into my dad about how this was an extremely rare and valuable animal, and he could have killed it, and for that matter it could have killed *him*, and what the hell was he thinking? My dad's position was: Fuck you, and I'm keeping the plum.

Now that you know what kind of guy my dad was, you probably know what he did when he found out about Artie Bermitt. First, he smacked me in the head, hard, for crying like a girl. Then he said, "Next time that punk starts with you, you hit him hard, right in the nose. If I find out you chickened out, I'll beat the living shit out of you myself."

So the next day, when Artie Bermitt came to my locker and told me to give him my lunch money, I hit him hard, right in the nose. And you know what happened? I'll tell you what: Artie Bermitt beat the living shit out of me *and* pissed in my locker. It's a lesson I never forgot.

This flashed through my mind when the crew started hitting me in the stomach. (I mean Artie Bermitt flashed through my mind, not the cassowary. I included that here just for background.) I knew there was only one way I was going to get out of that ship alive, and that was to fall on the floor and cry like a girl. If you think I'm a coward, you can eat me.

So I dropped down and curled up on the floor, eyes closed, whimpering, expecting to get yanked back to my feet or maybe kicked. Instead I heard this commotion, and then Horkman shook me and said, "Get up! We're being attacked by pirates!"

I opened my eyes and said, "What the fuck do you want me to do about it?"

He said, "We need to help repel the attack!" Those are the actual words he used: "Repel the attack."

I said, "Why, so those assholes can get back to punching us?"

"It's better than getting keelhauled by pirates."

I didn't answer that, because I didn't want Horkman to know I didn't know what "keelhauled" meant, although it sounded enough like "cornholed" that I had a pretty good idea. When you think about it, a lot of pirates are probably gay. Look at Johnny Depp.

We went up onto the deck, where most of the crew were gathered along a side rail. We joined them and looked down into the ocean. Next to our ship were two speedboats, carrying a dozen or so dark-skinned guys with guns. They were putting ladders against the side of our ship. Our crew didn't seem to be doing anything about this. In fact, our ship was no longer moving, which made it even easier for the pirates. It's like we had a big sign that said WELCOME ABOARD.

Horkman turned to the crewman next to him, a Dutch guy, and said, "Aren't we going to repel them?"

"Do *what* to them?" said the Dutch guy.

I said, "He means why don't we fight them."

"They have guns."

"Don't we have guns?"

"Yes, a few," said the Dutchman. "But if we shoot them, they shoot back at us, and somebody gets hurt." He spat on the deck. "Nobody wants to die for this piece of shit."

The pirates were climbing over the rail. They waved their guns and yelled at us to line up, move inside and sit on the floor. They left a couple of guards watching us, then went out. Pretty soon we felt the ship moving again.

We'd been sitting there for a couple of hours when three pirates came in, including one who I figured was the leader. He walked around the room, looking at the crew. When he got to me and Horkman, he stopped and looked at us hard. He said something in a foreign language to his two lieutenants, and they all laughed. A chill went down my spine, or up my spine, whichever way is medically correct. I whispered to Horkman, "I bet these faggots are picking out somebody to keelhaul."

He said, "You're disgusting, you know that?"

I said, "*I'm* disgusting? *They're* the ones looking to slam some ham."

He said, "What are you *talking* about?"

I didn't answer, because the pirate leader was now standing right over us. I frowned, trying to look as unattractive as possible, but you never know, with these perverts, what turns them on. A lot of them like back hair, which unfortunately I have a lot of. Once, for our anniversary, Donna gave me a gift certificate for laser hair removal, but I quit after two treatments, so all they cleared out was a patch of skin about the size of a business card, which Donna calls my mosquito landing zone.

The pirate leader pointed at me and Horkman.

"You two," he said. "Stand up."

We stood up. I kind of edged behind Horkman, so they would pick him. I'd made my mind up what I was going to do if these savages tried to violate me. I was going to cry like a girl and beg for mercy.

"Allow me to introduce myself," the leader said. He spoke pretty good English, for a savage. "My name is Ali. You are Mr. Horkman and Mr. Peckerman, am I correct?"

Horkman and I gave each other a *What the fuck?* look.

Horkman said, "How do you know who we are?"

Ali smiled. "Jon Stewart."

"Jon Stewart?" said Horkman.

"Yes," said Ali. "You're regulars on *The Daily Show*. Not you in person, of course. Your photographs. Jon's been doing a very funny running bit about two Jewish men from New Jersey being wanted international terrorists on the run, having to eat freeze-dried Chinese food on Sunday night, and so on. You're also mentioned regularly on Letterman."

"And Jimmy Kimmel," said one of the lieutenants.

"We watch on satellite," said Ali. "And of course we're among your many Facebook followers."

"Facebook?" said Horkman.

"You're huge," said Ali.

"Bigger than Snooki," said the other lieutenant.

"In any event," said Ali, "it's a pleasure to meet you in person. It would be my honor to offer you more comfortable accommodations, as well as transport to your ultimate destination, which I gather is Beirut."

"Beirut?" said Horkman.

"I assumed so, since that's where this ship was bound."

I said, "So you're not going to keelhaul us?"

Ali laughed. "Very funny!" he said. "Like we are Pirates of the Caribbean, eh?"

(So it's *true*, about Johnny Depp.)

"In all seriousness," continued Ali, "despite our image in the Western media, we are modern businessmen. We detain this ship; the insurance company pays us, let us say, twenty million dollars; we release the ship. The insurance company uses this as an excuse to increase its rates, thus making a tidy profit. The shipowners use that as an excuse to increase *their* rates. It's win-win-win!"

Horkman, solidifying his title of World's Biggest Asshole, said, "But isn't it *wrong*?"

Ali looked at him for a few seconds, then burst out laughing and said, "You had me for a second there!"

They moved us up to the captain's quarters, which were decent, and gave us some food. Also they had Cuban rum. We hung out there, mainly sitting around. Every now and then Ali would stick his head in the door and shout, "But isn't it *wrong*?" Then he'd crack up.

A few hours later, we were approaching the coast of Africa.

CHAPTER 40

Philip

You know that expression "Bucket List"? When people write down things they would like to do or the places they would like to visit before they die? Before they kick the (pardon my language) bucket?

Well, being a man who always considered himself blessed and was eternally grateful for the good fortune that life has afforded me and my glorious family, I was never desirous of doing more than I'd already done, as I thought it would be greedy.

So, as far as I was concerned, if the Good Lord deigned that my time in this life should come to an end, with the possible exception of not having the opportunity to ask Francis Ford Coppola what he was thinking when he made *Godfather III*, I would pass away wanting nothing. And with no regrets.

Until now. Until Peckerman started drinking the rum that the pirates placed on the table in the captain's quarters. And until it induced him to start singing the pirate song I used to sing along with the other kids on the bus that took us to day camp the summer between third and fourth grade.

Fifteen men on a dead man's chest,
Yo ho ho and a bottle of rum . . .

The song that all of us had outgrown and no longer sang the summer
between fourth and fifth grade.

Drink and the devil had done for the rest,
Yo ho ho and a bottle of rum . . .

So it was at that exact point that my bucket list was created.

Fifteen men of the whole ship's list . . .

With only one item on it.

Yo ho ho and a bottle of rum . . .

Which was to take karate lessons and have the sensei teach me how
to thrust my hand into Peckerman's chest, remove his heart, and
throw it at him before he died.

"Shut up, Peckerman," I told him.

Dead and be damned and the rest gone whist . . .

"I'm warning you, Peckerman!"

Yo ho ho and a bottle of rum . . .

The door opened again, Ali leaned in again, shouted, "But isn't it
wrong?" again, and laughed as hard as he did the first time again. And
when Peckerman stopped singing and joined him with a ridiculous
laugh of his own, I started wondering if that sensei could teach me
how to extract my own heart and throw it at myself.

"What's your problem?" Peckerman asked after Ali left.

"My problem, Peckerman? My problem is that no matter how they
describe themselves as businessmen, these pirates are ruthless people
and you're acting like we're on a ride at Disney World."

"Yeah, but they think we're just as ruthless. So why not kick back
and enjoy ourselves a little? I think we deserve a little RxR considering what we've been through," he said before taking still another swig.

"RxR?" I asked.

"Rest and relaxation."

"That's R&R, you moron. RxR is a railroad crossing."

He took another gulp, which emptied his bottle. He then picked up the untouched one meant for me and emptied about a third of it into that bottomless gullet of his.

"I have a great idea!" he then shouted. At least that's what I think he said as he was now slurring like a cast member of *Jersey Shore*.

"What's your great idea?"

"Well, this boat is carrying bananas, right?"

"About twelve tons."

"Then what do you say I mix some of them with this rum and make us a couple of banana daiquiris?"

I didn't even answer. All I knew was that I couldn't bear to be in the same air space as him anymore. So I left the captain's quarters and went outside.

It was night. I looked out as we bore down on what I assumed was the coast of Somalia, when I heard a voice cutting through the darkness.

"Why not join me?"

It was coming from above. I looked up and saw Ali, who motioned for me to climb the small ladder that connected the deck I was on to an upper level. I did and now found myself on the bridge where Ali was piloting the freighter.

"Nice night," he said.

"Balmy," I answered nodding.

"Balmy?"

It was the nerves talking. Had to be. I had never used the word "balmy." Only the weatherman used the word "balmy." But now I did, too. And in front of a pirate, no less.

He said nothing for a few moments as his look remained fixed on wherever he was steering the freighter. He seemed lost in thought. The silence was awkward. Especially when he shook his head.

"I wouldn't call it balmy," he finally said. "I think it's more . . . temperate."

I'm a Jew from New Jersey who was standing on the deck of a freighter talking about the weather with a Somalian pirate. Though I'm not a mathematician, my guess was that the odds against that ever occurring were off the charts.

"Really? I don't know about that," I told him.

"Why not?"

"You feel that little breeze? I think that little breeze is what makes a temperate day become a balmy one."

"Temperate plus breeze equals balmy?" he asked.

"Absolutely."

He nodded his head in a way that meant he'd heard what I said but didn't necessarily agree with it. But our meteorological discussion came to an end when he pushed a button on the panel and I no longer heard the sound of engines.

"Ever operate one of these?" he asked.

"Of course," I said with a laugh that also said *Please don't insult me with questions like that.*

"Well, we're going to let this drift to those waters over there," he said, pointing to a place a few hundred yards or so off the shore of Mogadishu. He told me the plan was to let it sit there until the ransom was paid.

"And then we'll have Hamas get you to Beirut."

"Much appreciated," I said simultaneous to my large intestine dropping to a place about an inch above my ankles upon hearing that I'd be spending time with Hamas.

The door to the bridge opened. It was Peckerman holding a tray upon which sat a dozen cups filled with liquid he insisted were banana daiquiris. I took one, drank it, and thought it tasted like wet banana cement. Ali drank it, loved it and asked if he could offer the rest of the drinks to the other pirates.

So Peckerman handed him the tray and, confident that I'd indeed operated a freighter, Ali told me to keep an eye on things and said he'd be right back.

"My God, your breath can melt a fire hydrant," I told Peckerman. "Do you plan to ever stop drinking? You're reeling drunk!"

"Reeling? Is that so, Mr. Bow Wow Meow Tweet Tweet Pet Shop Owner?"

"Jesus, Peckerman . . ."

"Well, for your information I don't even know how to reel."

At which point, as if a fly fisherman cast him outward, he reeled backward and grabbed the handle of the open door behind him. And then, as if that same fly fisherman reeled him in, he pitched forward, slamming the door shut, and kept his downward trajectory, which caused his face to hit the button which restarted the freighter's engines before his entire body came to rest on the control board itself—more specifically, on top of the lever which put the ship in full throttle.

"Peckerman, we're supposed to be drifting!" I shouted to his inert mass.

I looked out the front window of the freighter and saw the coast of Mogadishu drawing closer. I first tried rolling Peckerman off the control board—like he was a huge blob of dough, which he indeed was. But that proved futile, as the lever itself was caught between two buttons on the idiot's shirt, so even when I rocked him and got a good momentum going, he couldn't roll completely off as he was now virtually tethered to that throttle.

I then attempted to slide Peckerman off the board by grabbing his ankles and tugging in small heaves. The downward slant of the panel helped a little, but even gravity, as great a force as it may be, wasn't able to prevent Peckerman's chin from hitting what I gathered was an important red button as a lot of horns started blaring.

As loud as they were, however, they were no match for the banging on the door made by an enraged Ali who'd just returned with the tray and was less than pleased to see that the freighter was maybe a minute away from making a personal appearance upon the shore of Somalia.

And though I tried my best to let him in, the door's lock was jammed and no amount of ranting and pointing by Ali through the door's window trying to convey what to do seemed to work.

So about the same time that Ali stopped banging on the door and took his pistol out of his belt, I took hold of what I figured was the steering wheel and turned it all the way to the right, with every hope that its forward motion would be stopped by turning it sideways. And though I wasn't naïve enough to think that this 62,700-ton vessel would turn on a dime, I held on to every hope that it would turn on a quarter or a half-dollar.

But all I succeeded in doing was to move the rudders or whatever there was underneath whose job it is to turn a large boat. So when the freighter ran aground (about the same time that Ali shot out the window, reached inside, unlocked the door, and came racing in) their angles caused the ship to tip over onto its side, sending the containers toppling from the deck and spilling about two million bananas (minus the ones Peckerman used for those daiquiris) onto the shore of Mogadishu.

CHAPTER 41

Jeffrey

I thought Ali was going to kill us. The reason I thought this was that he was pointing his gun at us and shouting, "I WILL KILL YOU! I WILL KILL YOU!"

I tried to point out that he didn't need to kill me, just Horkman, since he was the asshole who crashed the ship into Africa. But I had trouble making myself understood because of all the noise and confusion. The ship was leaning way the hell over and everything was sliding all over the place. Also to tell the truth, I was pretty hammered from the rum.

The ship is what saved us. Ali aimed the gun at Horkman and me, and he actually shot it, but right at that exact instant the boat lurched really hard and leaned even farther over, and Ali fell backward right out the broken window.

You know how, in comics, people are always slipping on banana peels, but you never see that happen in real life, so you wonder if bananas are really that slippery? It turns out they are. Ali fell onto this huge mass of bananas that had poured out of the ship and formed a pile all the way down to the ground. It was a giant banana slide, and

Ali went down that thing like an Olympic luge competitor, except he was holding a gun and going backward and not wearing a helmet, which was too bad for him because he had to be going fifty miles an hour when he got to the bottom of the banana pile and hit a big rock. I don't want to get graphic here, but his head exploded like a watermelon in a wood chipper.

I know you think I keep harping on what a complete douchebag Horkman is, but listen to what he wanted to do next: *He wanted to go down and help Ali.* I am not shitting you. He's like, "My God, he's hurt!" I pointed out that (a) Ali had just tried to kill us, and (b) even if we wanted to help him, the only thing we could do for him, first aid–wise, was collect pieces of his brain in a baggie. For once Horkman realized I was right.

The ship was still making lurching noises, so we decided we'd better get off. It turned out that everybody else—pirates and crew—had the same idea. They were hanging a big net down the side, and we all used it to climb down off the ship. We were milling around on this rocky shoreline next to about sixteen billion bananas and what was left of Ali when a dozen guys with guns, some kind of soldiers, came running toward us. They were yelling at the pirates, who were yelling back and pointing at Horkman and me. One of the soldiers, a big guy who apparently was the leader, came over and started shouting at us. Of course, we had no idea what he was saying, so I just stood there, but Horkman held his hands out like he was the pope and said—get ready—"We come in peace."

I looked at him and said, "Are you *serious*?"

Apparently the big guy also was unimpressed, because he aimed his gun at Horkman and yelled something that I assume was African for "Don't make peaceful gestures at *me*, dickwad who just turned this coastline into the world's largest fruit salad." He was really pissed, yelling and waving his gun around, and it looked pretty bad for us. I was edging sideways, trying to get behind Horkman in case the big guy started shooting, when one of the other soldiers shouted and pointed inland.

We all turned to look. Coming toward the ship was a really skinny woman and some really skinny little kids. Behind them were more women and kids, and behind them were even more, hundreds of them, all skinny as skeletons. They had their eyes on the bananas. Some of the kids started running toward the pile.

The big guy fired his gun into the air. Everybody stopped. The big guy yelled something to his soldiers. They formed a line in front of the banana pile and pointed their guns at the crowd. Some of the soldiers didn't look too happy about this, but you could tell they didn't dare disagree with the big guy.

Now the big guy was yelling at the crowd, waving his gun to tell them to stay back. The women were crying, holding up their hands like they were begging, but the big guy didn't budge. More women and children were pushing in from behind; the crowd was getting huge, everybody staring at the bananas, but nobody daring to get any closer to the guns. It was tense.

Horkman whispered to me, "We have to do something."

"Right," I whispered back. I figured that what he meant by "do something" was "get the fuck out of there while the soldiers are looking the other way." I now realize this was stupid on my part, seeing as how the asshole had never once in all the time I had ever known him had so much as one good idea. And sure enough, he was not having one then. Instead of sneaking *away* from the soldiers, he started walking straight toward the banana pile. The big guy yelled something at him. Horkman kept walking. He reached the pile and picked up a banana. He turned to the big guy and said, "These people are hungry. Let them have these bananas."

The big guy raised his gun and aimed it right at Horkman. He seemed to be enjoying this, wanting the moment to last. Everything got very quiet. Horkman didn't move; he just stood there holding the banana. It was like a movie, except it was real; Horkman was about to get killed.

You know how sometimes in life, something happens that makes you see things really clearly? For me, this was one of those times. Standing there, looking at Horkman, who didn't even know these starving people and yet was about to get himself killed trying to help them, I suddenly realized something very significant about myself. Specifically, I realized that this was an excellent opportunity to get myself the fuck out of there.

I took one baby step backward from the big man. Then I took another baby step. Then another.

Then I farted. Sometimes you just don't see them coming. This was a real pantsblaster, maybe four seconds in duration, like *bwaaaapppppppppp*. The big man spun around, saw me moving, and swung the butt of his gun right into my stomach. I went down at his feet like a sack of gravel.

I'm still not 100 percent sure what happened next. As best as I can re-create it, the timeline was as follows:

(1) The big man resumes getting ready to shoot Horkman.

(2) As a result of the severe blow to my stomach, I puke maybe a quart of semidigested banana daiquiri directly onto the big man's combat boots.

(3a) The big man looks down to see what the hell is happening at exactly the same instant that . . .

(3b) . . . I lurch violently upward to get away from the puke spatter, which means that . . .

(3c) . . . the top of my skull slams into the big man's chin.

(4) We both fall down, me with a sudden nuclear headache and the big man out cold.

So I'm lying on the ground, holding my head and going "shitshit-shit." Meanwhile, with the ranking officer unconscious, the soldiers don't know what the hell to do. Some of the women and children in the front of the crowd are inching forward toward the bananas. Some of the soldiers lower their guns, but some don't. The crowd comes a little closer. A couple of the soldiers are shouting at the crowd and waving their guns; it looks like they're about to shoot.

Then Horkman runs past the soldiers, so now he's between them and the crowd. He faces the soldiers. Standing in front of the hungry crowd, holding his banana over his head like he was the Statue of Fruit Liberty, he shouts—I swear to God—"LET THESE BANANAS GO!"

For a few seconds, nobody moves. Then Horkman, still holding the banana up, starts walking forward, toward the soldiers. The crowd is following him. Horkman walks right between two soldiers, guns aimed. They don't shoot. A kid, right behind Horkman, scurries to the pile and grabs a banana. He shoves it into his mouth and takes a bite, peel and all.

That was it. The crowd stampeded in, and thirty seconds later you could barely see the pile. There were thousands of people chomping bananas, with more coming. The soldiers didn't even try to stop them.

Horkman worked his way through the mob to where I was lying on the ground. "Are you all right?" he said. I could tell he was really concerned.

"Fuck you," I said.

I stood up. My skull felt like that sweaty Irish stomping guy was in there, the Riverdance asshole. I just wanted to get out of there, away from all these people. I took a couple of steps and almost fell down. Horkman grabbed me.

"Fuck you," I reiterated. But I don't think he heard me, because all of a sudden there was a big black helicopter over us, very low, so loud it drowned out the noise of the banana mob. I looked up and saw some guys in the doorway, pointing at Horkman and me. Ten seconds later, they were coming down on ropes, four of them, right on top of us. Two grabbed Horkman; two grabbed me. Horkman yelled, "What are you doing? Who are you?" But they didn't answer. Twenty seconds later, we were being hauled up into the chopper, which was already heading out to sea. The last I saw of Africa was a couple thousand skinny people looking up at us, waving bananas, which I guess was their way of saying thanks.

CHAPTER 42

The NBC Nightly News

BRIAN WILLIAMS: Good evening. They're calling it "The Miracle of the Bananas." It's an amazing story from famine-stricken Africa—a story of compelling human drama and international intrigue, with an almost unbelievable twist. That twist involves the two most wanted men in the world—Philip Horkman and Jeffrey Peckerman, the mysterious, now-legendary *Fantasmas de la Noche* who allegedly masterminded the recent terrorist attacks in New York City before spearheading the lighting-strike overthrow of the Cuban regime. After that, Horkman and Peckerman seemed to vanish from the face of the earth. Today they suddenly resurfaced in, of all places, Somalia, where in one astonishing stroke, they struck a major blow against three scourges that have plagued that nation for years—hunger, corruption, and international piracy. For more on these developments, we go to NBC News African correspondent Andrew Sable in Somalia.

SABLE: Brian, the story began early today aboard the cargo ship *Sonia*, which you see grounded behind me on the Somali coast. The *Sonia* was bound for Lebanon carrying a massive shipment of bananas when it was hijacked off the African coast by one of Somalia's most feared and brutal pirates, a man named Ali. Details on what happened next are sketchy, but it appears that Horkman and Peckerman were aboard the *Sonia* posing as crewmen, having apparently boarded in Cuba. Somehow they were able to turn the tables on the pirates, hijacking the ship and killing the pirate leader Ali. It appears that Horkman and Peckerman then deliberately steered the ship onto the coast, grounding it in such a way as to spill literally millions of bananas onto the shore less than two miles from a camp housing thousands of starving famine refugees. When word of the spill reached the camp, the refugees—mostly women and children—started walking toward the ship, only to find their path blocked by local militants, who for months have been preventing international aid from reaching the refugees. Somehow, Horkman and Peckerman—who, according to the refugee eyewitnesses I spoke to, were armed only with bananas— were able to defeat the militants and open the path to the spill. What followed, as you can see in this video, was a dramatic and heartwarming scene, as thousands of women and children, many on the brink of starving to death, were able, for the first time in weeks, to eat, and to hope. Brian, I've covered a lot of stories in my day, but I don't think I've ever covered one as moving as this.

WILLIAMS: Incredible. And what happened to Horkman and Peckerman?

SABLE: Brian, they have once again vanished. Witnesses say that only moments after defeating the militants, the two men were whisked away in a black helicopter. Evidently they had this operation planned right down to the second.

WILLIAMS: Does anybody know where the helicopter came from, or where it went?

SABLE: Not a clue, Brian. The *Fantasmas de la Noche*—the Ghosts of the Night—are truly living up to their name.

WILLIAMS: Indeed they are, and thank you, Andrew. Meanwhile, video of the Miracle of the Bananas quickly spread around the world, and the response has been overwhelming. In the words of the secretary-general of the United Nations, "If two men, acting alone, can do so much for so many in such desperate need, how can we, the nations of the world, stand by and do nothing?" The UN Security Council is meeting in emergency session, and is expected to approve massive new emergency aid to Somalia, with UN troops to ensure its delivery. The public response has also been extraordinary, as millions of ordinary citizens, in America and abroad, have flooded relief agencies with donations and offers of help. As for Philip Horkman and Jeffrey Peckerman, in the eyes of millions around the globe, they are now seen as heroes, almost superheroes—a fact that has put the U.S. government in an awkward position. For more on that story, we go to NBC Washington correspondent Jeffrey Berkowitz.

BERKOWITZ: Brian, officially Horkman and Peckerman are still tied for the title of America's Public Enemy Number One— wanted by the feds for their alleged role in the New York attacks. But behind the scenes, according to my sources, the administration is deeply conflicted about the mystery duo. Not only have Horkman and Peckerman become hugely popular, they've achieved this popularity for stunning achievements in Cuba and Somalia that are exactly in line with official U.S. policies. As one White House source told me, "We don't know what game these guys are playing. But whatever it is, they're playing it brilliantly." I'm told that the president himself wants to contact the two men, but sources tell me that nobody in the entire American intelligence community has any idea how to find them. The million-dollar question now is, will they strike again? And if so, where?

WILLIAMS: Already there have been reported sightings of Horkman and Peckerman in London, Moscow, Paris, Rome, Cairo, Mexico City, Buenos Aires, New Delhi, several upscale restaurants in Los Angeles, and Graceland. Although none of those reports turned out to be accurate, one thing is certain: Wherever these two men appear next, the eyes of the entire world will be on them.

CHAPTER 43

Philip

I had never been to Asia before. But that's where the helicopter took us. Over the Gulf of Aden. To an airport in the town of Aden.

We were in Yemen.

"Pretty smart of these Yemenos," said Peckerman. "Gulf of Aden, town of Aden. This way they only have to remember one name. Saves time."

This was one of the remarkable things about Peckerman. That he dealt with each moment as it came along with absolutely no residual effects from what had just occurred. As if depositing a literal boatload of bananas onto a beach, a pirate's head exploding on a rock, and being lifted into a black helicopter by four army guys who said absolutely nothing during a flight to a hostile country didn't matter. Or happen.

On the one hand, I envied him, because I was a nervous wreck. On the other hand, I knew he was displaying the behavior of the true sociopath that he was. The same way Jeffrey Dahmer would go to a movie shortly after he ate the limbs of a young man he'd been dancing with the night before.

The army guys showed us to an awaiting limousine at the edge of the small landing strip. Standing next to its open back door was a Middle Eastern man who was dressed the way, well, the way Middle Eastern men dress.

"Welcome to Yemen, Mr. Horkman!" said the man, before shaking my hand for a very long time, then grasping my elbows for an equally long time, and then hugging me to the right and then to my left.

Then it was Peckerman's turn.

"Welcome to Yemen, Mr. Peckerman!" said the man, before shaking his hand for a very long time, then grasping his elbows for an equally long time, and then hugging him to the right and then to his left.

Twenty minutes later, this interminable greeting mercifully behind us, Peckerman and I got into the limo and took a seat opposite the man.

"Roomy," said Peckerman, looking around.

I agreed. It was a rather large limo. Had a bar. Television. Retractable sunroof. The kind of limo used only by heads of state and suburban kids on prom night.

"Mr. Horkman, Mr. Peckerman," he said as the car pulled away. "It is indeed an honor to meet you both."

"The feeling is mutual, Your Royal Majesty," replied Peckerman.

"Are you sure about that 'royal majesty' business?" I asked under my breath.

"No."

"With all due respect," I finally said to the man, "what should we call you?"

"Call me Ishmael!" he said, with a hardy Middle Eastern laugh that seemed to last as long as his hug. But the close quarters gave me and Peckerman no choice but to laugh along with him. So we did.

"Why is that funny?" Peckerman sneaked in during an over-the-top guffaw.

"You know, because of *Moby-Dick*."

"Moby-Dick?"

"That's how the book starts."

"Moby-Dick the singing whale?"

"Please tell me you didn't really just say 'singing whale.'"

We rode the downward arc of this guy's laugh, and when calm was finally restored I asked him to elaborate.

"So your name is Ishmael?"

"Close enough," he answered.

His name was Ismail Haniyeh. And he was the Prime Minister of Hamas. The political party that governs the Gaza portion of the Palestinian territories.

"When Ali called to let us know you were on the freighter, I dispatched that helicopter to assure your safety."

"Thank you," we said in unison.

"No. Thank *you*, gentlemen. Thank you in advance for what you are about to do to help us settle this once and for all."

"You're welcome," we said reflexively—too afraid to ask what it was we were about to do or what the "this" was that we were going to settle once and for all.

When the limo suddenly left the main road, I looked out the window and saw sand. And some intermittent hills made from natural rock formations. The kind of desert terrain one would expect to be traversing in an ATV as opposed to a stretch limo.

"Where are we going, Ismail?"

He looked at me and smiled.

"It's probably best you don't know."

"And why's that?" I asked.

"For your own security."

"Of course," I said. This time Peckerman didn't say anything. He was too busy wetting the seat we were sitting on to be bothered with talking.

It didn't really matter, though. Ismail did all of the talking. Telling us, or should I say confiding in us, the frustrations that the Arab governments were having. Within their own borders where it was becoming increasingly difficult to maintain tight grips on populations who saw the downfall of rulers like Mubarak and Qaddafi and wanted to seize control of their destinies as well.

And of the trouble those nations were having with each other as enmities between militant power groups like Hamas, Hezbollah, al-Qaeda, and Fatah was a constant threat to the stability of the region.

However, he said, they were united by one common sentiment. That Israel should no longer exist.

"And that's where the two of you could be of help to us," he said.

"Excuse me?" I said.

"You don't want us to be suicide bombers, do you?" asked Peckerman, who then burst out crying like the day he was born—after the doctor who delivered him kicked him in the face.

"Calm down, Peckerman," I said, though I could hear my own voice cracking.

Ismail looked at the two of us. A curious stare I had trouble reading and scared me even more than I already was, until he burst out laughing again.

"Ali told me how funny you two are," he said. "And that's exactly how we would like to use you."

"I'm afraid I don't understand," I told him.

Again I glanced out the window and saw the same nothingness as before. I remember wondering how the driver knew where we were, given there were no signs or landmarks or *anything*, for that matter, to differentiate one mile from the next.

I looked back at Ismail, when he started to explain.

"The way I see it, Mr. Horkman, laughter's a language that transcends culture and unites people the world over," Ismail answered. "And it is while people are disarmed enough to sit back and laugh that they are most receptive to whatever message's being conveyed— whether they realize it or not. It's subliminal. Done in advertising all the time. Enjoy the commercial and they'll buy the product."

The driver steered the limo to the right.

"Same thing with propaganda," he continued. "Keep their attention long enough and you'll change their minds."

The limo was slowing down.

"So our thinking is that while the entire Arab population is laughing at the comedy of two funny people, two funny Jews no less, whose message is that Israel is the common enemy, it won't be too long before everyone unites and jihad can begin."

"Jihad?" I whispered to Peckerman.

"What the fuck?" he whispered a little too loudly.

"Is everything okay, Mr. Peckerman?" asked the Prime Minister of Hamas.

"Absolutely!" he responded a little too loudly. "We love jihads!" he added with a raised clenched fist, which I made a mental note to shove up his butt if the opportunity ever arose.

The car came to a stop next to the base of a hill. Our doors were opened by two soldiers with rifles who nodded their greetings and flanked us as we climbed the rocks to a flat level where we entered a cave. Dark. Cold. Damp. The adjectives people generally use to describe the inside of a cave.

We walked farther into the belly of the mountain, turned a corner and came upon an open area with, of all things, lights. Big overhead klieg lights like they would have in a television studio. And cameras. Three broadcast cameras like they would have in a television studio.

"What is this place?" asked Peckerman.

"It's a television studio," said Ismail.

"And why are we here?" I asked.

Ismail said this is where Peckerman and I would be uniting all Arab nations in laughter with our own show on the Al Jazeera network. Followed by jihad.

CHAPTER 44

Jeffrey

I'm not saying I'm Jay Leno. But I have done some television. You might have seen me, if you ever caught a show I hosted called *Forensic Plumbing!*, which ran on local-cable-access TV in parts of northern New Jersey.

The problem was, they gave me a shitty time slot. I asked for prime time, like eight p.m. on a weeknight, but the asshole station gave me, get this, *six a.m. Sunday morning*, when there's nobody in front of a TV except three-year-olds and drunks passed out from Saturday night. Here are some of the shows that had better time slots than I did:

— *Candle Dipping for Seniors*, which was one solid hour of this guy who talked like Mister Rogers on quaaludes dipping a string into a pot of hot wax over and over and over and over until you wanted to just shoot the fucking television.

— *Ask the Rhododendron Doctor*, which was this guy who fielded calls from the public about rhododendron diseases. Except the public never called. All the calls were from the guy's wife, who tried to disguise her voice—like she'd try to talk in a low pitch and claim her name was Steve—but you could still tell it was her. Plus every now and then the asshole would slip up and call her "honey," even when she was allegedly a man.

— *Compost It!*, which was a bearded hippie dipshit going through his neighbors' garbage cans and pointing out what they could have put in a compost pile. He'd find, like, a grapefruit rind, and get all excited, like it was the fucking Hope Diamond. The only time the show was any good was when people would come out of their houses and yell at the hippie to get away from their garbage cans, and he'd brandish the grapefruit rind at them and yell that they were raping the Earth. I admit, I got the idea for putting an exclamation point at the end of *Forensic Plumbing!* from *Compost It!* But the guy really was a dipshit.

— *Hilda and Gloria's Wide Universe of Books*, which was these two fat old broads talking about a book they supposedly read that week, only half the time you could tell neither one of them had finished it, so most of the show consisted of one of them, Hilda I think, talking about medical complications arising from her hysterectomy, which she claimed was botched, and the other one going, "Oh my God, that's *awful*!"

These were the kinds of assholes who were getting better time slots than I got, which was a total joke because *Forensic Plumbing!* had some real meat to it. The set was me sitting in a chair next to a potted tropical plant. I opened the show every week by breaking the ice with a couple of plumbing-related jokes. Like: "Did you hear that somebody broke into the police station and stole the toilet? Police have nothing to go on!" Then I'd move on to that week's Plumbing Whodunit, which would be an actual forensic plumbing case.

Like there was one fascinating case where a forensic plumber was called in to investigate how come a high-rise building got flooded.

His investigation determined that a plumbing contractor had been called in to unclog a toilet on one of the middle floors. This guy ran a cable through the carrier and the four-inch horizontal waste into the six-inch vertical stack, where it got stuck. So the plumber, assuming the cable went down the stack, went looking for it on a lower floor, where he tried to cut into the riser with a band saw. But his blade got jammed, so he gave up and just left the blade there, if you can believe that, with a come-along still attached to the riser. The other end of the come-along was attached to a two-inch galvanized cold-water header in the pipe chase, which was what broke and caused the actual leak. But here's the kicker: The cable never went down the vertical stack in the first place! It got turned around in a tucker fitting and actually went *up*. Seriously. You can't make this shit up.

Every week on *Forensic Plumbing!* I would take the viewers through cases like that. Midway through my presentation, to add variety and action, I'd get up from the chair and go to a dry-erase board, where I'd diagram some of the key points. What made that a little tricky, productionwise, was that my camera operator was this older Italian guy from my neighborhood, Joe Stampone, who was legally blind. To be honest, you didn't really even need the "legally" part: He was blind as a bat with a bag over its head. The funny thing was, he still insisted on driving, being Italian, so his wife, Marie, had to ride with him and yell "It's turning yellow! Slow down! Now it's red! Stop the car stop stop forgodsake Joe *STOP*!!"

The thing was, Joe was the only person I could find who would go with me to the studio at six a.m. on a Sunday, so I had to use him on the camera. He was okay when I was sitting at the desk, but when I made the move to the dry-erase board, his aim was sometimes off, so if you were watching you'd hear me talking, but what you'd see on the screen was the tropical plant. So I came up with a system where I'd signal him to move the camera by snapping my fingers. If I snapped once, that meant move the camera left, and two snaps meant move it right. But Joe's memory wasn't much better than his eyesight, so sometimes I'd snap and you'd hear him saying, in what he thought was a whisper, "Wait, is it *your* left, or *my* left?"

But the point is, I had some experience in front of the camera, so when the Hamas guy, Ismail, told us we'd be doing a live international broadcast on Al Jazeera, which is a major network I have heard of, I right away had some ideas. My thought was a talk-show format, with me as the host, maybe opening with a monologue and interviewing guests. I saw Horkman in more of the Ed McMahon role—his job would be to laugh at the monologue, then shut the fuck up, move down the sofa, maybe get off camera altogether.

I explained my concept for the show to Horkman while Ismail was talking with the TV people in the cave. I expected Horkman to argue for more airtime, but instead he told me he didn't want to do the show at all. He didn't want me to, either.

"Don't you see?" he said. "They're just using us for propaganda, like Tokyo Rose, because we're American Jews, and they want to . . ."

"Who the fuck is Toyota Rose?"

"*Tokyo.* I said *Tokyo*, you idiot."

"Okay, so what the fuck does Japan have to do with . . ."

Horkman grabbed my shoulders and leaned in close. "Will you just *listen* to me?" he said. His breath smelled like bananas. "We *cannot do this*. They're going to use us to promote jihad."

"So we promote a little jihad," I said. "What's the harm?"

"A *little jihad*?" Horkman said. "What's the *harm*?" He took a deep breath, looked at the roof of the cave, then back at me. "Listen," he said. "You have to get this into your tiny brain. We can't do this. We have to figure out a way to . . ."

He shut up then, because Ismail was coming back.

"All right, gentlemen," Ismail said. "If you'll come this way, we're ready for you on the set."

He led us over in front of the cameras. It turned out the "set" was just an area on the cave floor, totally empty except for a dead scorpion.

"You will stand here," said Ismail, "and speak into the camera."

"Waitwaitwait," I said. "All due respect, this is not a good visual. It looks like we're in a fucking cave here."

"We are in a cave," said Ismail.

"Exactly," I said. "That's the problem. It's called production values. Are you familiar with an American TV show called *Forensic Plumbing!* by any chance?"

"What kind of plumbing?"

"Forensic. The show is *Forensic Plumbing!*, with an exclamation mark."

"No."

"Okay, anyway, it's a show that's been on for a while, and I happen to be the producer, so I know a little something about the medium of television, okay? It's all about creating an image. Now with this set here, the image you're creating is, you're a cheap half-ass operation that can't even afford a studio. That's not going to impress your viewers. They're going to tune in and see two guys standing in a shithole cave. They're going to think, 'This outfit can't even afford chairs! I don't want to buy whatever these losers are selling!' They're going to change the channel. But if you dress this set up a little, get some curtains, some nice chairs, maybe a plant and a desk I could sit behind as host, then you have some credibility. The viewers will be like, 'This is obviously a first-class operation! Maybe I'll give this jihad thing a try!'"

Horkman made a sound like a bullfrog trying to give a blow job to a buffalo.

Ismail shook his head. "We prefer the image of a cave."

Not to stereotype, but this is exactly why these ragheads are still riding around on fucking camels.

"So gentlemen," said Ismail, "as I said, we want you to stand here"—he pointed basically at the dead scorpion—"and speak to the camera."

"Okay," I said, "but what's the format?"

"As I said in the car," said Ismail, "we just want you to be yourselves—two humorous Jewish American men, respected international terrorists, bantering in an amusing fashion, perhaps making a few jokes about how Israel is an oppressive racist state that must be destroyed."

Horkman's face was now the color of a baboon's ass.

"Also," continued Ismail, "at a certain point, which I will indicate to you by raising my hand, we would like you to read a brief statement, which we have printed on a card for your convenience." He held up a white card. On it, handwritten, were these words:

SOMEONE LEFT THE CAKE OUT IN THE RAIN.

"What the fuck?" I said.

"It's a code," said Horkman. "To trigger the jihad."

"I hate that fucking song," I said.

"I'm sorry to hear that," said Ismail. "Nevertheless, I must insist that you read it exactly as it is written, when I give the signal."

"What if we don't?" said Horkman.

"Yeah," I said. "What if we don't?"

"We will decapitate you on camera," said Ismail.

"Okay, then!" I said. "Not a problem. We were just curious."

"Very good," said Ismail. "We will start the broadcast in"—he looked at his watch—"ninety seconds. To summarize: We want lighthearted banter—easygoing, joshing camaraderie between two humorous friends, interspersed with playful references to the need to exterminate all Jews from the planet. When I give the signal, you will read the card precisely as written. If you do not, I will have to call upon these men to intervene." He nodded toward the far cave wall. Two men I hadn't seen before were standing there. They had black hoods over their heads. And they were both holding swords.

Ismail said, "Do you understand?"

"Absolutely!" I said.

Horkman didn't say anything.

"Excellent," said Ismail. He looked at his watch again. "Fifteen seconds." He stepped out of camera range.

"Have fun with it, gentlemen," he said. "You're on."

Philip

I had been on television only once in my life. I was four-teen years old and my parents took me and my sister into New York City to see a taping of *The Price Is Right*. My seat was on the aisle, so if you were watching at home you got to see the left half of my face when they showed the audience after Bob Barker yelled "Come on down!" and that contestant was actually coming on down.

That was the extent of my resume as a performing artist.

So when the Hamas stage manager started counting down the seconds until we were on the air, I was nervous, thanks to the combo platter of performing comedy on live television, the message we were to deliver on live television, and the threat of having our heads separated from our bodies on live television by those two black-hooded gentlemen brandishing very large swords.

Very large swords with very dull blades, mind you. Back in the days when my parents forced me to go to Hebrew school, I remember learning that what made a kosher chicken kosher was that it was killed with a knife so sharp that when the rabbi cut the chicken's head off, it actually felt no pain. It was that quick.

But dull blades? A dull blade is used by a decapitator to make the decapitatee feel as much pain as possible when they take their time sawing his head off. Lovely.

So, while Peckerman and I stood there side by side looking into camera, I resigned myself to do all I could to not screw up and to be as funny as possible.

"Five, four, three, two, one . . ." said the stage manager, before pointing to us. We were on television. Peckerman lead the way and I followed.

"Good evening, fellow jihadists. Welcome to *Peckerman and Horkman.*"

"Why is your name first?" I asked.

"Because I spoke first," he said.

"So if I spoke first, the name of our show would be *Horkman and Peckerman*?"

"That's right."

"Then can we start the show over and I'll speak first?"

Peckerman looked into camera and pointed to me.

"Typical Jew," he said.

Ismail, the stage manager, and the cameramen started laughing.

"How does that make me a typical Jew?" I asked.

"Because you're whining like a Jew when he doesn't get what he wants."

"You mean like the Gaza Strip?"

They laughed some more.

"Yes," answered Peckerman.

"And the Left Bank?" I asked.

"You mean the West Bank, don't you? The Left Bank is in Paris."

"I know. But Jews want that, too."

More laughter.

"Really?" asked Peckerman.

"Oh yeah. We Jews want all the banks."

Even more laughter. From everyone. Including, I assumed, the decapitators because their black hoods were now bobbing like turds in the ocean.

Encouraged by the appreciative audience, Peckerman and I kept going.

"So tell me, Horkman, did you hear the one about the old Jew who was walking down the street in Nazi Germany?"

"No, I don't think I have."

"Well, this old Jew was walking down a street in Nazi Germany when a car pulls up and Hitler steps out. Hitler sees a pile of dog shit on the sidewalk, takes out his gun and orders the old Jew to get down and eat it. So the old Jew bends down, eats some of it, looks up, grabs the gun away from Hitler and orders *him* to get down and eat the dog shit. So Hitler gets down and eats some of it. Later the old Jew went home and said to his wife, 'You'll never guess who I had lunch with today.'"

This brought the room to the brink of hysteria. Loud sustained laughter. High fives. Clapping as if they could already taste the victory that would assuredly ensue thanks to this barrage of anti-Semitic jokes.

"If we're all laughing," Ismail said to one of the cameramen, "I can only imagine how jihadists everywhere are united in laughter as well."

Thrilled that his instincts were correct in having me and Peckerman do this little dog and pony show, Ismail then reached down and picked up the card that had that inane lyric from that dreadful song written on it.

But Peckerman and I pretended not to see it, knowing full well what the result would bring. So we stalled.

"You know, Horkman. There must be literally thousands of Jewish jokes we can tell on our new show."

"Thousands?" I said. "I'd bet there's *tens* of thousands."

Ismail, giving us the benefit of the doubt that we hadn't seen the card, started waving it while clearing his throat to get our attention.

"Tens of thousands?" said Peckerman. "Okay, let's tell them all."

"Sounds good to me."

But after I said that and we both turned forward, Ismail knew it was impossible for us not to have seen the card and deduced that we were defying his orders. So he looked over at the two black-hooded gentlemen, who instantly took a step toward us.

"Let's start by making fun of Jewish women, shall we?"

Exactly what we expected to happen by delaying the inevitable is anyone's guess. A miracle? One that would save both Israel and our necks as well? Probably. Yet it did cross my mind that any shot we had with the God of the Chosen People intervening on our behalf was becoming less and less likely with the riddles we were now telling.

"What's the difference between a Jewish woman and Jell-O?" Peckerman asked.

"I give up," I answered.

"Jell-O moves when you eat it."

Aside from our own nervous giggles, there was no other laugher in that cave. Apparently the comedy portion of our show was over, as Ismail glared at us and the two decapitators-in-waiting took another step in our direction.

"What should we do?" I asked under my breath. And when I heard the sound of my voice cracking, it scared me more than I already was.

But that was nothing as compared to how scared I became about a second later when a seething Ismail held the white card up for what I knew was going to be the last time and Peckerman looked up and blurted.

"Someone left the kike out in the rain!"

"Huh?"

"Kill them!" yelled Ismail.

Pandemonium broke out as the hooded guys raised their swords and rushed toward us. Having no desire to see just how far our heads would fly before hitting the ground, we knocked over two of the cameras that were between us and the black-hooded guys, and started running.

Because the mouth of the cave was crowded with members of Hamas who we felt would be less than willing to aid in our escape, we went in the opposite direction, which took us deeper into the base of the mountain with the black-hooded guys already bearing down on us.

"Good going, Peckerman!"

"What's your problem now, dickstroker?"

"Ismail said to read exactly what was on that card."

"And that's exactly what I did."

"Someone left the kike out in the rain?"

"That's what it said!"

"He showed us the card, Peckerman. It said cake."

"I'm telling you. Someone must've changed it."

"He's right, Horkman. We changed it," shouted one of the black-hooded guys.

"You could both stop running now," shouted the other black-hooded guy.

"Are you going to stop running?" I asked Peckerman, while we were still running.

"Not a chance in hell!" he said while we were still running. "How about you?"

"I may have to," I told him.

"Why?"

"Because one of them has his arm around my neck," I managed to eek out as I was being forced to the ground by a forearm larger than the house I grew up in.

"On second thought, I may have to revise what I said about stopping," Peckerman said on his way down to the same ground.

We were lying there for maybe a second, before being yanked back up to our feet and pushed against the cave wall.

"Are you going to stand still or not?" asked the black-hooded guy who had his hand around my throat.

I nodded. Then he let go of me.

"And how about you?" the other black-hooded guy asked Peckerman. "Jesus, what's that smell?" he then asked.

For those of you who guessed that a terrified Peckerman soiled himself again, you're right.

"I'll take that as a yes," said Peckerman's black-hooded guy.

Then they both took off their black hoods.

"Who are you guys?" I asked.

"We're with Mossad," said my guy.

"Moe Sod?" asked Peckerman. "Who's that? A tailor?"

"Mossad, you ignoramus. It's the Israeli intelligence agency," I told him. "What's this all about?" I then asked the commandos.

"We've been tracking you two," said my guy.

"And we did switch that card when Ismail and the others weren't looking," said the other one.

"Why?"

"Because whenever a code isn't recited exactly as planned—if a *single word* is changed—it's a signal to the jihadists that the jihad has been aborted, permanently, and they should lay down arms," my guy explained.

"Now we have to get you two out of here," said the other commando, "before Hamas finds out that we didn't kill you."

CHAPTER 46

The NBC
Nightly News

BRIAN WILLIAMS: Tonight, a stunning development in the Middle East, where there is suddenly real hope for an end to the conflict that has spawned decades of hatred, violence and death. And as unbelievable as it seems, the architects of this historic breakthrough are the same two men who seem to have turned the entire planet upside down in recent weeks: Philip Horkman and Jeffrey Peckerman, the now-legendary international masterminds with an uncanny ability to show up in critical world hotspots at exactly the right moment, perform some seemingly impossible feat, then vanish—which is how they have become known to millions as the *Fantasmas de la Noche*, or "Ghosts of the Night." Today the duo appeared in Yemen, where, executing the kind of exquisitely planned, split-second operation that has become their trademark, they essentially dismantled the world's largest terrorist organization, and in doing so created a pathway that many observers believe could lead to lasting peace. For more on this astonishing story, we go to NBC Middle East correspondent Elizabeth Burger in Yemen. Elizabeth, how did Horkman and Peckerman pull this off?

BURGER: Brian, as you recall, the two men were last seen in Mogadishu, where they staged a lightning-strike operation that not only fed thousands of refugees, but also struck a critical blow against government corruption and international piracy. Horkman and Peckerman were last seen leaving the scene of that operation in a mysterious black helicopter. That helicopter, we now know, brought them here, to Yemen, where they made contact with this man, Ismail Haniyeh, the Prime Minister of Hamas, who took them to a secret cave equipped with a TV studio. Horkman and Peckerman, who now have a huge international following, had apparently led Hamas to believe that they would make a propaganda broadcast. In it, they were to deliver a coded order that, according to intelligence sources, would activate a network of terror cells throughout the United States and Europe, and trigger "the final jihad"—an all-out terror attack on the West, combined with a full-scale military assault on Israel. Instead, after a comical monologue, they—or specifically, Jeffrey Peckerman—delivered a coded order that had a radically different effect.

WILLIAMS: We're going to play the video of Peckerman delivering that phrase now. We warn you that the content is offensive. But because of the historic significance of this event, *NBC Nightly News* has decided to play it exactly as it was broadcast on Al Jazeera.

PECKERMAN: Someone left the kike out in the rain!

(Shouting.)

WILLIAMS: The phrase, of course, is a variation of a line from the song "MacArthur Park." Any idea why the terrorists picked that particular song, Elizabeth?

BURGER: Brian, one theory is that it was chosen specifically to demoralize the United States, because it gets stuck in your head and everybody hates it. But whatever the reason, the key fact is that when Peckerman, who is Jewish, changed "cake" to the anti-Semitic slur we just heard, he completely changed the coded meaning of the phrase. Instead of triggering the final jihad, Peckerman was sending out the opposite order, commanding the sleeper cells in the terrorist network to abort the jihad altogether. Not only that, but many of the cells interpreted the code to mean that they were actually supposed to surrender.

WILLIAMS: What happened next was a sequence of events the likes of which has never before been seen in the history of counterterrorism. In dozens of locations throughout the United States and Europe, terrorist agents, believing they were following orders from the highest levels of their organization, turned themselves in to local police and federal authorities. With the information obtained from these terrorist groups, the authorities were able to quickly locate and apprehend many other terrorists. The extent of the sleeper-cell network came as a shock to the authorities. It turns out that terrorists had penetrated deep into some of our most trusted institutions. For more on that, we go to NBC News national security correspondent David Golia. David?

GOLIA: Brian, the list of compromised organizations is almost unbelievable. According to FBI sources, terrorists had infiltrated—among many other entities—the U.S. Department of Commerce, the Home Shopping Network, the Audubon Society, the Florida Department of Motor Vehicles, the League of Women Voters, at least fifty Waffle Houses, the University of Alabama cheerleading squad, Up with People, a national chain of Pilates studios, the Kansas state legislature, and an entire touring company of *Rent*. Perhaps most shocking of all, it is now estimated that terrorists made up at least 15 percent of the Transportation Security Administration workforce.

WILLIAMS: David, are you saying that the TSA—the federal agency responsible for screening airline passengers for potential weapons of terrorism—has *itself* been infiltrated by terrorists?

GOLIA: That's what I'm told, Brian. Every year they confiscate millions of containers of seemingly harmless shampoo, perfume, hair spray, cosmetics and other personal hygiene products from airline passengers. Have you ever wondered what they *do* with all those products?

WILLIAMS: I have, David.

GOLIA: Well, according to my sources, these undercover TSA terrorists have been funding their operations by selling these confiscated items to the Amway Corporation, which in turn repackages them for sale to the very same public from which they were confiscated in the first place.

WILLIAMS: *Amway* is involved in this?

GOLIA: Brian, I'm told that Mary Kay is also heavily implicated.

WILLIAMS: Truly shocking. For more on the international implications of this story, we go to NBC United Nations correspondent Ronald Ungerman. Ron?

UNGERMAN: Brian, the Horkman-Peckerman takedown of the international terrorist network had an immediate impact on the stagnant Middle East peace process—but not the impact you would expect. It seems that Hamas, unwilling to admit that two men— two *Jewish* men—were able to foil the jihad, is now claiming that the whole thing was planned.

WILLIAMS: Hamas is claiming it *deliberately sabotaged* its own terrorism network?

UNGERMAN: That's right, Brian. Here's a statement made earlier today by Hamas Prime Minister Ismail Haniyeh.

HANIYEH: Of *course* it was planned. Do you think we are idiots? We had decided that the time had come to end this cycle of senseless violence. But to accomplish that objective, we needed a dramatic gesture, and it had to be made by men of such international stature that both sides—Palestinian and Israeli—would listen to them. That is why we chose Horkman and Peckerman for this mission. They carried it out flawlessly. I love those two crazy guys.

WILLIAMS: Ron, is anybody buying this?

UNGERMAN: Not really, Brian, but at this point it doesn't seem to matter. The logjam has been broken, and I'm told that even as we speak, rapid progress is being made in secret, high-level Mideast peace talks brokered by the United States. A deal is being hammered out involving a complex series of land transfers under which Israel will give up a substantial portion of the disputed West Bank, in return for which it will be granted a parcel of land from Lebanon, which will be compensated by a comparable parcel from Syria, which in turn will be ceded land by Iraq, which will receive land from Iran, which will in turn be granted land by Azerbaijan, which will for its part be granted full access rights, in perpetuity, to what I am told is a very nice time-share property in the Hamptons. The Gordian knot has been cut, Brian, and within a matter of days we may finally see, for the first time, lasting peace in the Middle East.

WILLIAMS: Incredible. Thank you, Ron. Meanwhile, the big question, once again, is: Where are Philip Horkman and Jeffrey Peckerman? For more on that, we go to NBC correspondent Richard Hanft, who has been following the two men since they liberated Cuba. Richard?

HANFT: Brian, once again Horkman and Peckerman have disappeared like, well, like ghosts in the night. They are still officially wanted by the United States government for, among other charges, committing acts of terrorism in New York City, endangering zoo animals, hijacking a cruise ship, extorting hundreds of millions of dollars, and seriously damaging a valuable flamenco guitar belonging to the singer Charo. It is safe to say, however, that because of their spectacular string of daring humanitarian acts, they would be treated very leniently by the Justice Department, and almost certainly would be granted presidential pardons. Right now they are, without question, the two most popular human beings on the planet. Street vendors are selling *Fantasmas de la Noche* T-shirts as fast as they can get their hands on them. Already at least four movies about their lives are being rushed into production, including one featuring George Clooney as Horkman, Brad Pitt as Peckerman, and Charo as herself. Virtually every head of state, religious leader and news organization on the planet is trying to get in touch with Horkman and Peckerman; it's also safe to say that the opportunities available to the two men would make them fabulously wealthy. The world is at their feet, Brian. The question is, where in the world are they?

WILLIAMS: Where, indeed?

CHAPTER 47

Jeffrey

Here're some things you never hear anybody say:

— "Guess where we're going on vacation? Yemen!"

— "There's no place like Yemen!"

— "Yemen? Count me in!"

The reason nobody says these things is, Yemen sucks. If nations were Kardashian sisters, Yemen would be whatshername, the one who looks like Herman Munster. Compared to Yemen, Haiti is the Magic Kingdom. I'm not saying this just because Yemen is hot. Hot, I understand. It's a fucking desert. But *mosquitoes*? What the fuck are mosquitoes doing in a fucking desert? That's what I wanted to know.

"What the fuck are mosquitoes doing in a fucking desert?" I asked.

"As I have repeatedly informed you," said Moishe, "the mosquitoes breed in the salt marshes near the coast. And if you ask me that question one more time, I'm going to rip out your larynx with my bare hands."

"He is capable of doing that," said Shlomo. "He is *trained* to do that."

"Don't let me stand in the way," said Horkman.

Moishe and Shlomo were the Mossad agents. Those aren't their real names; that's just what I called them. They wouldn't tell us their real names. They wouldn't tell us hardly anything, except that we had to do exactly what they said or the Hamas assholes would kill us.

They did get us out of the cave, I'll give them that. They took us down a bunch of dark tunnels, and after a couple of hours of creeping around in there we finally got outside. I figured they'd have a car waiting to take us out of there, but they said no—no car, no roads, we were going to walk. They also gave us some garments and told us to change into them. I held mine up; it was one of those bathrobes the Arabs wear.

"What the fuck is this?" I said.

"It's a thob," said Shlomo.

"A *what*?"

"A thob. It's traditional Yemeni attire."

"Well, I'm thorry, thir," I said, "but you can thtick your thob where the thun don't thine."

Pretty good, right? Those assholes didn't even crack a smile.

"Just put it on," said Moishe.

"Why?" I said.

"Because we cannot be conspicuous," said Moishe.

"And because you shat your pants," said Shlomo.

Like they never shat their pants.

"Okay," I said. "But I'm not wearing one of those douchebag camel-jockey head things."

"You mean like this?" said Moishe, handing me one of those douchebag camel-jockey head things.

So that's how we ended up walking—*walking*—across the fucking desert, four Jews dressed like Lawrence of fucking Arabia, getting eaten by mosquitoes, which is why I periodically felt the need to raise the question of what the fuck were mosquitoes doing in the fucking desert, which is why Moishe threatened to rip out my larynx.

My point, as I mentioned earlier, is that Yemen sucks, and it *really* sucks if you're walking in sixty-seven-million-degree heat swatting little vampire Arab bugs.

Guess what Planet Horkman thought about it.

He thought it was moving.

"This is moving" were his exact words.

I said, "It's *what*?"

"Peckerman," he said, "this is our Exodus."

"What the fuck are you talking about?"

"Haven't you ever been to a seder?"

The true answer was yes and no. When I was a kid, our family had seders, but they almost always ended early because of my dad. Like for example, one year he accused my Uncle Harvey of deliberately hiding the afikomen where he knew his kids would find it and get the five dollars. Uncle Harvey told my dad he was being ridiculous, so my dad threw the shank bone at him. My dad later claimed he meant it as a joke, but the truth is he threw the bone overhand from fairly close range and it hit Uncle Harvey in the eye and detached his retina, so between Aunt Janet screaming and the paramedics coming, that seder was pretty much down the toilet.

I didn't tell Horkman any of this. What I said was, "Of course I've been to seders. You eat a hard-boiled egg, talk about Moses and the Pharaoh and the ten plagues of Egypt. Boils, hail, snakes, blood, yadda yadda."

Moishe said, "No snakes."

"What do you mean, no snakes?" I said.

"There was no plague of snakes," said Moishe.

"You're probably thinking of frogs," said Shlomo.

"Seriously?" I said. "*Frogs* were a plague of Egypt?"

Moishe, Shlomo and Horkman all nodded.

"So," I said, "you're telling me that the Pharaoh, who's the king of Egypt and has this big-ass army, he's supposed to be scared of *frogs*? He's supposed to go, 'Ohmigod! Frogs! They might flick their tongues at my ankles! I better let these Jews go!'"

"It was a lot of frogs," said Moishe. But he definitely sounded defensive.

"*Anyway*," said Horkman, "until now, the story of Exodus was just words to me. But now, being here"—he gestured toward Yemen in general—"I find it very moving. It's *real*, Peckerman. We're crossing the desert, just as our people did more than three thousand years ago. We're fleeing the forces of the Pharaoh. And these men"—he pointed at Shlomo and Moishe—"are our Moses."

Shlomo and Moishe gave each other a look that said *douchebag*.

"Okay," I said. "If they're Moses, where are they leading us?"

"To the Promised Land, of course," said Horkman. He looked at Shlomo and Moishe and said, "Right? I assume we're going to Israel?"

They shot each other another look.

"Not exactly," said Shlomo.

"What do you mean, 'not exactly'?" said Horkman.

Shlomo took a few seconds, then said, "At the moment, Israel is involved in some very sensitive negotiations. If you two were to be seen in our country, or are in any way seen as acting as our agents, it could jeopardize our position."

"So where *are* you Moseses leading us?" I said.

"Our immediate destination," said Shlomo, "is Sana'a."

"Where?"

"The capital of Yemen."

"And we're going there because . . ."

Another look between them.

"You don't need to know that right now."

We walked for a couple of hours, until finally we came to a little dirtball town, where we got on a prehistoric bus full of Yemen people. The bus went maybe four miles an hour and smelled like a Porta-Potty at a Metallica concert, but at least there were no mosquitoes. Moishe and Shlomo told us to keep our mouths shut and let them do all the talking, because they spoke Yemish, or whatever you call it.

After about four million hours on this bus, we finally got to a city. We got off at an airport, which I was pretty happy about, because I figured it meant we were getting the fuck out of Yemen. Outside the terminal, Moishe and Shlomo handed me and Horkman Yemeni passports, which looked real. I opened mine and—I don't know how they did this; Photoshop, I guess—inside there was a picture of me wearing the douchebag camel-jockey head thing. Next to my picture it said "Yasser al-Fakoob."

"Yasser?" I said.

"It's a common name in Yemen," said Moishe.

"What's his name?" I asked, pointing at Horkman.

Horkman looked at his passport and said, "Murad Fazir."

"You want to trade passports?"

"No."

"Why not?"

"I don't want to be Yasser."

"Well, why the fuck do *I* have to be Yasser?"

Moishe stepped close, and I could feel something pressing into my stomach, which I figured was a gun.

"Listen," he said. "If you don't stop talking right now, I will shoot you. It will be the end of my career, but I will do it anyway, purely for the enjoyment."

Asshole.

We went into the terminal. Moishe and Shlomo also had Yemeni passports, so we acted like a traveling party of four, with them doing all the talking. We went through security, which was a joke, especially when you consider that at least one of us had a gun.

We got to our gate. The flight was boarding. Shlomo and Moishe handed each of us a ticket.

"Stick out your left hand," Moishe told Horkman.

Horkman did, and Moishe snapped a handcuff around it.

"What's that for?" said Horkman.

"So you will not lose this," said Moishe, handing Horkman a brief-case, which was attached to the handcuff with a chain.

"What's in this?" said Horkman.

"You don't need to know that now," said Moishe.

"You will board the plane now," said Shlomo. "We will wait here to make sure you leave with the flight. You'd be fools to get off the plane, anyway; if you stay in Yemen, you would be dead men."

"What do we do when we get there?" said Horkman.

Moishe and Shlomo looked at each other, not quite smiling, but close.

"Just do what you do best," said Moishe.

Whatever the fuck *that* meant.

I said, "Why don't *I* get a fucking briefcase?"

"Go," said Moishe, pointing toward the jetway.

And so we got on the daily Air China flight from Sana'a to Beijing.

CHAPTER 48

Philip

"**You've never flown** first-class before?" I asked Peckerman.

"Are you kidding? It's the only way I travel," he answered. "Why?"

"Just curious," I said, shrugging. "I mean, first class does offer a lot of amenities that aren't available back in coach—but I don't remember taking off your clothes and sitting in underpants the color of a wooden salad bowl as being one of them. What airline do you usually fly?"

"Fuck off, thimble dick!" he said under his breath. "As long as my name has to be Yasser, that thob stays off my body."

"And hangs down from the ceiling in the front of the cabin?"

"Yep."

"As opposed to, let's say, stowed in the overhead compartment?"

"The overhead compartment is not a statement."

"Just so I know, exactly what statement are you trying to make?" I asked.

"That I will not be pushed around," he said emphatically.

I must say that I admired Peckerman's resolve in wanting to remain his own person. A fascinating stance, I thought, for someone who'd just been given a new name and deposited by gunpoint on a plane to China.

"Besides," said Peckerman continuing a conversation I had every reason to believe was over, "if you're such a fan of the overhead compartment, why don't you stow that briefcase Moishe gave you up there?"

"Because it's handcuffed to my wrist? Because if I put it up there, I'd have to lie next to it for the next twenty-three hours?"

That's right. The flight from Sana'a to Beijing was going to take twenty-three hours. Ordinarily, during a long flight, I pass the time reading. I usually pack three books—the one I'm almost finished with, a new one to start, and then a third after I finish that one on the return trip.

For example, I recently discovered classics that I never got around to reading in my school years. In particular, Jane Austen—the nineteenth-century English novelist whose works of romantic fiction, set among the landed gentry, highlight the dependence of women on marriage to secure social standing and economic security.

So on my last trip to Portland, Oregon (to visit my wife's half sister's brother's son after he became the recipient of a compatible kidney from my wife's half sister's brother's son's brother), I made sure to pack *Emma*, *Mansfield Park* and *Sense and Sensibility*.

But since the flight we were now on was far from anticipated, I obviously didn't have any reading material with me.

"Just as well," said a yawning Peckerman. "Why you'd want to read anything written by that dead goybox is beyond me."

"Goybox?"

"This thing has a huge selection of movies and TV shows," he said, pointing to the screen he was lifting from the depths of the armrest between us. "Get with it, asshole. No one reads anymore. Reading is for the uninformed."

"Goybox?"

I guess at this point I could tell you what the ensuing twenty-three hours were like. But, with all due respect, I refuse to. Partially for your sake, mostly for mine.

Because in the interest of preserving my own sanity, I couldn't bear to revisit what it was like for me to be sitting next to someone who watched the movie *Jackass* fourteen consecutive times during the flight.

How he would lie curled up in the seat, his bloated body quaking with muted laughter under the blanket the flight attendant gave him. How, each time the movie was over, he'd peep out from under that blanket, shake his head and say, "One of the three greatest American films ever made! This, *The Godfather*, and *Jackass II*," and then go back under that blanket for another viewing. Or how my jaw dropped each time I reminded myself that the characters in the movies on this particular flight from Sana'a to Beijing were speaking Chinese with Arabic subtitles—two languages that Peckerman didn't speak.

So in essence, he was enthralled with moving pictures the way an imbecile is mesmerized by shiny objects. On second thought, it's worse, because an imbecile just sits and stares in wonderment at shiny objects. He doesn't laugh and make loud snorting sounds while doing so. Therefore, I apologize to all you imbeciles out there for making such a comparison and clumping you into Peckerman's category when you already have enough problems of your own.

And while I'm at it, I may as well apologize to all of you because I've gone into vivid detail about all of this after promising I wouldn't. So, in the spirit of trying to regain your trust, I'll spare you how Peckerman ordered meals from the unassuming flight attendant who didn't speak English by pointing to a selection on the menu and saying, "I'd like one of these, and both of your Moo Goo Gai Tits."

As for me, I couldn't do much of anything other than sit there wondering what was inside the attaché case dangling from my wrist like a huge charm bracelet. Noticing that the lock had three numbered tumblers, I was fairly confident that during a long flight like this I might have enough time to ultimately come up with the correct combination to open it.

So I decided to do this systematically.

"Can I please have a pencil and a pad?" I said, as if it was the English translation of what I was motioning to the flight attendant.

When she handed them to me, I wondered if the pad had enough pages in it given the number of permutations I might have to try. And I was going to ask for a second and maybe even a third pad, but she was waiting on other passengers at that point so, if need be, I could always get more pads from her later.

I looked at the lock. The tumblers were showing "0-0-0" so I wrote that down in small numbers at the top of the first page and then tried the switch on the attaché case. It slid and the lock popped up.

Huh?

I couldn't believe I'd gotten it on my first try! Couldn't believe that Moishe and Shlomo were actually that naïve to set such a simple combination as that! Maybe they weren't as smart as we thought they were!

It then became a matter of where I would open the case. There in my seat? Or should I take it into the restroom and open it there, lest one of the other passengers get a glimpse of whatever was inside?

But since it was still daytime and probably a number of hours before they would dim the cabin lights so people could sleep, I decided to stay put and not risk arousing curiosity by being seen entering a bathroom with an attaché case.

So while the idiot Peckerman was under his blanket laughing his butt off at the Algonquin Round Table–type wit of one of the three greatest American movies ever made, I laid the attaché case across my lap, slowly lifted its top half with my untethered hand, stopped to peer inside after every inch or so, and didn't see a thing until it was finally open all the way.

And there, in the bottom compartment, was a baseball card. A Mickey Mantle rookie baseball card that looked like it was in mint condition, which even the most casual baseball fan knows is worth upwards of $250,000.

I then sat there for what must've been six hours until it was dark outside. Night. When I was confident that not only the other first-class passengers but also the flight attendants were asleep. I went into the restroom, where I had my first experience with trying to wash and dry my hands with an attaché case linked to my wrist banging against the walls.

I then went back to my seat and, as if I were a surgeon removing a delicate organ from its assigned location inside of a body, carefully lifted the card by its edges. I was able to easily detach the gummy substance that made it adhere to the bottom of the case by rolling it with my fingers and then I examined the back side of the card, which also looked pristine.

At this point I wasn't sure if I was more relieved that it wasn't a bomb or more baffled as to why Moishe and Shlomo would make such a big deal about a baseball card, albeit a valuable one.

In retrospect, I guess I was more relieved, because after I put the gummy substance back on the bottom of the card before placing it into its original position and closing the case, I was actually comfortable enough to fall asleep. For eight hours. Until we landed at Beijing Capital International Airport. Where, right after Peckerman said "Thanks for the smooth ride, pan-fried vaggies" to that same flight attendant as we were disembarking, we entered the terminal and were met by Chinese soldiers.

CHAPTER 49

Jeffrey

I don't mean to generalize, but the Chinese are assholes.

I'm not just saying that because of what happened to me in Beijing. It's a lot of things. Like—this is just one example—when you get Chinese takeout, why do they give you sixty-three tiny packets of soy sauce containing maybe three molecules of soy sauce apiece, which you end up throwing away because they're such a pain in the ass? Give us *one* container of soy sauce, but MAKE IT BIG ENOUGH THAT WE CAN ACTUALLY FUCKING USE IT, OKAY, CHINESE PEOPLE? That's all I'm saying.

And don't get me started on Communism.

The point being I already had a few bones to pick with China before I even got there, and the flight over did not help. The Air China stewardess was a total bitch. I tried making a few jokes with her, lightening things up a little on a long flight, and, every time, she gave me a look like I puked on her tea tray. She also didn't like it that I took off the thob. Horkman didn't like it, either.

"Peckerman," he said, "hygiene aside, do you realize how ridiculous you look wearing just underpants and a headpiece?"

Yes, he actually said "hygiene aside." To be totally honest, I'd for-gotten I was wearing the camel-jockey head thing, but I decided to keep it on because it pissed Horkman off.

At least they had video on the plane. This is off topic, but: It's really amazing, the way *Jackass* holds up. You know the scene where the guy goes into a plumbing supply store, and he takes an actual dump in a display toilet? Believe it or not, that scene is *even better in Chinese.*

So anyway, after, like, nineteen million hours of flying, we finally got to Beijing. When we landed, the stewardess bitch brought me the thob, but as a protest I left it in the plane and walked off wearing the Air China blanket. Horkman was right behind me with the brief-case, which I was hoping had money in it. My plan at that point was:

(1) Find someplace quiet at the airport where we could figure out how to open the briefcase;
(2) split the money, or better yet find some way to
(3) dump Horkman and
(4) keep all the money, then
(5) buy a plane ticket and get the fuck out of China.

But right away there was trouble. There were soldiers in the termi-nal, and as soon as we got off the plane, a couple of them started walk-ing toward us. We tried to walk away, but the soldiers blocked us. They held us by the gate until finally another Chinese guy showed up. Actually, to save words here, I'm going to stop describing people in China as Chinese, because basically everybody over there is Chi-nese. From now on, if I tell you about a person in China, you can just assume that person is Chinese.

So anyway, this guy showed up, wearing a suit. He looked at our passports, then started talking to us, not in Chinese, but also not in English, so we had no idea what he was saying. I finally figured out that, because of our passports, he was talking Yemish. So I held up my hand and said, *"No comprendo."* I pointed at Horkman and me and said, *"No hablo Yemen-o."*

"Why are you talking to him in Spanish?" said Horkman.

"Because it's a foreign language," I said.

"But that doesn't make any *sense*," he said.

"Maybe not to *you*, asshole," I said.

The suit guy, who'd been listening to this discussion, said, in English, "You speak English."

We agreed that we did.

He looked at our passports again and said, "You are Yasser al-Fakoob and Murad Fazir, citizens of Republic of Yemen?"

"That's what our passports say," I answered. Technically, this was true.

"But you do not speak Arabic?"

"We're not originally from Yemen," I said.

"Where are you from?" he said.

"Hungaria," I said.

"Hungaria?" he said.

"Hungaria?" said Horkman.

"Shut up, asshole," I whispered. "I'm creating a backstory here."

"I know," he whispered back. "But *Hungaria*?"

Of course by then the asshole had completely blown it. The suit guy said something to the soldiers, then told us, "You will come with me, please."

Fifteen minutes later, we were in a speeding black Mercedes with a police escort. The suit guy sat in the front next to the driver; Horkman and I were in the back. Horkman wasted some breath demanding his rights, which the suit guy ignored. His attitude was, hey, this is China, *nobody* here has any fucking rights.

Finally, Horkman gave up on the suit guy and leaned over to me. "Listen," he whispered. "Whatever we do, we can't let them get what's in the briefcase."

"You know what's in the briefcase?" I whispered.

"Yes. I opened it on the plane. It's a baseball card."

"*What?* A fucking—"

"Shh. Listen! It's a very rare card. Mickey Mantle's rookie card. It's worth a fortune."

"Why would the Israelis give us that? Do they even *play* baseball? Aside from Sandy Koufax, I mean."

"Peckerman, just *listen*, okay? The card could be the only bargaining chip we have to get out of here. We can't let them take it away."

"So what do we do?"

"We play it by ear."

Which is what people say when they have no fucking clue.

We drove for maybe forty-five minutes in ridiculous traffic to downtown Beijing, which is not an attractive city unless you are attracted to a lot of big-ass buildings jumbled together under a daytime sky the color of infant diarrhea. We turned into a driveway guarded by soldiers and went down a tunnel into some kind of underground complex. There were more soldiers waiting for us underground. They hustled us out of the Mercedes and down some hallways and into a room with a couple of chairs, which they pointed to. We sat down. The soldiers punched a code in a keypad next to the door, opened it, and went out.

After a few minutes, the keypad beeped and the door opened. In walked a guy I'll call Lieutenant Sulu because he looked like the *Star Trek* guy, and before you tell me that Sulu was Japanese not Chinese and I'm a racist who thinks all Asians look alike, allow me to inform you that you should go fuck yourself, because this guy looked *exactly* like Lieutenant Sulu, okay?

He asked us what we were doing in China. Horkman and I looked at each other for a second, and then, at the same time, Horkman said "tourism" and I said "business."

"So, which one is it?" said Lieutenant Sulu. "Business, or tourism?"

"It's basically a tourism business," I said.

"What kind of tourism business?" said Lieutenant Sulu.

"You know," Horkman said, waving his arm to indicate China in general. "Arranging tourist visits to the many sights of your great country. The Great Wall, the Forbidden City . . . the, uh, Great . . . Wall . . ."

I could see he was stuck, so I added, "All the main popular Chinese tourist shit."

Horkman gave me a look that said *Shut up*, and I gave him a look that said *Fuck you, asshole, at least I didn't say the Great Wall twice.*

Lieutenant Sulu was frowning at us. He pointed to Horkman's briefcase and said, "What do you have in that briefcase?"

"Personal effects," said Horkman.

"What kind of personal effects?"

"Just . . . the usual," said Horkman.

"The *usual*?" I said.

"Shut up," said Horkman.

"Mr. Fazir," said Lieutenant Sulu, speaking to Horkman. "Please open the briefcase."

"I'm afraid I can't do that," said Horkman.

"May I ask why not?"

"I don't know the combination."

"You don't know the combination to the briefcase of personal effects you have handcuffed to your wrist?"

"Correct."

"I see. Do you have the key to the handcuff?"

"No."

Lieutenant Sulu sighed. "All right," he said. "I will have the briefcase removed, then." He stood up and went to the door. He punched the keypad, opened the door and stepped out; we heard him talking to somebody in the hallway. Horkman quickly put the briefcase in his lap, worked the combination lock and opened it.

"What are you doing?" I said.

"I'm going to give you the card," he said.

"What am I supposed to do with it?"

"Hide it," he said.

He reached into the briefcase and, using his fingertips, carefully took the Mickey Mantle card out. He handed it to me, then quickly shut the briefcase. Lieutenant Sulu was coming back in. I stuck the card under my Air China blanket.

"Mr. Fazir," said Sulu. "You will come with me. Mr. al-Fakoob, you will stay here."

"Why don't you go fakoob yourself," I said, although not too loud.

As Horkman stood up, he leaned over and whispered, "Don't let them get the card." Then he followed Sulu out of the room.

For once I agreed with Horkman; no way was I going to let the Chinese get hold of the card, which I figured was worth a lot of money, at least half of which would be mine, and maybe all of which would be mine, depending on what happened to Horkman, which frankly was not my concern. My concern was where to hide the card. All I was wearing was underpants, an Air China blanket and Arab headgear. I had no pockets. I tried tucking the card into my headgear, but it wouldn't stay. I could hear noise in the hall, people coming my way. They were getting close. I had to make a decision. So I did.

I stuck the card up my ass.

I had to roll it up first, which probably is not ideal treatment for a rare mint-condition baseball card, but put yourself in my position and ask yourself: What would you do? I'll tell you what: You would stick the card up your ass.

I was just finished when the door opened. In came Lieutenant Sulu and Horkman. I could see soldiers behind them. Horkman's handcuff was gone, and so was the briefcase. Lieutenant Sulu did not look happy.

"You will come with us," he said to me.

I stood up and started walking toward them. I got maybe two steps. Then the whole building went batshit.

I mean *batshit*. Alarms started going off everywhere. The lights went off, then back on again. Chinese voices started shouting from speakers in the wall and walkie-talkies carried by soldiers.

Lieutenant Sulu, looking worried, told me and Horkman to stay in the room. He left, slamming the door shut behind him.

"What the fuck is happening?" I said.

"I don't know," said Horkman.

"Let's get the fuck out of here."

"How?" said Horkman. "We're locked in."

Exactly when he said that, the lights went off, then on again. Then the keypad by the door beeped.

Then the door swung open.

We went to the doorway and looked out. There were people in the hall walking fast in both directions, but at the moment no soldiers, and no Sulu. Horkman and I looked at each other.

"Okay," I said, "*now* let's get the fuck out of here."

We went out into the hall and started walking. We passed a lot of people, a lot of them running now, everybody looking really worried. Some of them stared at us, but nobody tried to stop us. The loudspeakers were still shouting in Chinese, alarms were going off everywhere. The lights kept going off and on.

We came to a big corridor, where there was a steady flow of people heading in one direction, which we figured was out. So we got into the flow, and pretty soon we came to a building exit, with everybody pouring out past a bunch of soldiers, who were shouting, but nobody was paying any attention.

Now we were outside in a huge mob, everybody yelling and shoving everybody else. There were helicopters overhead, and more sirens, and more loudspeakers blaring. Horkman and I had no idea which way to go, and it wouldn't have mattered if we did, because all we could do was get pushed along by the crowd. We got swept into a wide street next to a huge open area containing approximately the entire fucking population of China.

That's when it got bad.

First, I heard screaming in front of us. A *lot* of screaming, really loud.

Then, all of a sudden, all the people in front of us, who had been surging forward, suddenly turned around and started surging back in our direction.

Then I got my fucking foot stuck. I don't know how I did it, but all of a sudden my left foot was jammed way down into a wide crack in the pavement, and I could *not* get the fucking thing back out, at least not with all these asshole Chinese people pushing against me and screaming.

"HORKMAN!" I yelled. "HELP ME OUT HERE! I'M STUCK!"

"I CAN'T GET TO YOU!" he yelled back from the crowd, which was dragging him away. Right then I decided I was definitely keeping all the Mickey Mantle card money.

So the situation was, I was in this insane mob, leaning over, yanking on my foot, which was not budging, with all these screaming people running past me, bumping into me. Then I heard a new sound, a motor. A *big* motor, really close. And a noise like *clank clank clank*.

So I stood up, and there it was, right in front of me, just a few yards away.

A fucking tank.

The size of a three-car garage.

Coming straight at me.

Clank clank clank . . .

The crowd was now completely cleared out of the way. It was just me and the tank, which was close enough that I could reach out and touch it.

"HEY!" I said, banging on the hood, or whatever you call the front part of a tank. "STOP!"

The tank kept coming.

Clank clank clank . . .

Now I'm pounding like a maniac and shouting, "STOP! PLEASE! STOPSTOPSTOPSTOP*STOPPPPP*!!"

The tank bumped against my chest. I was absolutely sure I was about to become a human tortilla. All I could think, in what I truly believed were the last seconds of my life, was, *Why couldn't it be Horkman who got his foot caught?*

And then, all of a sudden, the tank stopped.

For a few seconds, nobody moved. It was just me standing there with the tank touching my chest, and all these Chinese standing around in a big circle, watching. Nobody said a word. It was totally silent, except for a sound like *prrbbbt*, which was the Mickey Mantle rookie card squirting out of my ass. Go ahead, judge me. Let's see how *your* bowels handle a fucking tank.

The silence went on for maybe ten seconds, until it became clear the tank wasn't starting up again. And then the crowd went nuts. They all came charging forward, smiling and shouting, swarming around me and the tank. A bunch of hands grabbed me. I yelled, "HEY! MY FOOT IS STUCK!" But they lifted me straight up, and the way they did it yanked my foot loose.

Next thing I knew they were carrying me over their heads. I was yelling, "PUT ME DOWN! PUT ME DOWN, GODDAMMIT!" But they paid no attention. They were like a bunch of ants carrying a dropped particle of corn dog. I don't mean that in a racial way, the ants thing. I mean it in the sense of, even if a corn dog particle doesn't want to be carried, the ants don't give a shit.

I heard a voice yelling, "PECKERMAN! PECKERMAN!" I looked down and saw Horkman reaching for me. The crowd realized we were together, but instead of putting me down, they lifted *him* up, too. Now we were both bouncing around up there like the bride and groom at some kind of nightmare Jewish wedding where the guests were all Chinese and batshit crazy. From that height I could see that the tank that almost ran me over was the beginning of a long line of tanks, which were all stopped and being swarmed over by thousands of people. There were people in every direction, no end to them, all waving and yelling at me and Horkman.

The crowd started passing us along overhead, from one set of hands to the next. They also started chanting something—something about a phantom, it sounded like, but I couldn't make it out. I also couldn't figure out how to make them put me the fuck down.

I looked back at Horkman, bouncing along on top of the crowd behind me. Believe it or not, he was *smiling*.

"Isn't this *exhilarating*?" he shouted.

Seriously, could there possibly be a bigger asshole?

CHAPTER 50

The NBC
Nightly News

BRIAN WILLIAMS: Good evening. After their brilliant triumphs in Cuba, Somalia, and the Middle East, it seemed impossible that international activists Philip Horkman and Jeffrey Peckerman would be able to top themselves. Now, incredibly, they have. This time the *Fantasmas de la Noche*—the Ghosts of the Night—struck in China, and the result is nothing short of world-changing. What you're looking at now are live images from Tiananmen Square in the heart of Beijing, where a crowd estimated in the millions— that's right, *millions*—has been celebrating all night, with no sign of stopping. There are joyful throngs like this gathered in cities all over China, which is experiencing a peaceful pro-democracy up- heaval at a speed and on a scale unprecedented in modern his- tory. And it all began with a single act—an act of great courage; an act that resonated deeply with the Chinese people; an act that inspired what is being called the Blanket Revolution. For more on this astonishing story we go to NBC China correspondent Judith Smith, in Tiananmen Square. Judith?

SMITH: Brian, yesterday began as an ordinary day in Beijing, but it took an extraordinary turn. At about two p.m. local time, China was attacked by a fast-spreading computer virus that, among other things, severely disrupted the power grid and wiped out the government's ability to monitor and control Internet and telephone communications. In a matter of minutes, China's vast military and police surveillance apparatus was rendered completely blind, and virtually powerless. This triggered an official panic, as the authorities, fearing an attack, ordered troops, tanks, and armored vehicles into the streets of Beijing, which at the same time were rapidly filling with masses of nervous civilians scared out of buildings by the alarms and commotion. And that, Brian, is when it happened: A confrontation between a man and a tank, evoking the iconic encounter that took place here during the 1989 protests. This video, shot on an onlooker's cell phone, shows a man standing alone, directly in front of a line of Chinese army tanks, refusing to move and pounding defiantly on the lead tank. It was a game of chicken with deadly stakes, and in the end, this man, armed only with his courage, triumphed. The tank stopped, the balance was tipped, and a revolution was won. The man who took on that tank—the brave man who would not be moved—has since been identified as none other than Jeffrey Peckerman.

WILLIAMS: Judith, do you have any information on the odd costume he's wearing?

SMITH: Brian, the headpiece he's wearing seems to be a traditional kaffiyeh, worn by Arab men. His body is covered by a blanket with the logo of Air China, the official Chinese airline. Experts I've talked to believe this costume is meant as a political statement, symbolizing unity between the people of China and the people of the Middle East in their struggles for democracy.

WILLIAMS: Fascinating. And what about the other "Ghost of the Night," Philip Horkman?

SMITH: He must have been very close by, Brian. This video, taken moments after Peckerman stopped the line of tanks, shows both men being passed hand to hand over the cheering crowd, which at that point had recognized the *Fantasmas de la Noche* and was chanting their nickname. Inspired by Peckerman's display of bravery, the crowd then stormed into and took over government facilities throughout Beijing; they were joined by soldiers and police officers, who put down their weapons and joined the fast-spreading movement. By nightfall, the entire country had been swept up in what the Chinese are now calling *Tan Geming*, or the "Blanket Revolution." As you can see in the crowd behind me, tonight thousands of people are wearing blankets and homemade kaffiyehs as a tribute to Peckerman and Horkman.

WILLIAMS: Judith, what about the computer virus? Was that also the work of Horkman and Peckerman?

SMITH: Nobody knows for certain, Brian, but it certainly seems likely, given the timing, and the level of technical proficiency displayed by these men in their previous operations.

WILLIAMS: For more on that aspect of the story, we go now to NBC News science and technology correspondent Robert Pearson in Washington. Robert, what can you tell us about the virus that brought China to its knees?

PEARSON: Brian, nobody here will speak on the record, but sources in the intelligence community tell me that this appears to be the work of a new supervirus that has been rumored to exist, but never seen in action before, called Fruxnet.

WILLIAMS: Fruxnet?

PEARSON: Fruxnet, Brian. It's believed to be an extremely sophisticated, highly adaptable virus that inserts itself into target networks wirelessly. It's carried on a tiny microchip incorporating a

miniaturized radio receiver/transmitter and power supply so
thin that the entire device can be concealed inside something
as small as a business card. The device could be activated in a number of ways; for example, by simply bending the card, or warming
it to body temperature. When activated, the virus immediately
senses and penetrates any nearby networks. Once it gets inside, it
quickly replicates itself and mutates as necessary until it has totally
taken over. The effects, as we saw in China, are swift, and utterly
devastating.

WILLIAMS: Do we have any idea who developed this virus, and how
Horkman and Peckerman would have obtained it?

PEARSON: That's a murky area, Brian. All we really know is that
whoever developed it must have extremely advanced programming capabilities. The U.S. is believed to be doing top-secret work
in this area, as are Israel, North Korea, Russia, Japan, and no doubt
other nations as well. It's also possible that another kind of sophisticated, extremely powerful and obsessively secretive international
entity is behind this whole thing.

WILLIAMS: You don't mean . . .

PEARSON: That's right, Brian: Google.

WILLIAMS: My God.

PEARSON: I'm told Apple may be working on something similar,
but with a cleaner design.

WILLIAMS: Thank you, Robert. As news of the developments in
China spread, spontaneous demonstrations of support broke out
in cities around the world. You're looking now at live video from
Times Square, where a huge crowd has gathered, many people
wearing blankets and traditional Arab headpieces. Many are also
carrying photographs of Horkman and Peckerman, who are now
unarguably the two most famous men on Earth, with worldwide
legions of worshipful followers. Their faces are everywhere; their

names are on everyone's lips—and yet no one knows where they are. For once again, as they have after each previous exploit, the *Fantasmas de la Noche* have vanished. They possess a seemingly magical ability to turn up where they are needed. The question is, where will they be needed next?

CHAPTER 51

Philip

We were inside a crate.

I think that bears repeating. After the events that took place in Tiananmen Square, Peckerman and I spent the next two days inside a large wooden crate.

Allow me to explain.

Once those tanks sputtered and died, the mounting excitement of that crowd swelled to the point where the air was charged with the energy of celebration. And though we were in the midst of it all, we couldn't figure out what they were celebrating.

"It's probably New Year's Eve!" shouted Peckerman above the mass hysteria.

"Can't be," I yelled back. "It's summer."

"I meant the Chinese New Year!"

"Nope, that's in late January!"

"How about Presidents' Day?"

"China doesn't have presidents."

"How about go fuck yourself?"

It was during this Talmudic exchange that I noticed the people who were now passing Peckerman from one set of hands to another were wearing red caps. And that they were moving him faster than I was being moved—most likely because none of them, despite their unbridled glee, wanted to be in contact with a bloated body covered only by a pair of fetid BVDs, a turban, and an Air China blanket a millisecond longer than was absolutely necessary.

But then the folks who were passing me along, now curiously sporting red hats as well, started moving me faster. And when I took a slight lead, the Peckerman handlers stepped up their speed and an impromptu race was on—with me and Peckerman now being batted like beach balls from one group of revelers to another and spending more time aloft than in their hands.

But where are we headed? I wondered, because it now felt like this crowd was sending me and Peckerman in a particular direction. As if this race had a finish line.

So I looked ahead and saw, at the north end of the square, beyond the sea of people and stalled tanks, a gate that we were now bearing down on at an accelerating speed. And that we arrived at precisely the same time that a rather large truck pulled up with its rear doors open and, after we were thrown inside, pulled away.

We were now both lying facedown. In the back of a speeding rather large truck. Not knowing where we were going. I just assumed that, once again, we were being kidnapped.

To say the least, I was upset. A person can be abducted just so many times before it starts wearing on him. He's overcome by fear. Anger. And a depression resulting from the helpless feeling of not having any say in where you're going or what you'll be doing once you get there. Fact was, I no longer controlled any aspect of my life and I felt empty. Sapped of all physical and emotional strength. On the verge of tears, but too weak to cry.

My guess is that *any* human being who'd experienced what I'd been through since this ordeal began would feel similarly. On the other hand, what does someone who isn't a human being feel?

"I'm so hungry I can eat a sorority."

"Jesus, Peckerman . . ."

"Maybe you'd like some Moo Goo Gai Tits," said a female voice that sounded vaguely familiar.

So I pushed myself up from the floor of the rather large truck and found myself looking into the face of our Air China flight attendant.

"Huh? Why are *you* here?" I asked her.

"Why is *who* here?" asked Peckerman, who was turning the act of getting off the floor into a Kabuki art form as his unfortunate head was now between his legs.

"You speak English?" I asked her.

"My name is Julie," she answered, nodding.

Finally, when Peckerman was geometrically able to look in our direction and see who the woman was, his face lit up the way I imagined it did every time he discovered there was more custard than usual in his morning donut.

"I believe this is yours," he said while removing his Air China blanket and attempting to hand it to her.

Now, to my mind, her reaction (drawing a Luger and threatening to blow Peckerman's head off if he didn't immediately take back the blanket and cover those underpants "with stains dating back to the Ming Dynasty") was not at all over the top. If anything, I applauded her restraint.

I then asked her to please explain who she really was and to tell us what this was all about.

"I work with Moishe and Shlomo," she said. "My assignment was to track your movements in China. Those folks in red caps were planted to protect you from the authorities, who were less than thrilled about that little party in Tiananmen Square. And now I'm supposed

to make sure your exit from the mainland is swift and without incident. So . . ."

She raised a thumb, and in a hitchhiker's motion indicated an extremely large wooden crate behind her.

"What are you saying?" I asked.

"Get inside," she said, pointing to the crate again, this time with
the Luger.

Peckerman and I stood and walked toward the crate which, according to a manufacturer's label on its side, was for Sub-Zero refrig-
erators. Its door was wide open, and a vertical plank down the middle
divided the inside into equal halves.

I took the compartment on the left, Peckerman the right, and we
stood there looking outward as Julie started to close the side that
would box us in.

"What are you doing to us?" I asked.

"Not to worry. In twenty-four hours, you'll be thanking me. In the
meantime, try to stay as comfortable as possible. There's some food
and water in there. If it gets cold, you can cover yourselves with these,"
she said, tossing us fresh Air China blankets.

She also handed us pharmaceutical vials that had pills inside. "And,
if either of you gets claustrophobic, just take some of these."

She then closed the side all the way and we heard her nailing
it shut.

What happened after that? Well, I'll tell you as much as I can remember. Which means the time before I took a pill and then after I
awakened.

Before I took the pill . . .

Just know that I didn't take it to deal with the confined quarters.
Fact is, the airholes in the roof of that box were big enough not only
for purposes of breathing but allowed me to catch a glimpse, after we
were wheeled off the rather large truck, along a flat surface, and then
up a ramp, of a few dozen crates that looked just like ours.

And then, everything turned dark. Pitch-black following the sound of a heavy door closing. Followed by more movement and then (I could tell by a new angle that sent me slamming into the side wall of the crate) a liftoff.

It took a few seconds to shake it off, but I was okay.

"We must be on some kind of cargo plane," I said to Peckerman through the wall that separated us.

No response.

"Peckerman?" I said louder.

Still no answer.

"Peckerman?" I said even louder, as I pounded on the wall.

I wondered if he was hurt. That perhaps when the plane suddenly tilted upward, he was caught off guard, his head hit the wall, and he was knocked unconscious.

"Peckerman! Peckerman! Peckerman!"

Or that he was dead.

"Peckerman! Peckerman! Peckerman!"

I then pressed my ear against the dividing wall and heard the following coming from the other side.

"Jesus, Horkman. Show some fucking respect, will you? I wouldn't make that kind of racket if *you* were shaking hands with the sheriff."

This was followed by the sounds a man makes during the act of self-induced pleasure. Followed by him shouting "Oh, the humanity!" to herald the arrival of that pleasure. Followed by the words "Good job, Mr. Wigglestick" in its aftermath.

This was then followed by me taking my ear away from the wall and swallowing one of the pills Julie gave me.

Exactly how long I was asleep is hard to say. However, I do know from my experience as a pet store owner that when a caged animal that's been given a tranquilizer to quell its nerves arrives at The Wine Shop, it tends to drift in and out of consciousness until the calming agent is totally out of the system.

So all I could really recall were the intermittent patches of hazy sound bites. A plane door opening. A man saying, "Change of plans for this one, customer needs a replacement a.s.a.p. Put it on that truck over there."

The next thing I remember is the sound of the crate being opened.

CHAPTER 52

Jeffrey

To be honest, I didn't mind the crate. I'll tell you why.

When I was a kid, we had a Weimaraner named Jimmy Carter. Seriously. My dad named him that because Jimmy Carter was the president at the time, and my dad thought he was a douchebag. He named the dog after him specifically so he (my dad) could say stuff like, "Look, Jimmy Carter is licking his balls again." Or, "Look, Jimmy Carter is dragging his ass on the carpet." Or, "Look, Jimmy Carter puked on the bed." My dad really didn't care what Jimmy Carter (the dog) did, because (a) he got to say, "Look, Jimmy Carter did whatever," which he always thought was funny no matter how many times he said it; and (b) whatever it was that Jimmy Carter did, my dad never cleaned it up. My dad believed cleaning was a woman's job, along with food shopping, cooking, laundry, yard maintenance, minor home repairs, and anything involving children, except teaching them to throw like a fucking man.

Anyway, in warm weather we used to keep Jimmy Carter outside on this deck we had over the carport. So one day, we were going to go to the mall, and when we got outside, Jimmy Carter, who like basically every other dog in the world had the IQ of a glazed donut, decided he wanted to join us, so he jumped off the carport. The problem was, he was tied to the doorknob by a piece of rope, which was supposed to keep him from jumping off the carport, so all of a sudden he's hanging by his neck with his legs about seven feet off the ground, making really high-pitched noises for a dog his size, sounding more like a squirrel.

So we're all yelling, and my dad runs over and gets underneath Jimmy Carter and is trying to hold him up, and meanwhile he's shouting for somebody to forgodsake go inside and untie the fucking dog. So my brother runs to the door, but it's locked, so he runs back to my mom to get the keys, and just then—it was probably some kind of nervous digestive reaction to being choked—Jimmy Carter releases a serious load all over my dad.

For a minute there it was really quiet, and then my mom said, "Look, boys, Jimmy Carter pooped on your father." Which was probably the funniest thing my mom ever said. The three of us busted out laughing so hard, we were crying. That went on for, like, thirty seconds, us laughing, my dad standing totally still while Jimmy Carter's stool dribbled down his head. And then Dad just let go and walked away, leaving Jimmy Carter hanging there making squirrel noises. My brother got the keys and ran upstairs and untied Jimmy Carter, and he dropped to the driveway and took off running, and we never saw him again, which to be honest was fine with everybody.

The reason I bring this up is that Jimmy Carter had this big crate that he used to sleep in, and after he ran away, my dad had this idea of using it for car trips to keep my brother and me from fighting. He'd put it in the back part of the station wagon, and the first time either one of us hit the other, which was usually while we were still in the driveway, my dad would make whoever he thought was guilty ride back in the crate. It was supposed to be a punishment, but I actually liked it. I could curl up in there and get comfortable, and it was farther from my dad, who was always in a bad mood when he was driving, because all the other drivers were such fucking assholes. After a while it got so whenever we drove anywhere, I just automatically got into the crate, and nobody even thought about it.

This caused a problem one time when we drove to Canada on vacation, and on the way back a Canadian border officer saw me in the crate, and he pulled my dad over because he thought maybe it was some kind of kidnapping. My mom tried to explain that I was their legal child who just liked to ride in a dog crate, but she was overruled by my dad, who preferred to explain to the officer, who my dad referred to as Dudley Do-Right, that who the fuck did he think he was, stopping an American citizen on his way to America, and was he aware that if it wasn't for America, Canada would have had its ass kicked in World War II? So we ended up spending an extra day in Canada, and my dad ended up on a special Canadian list of people not allowed to return. (He's on a similar list for Disney World because of the time he put Dale, of Chip 'n' Dale, into a chokehold because of what my dad claimed was a clearly anti-Semitic gesture, but I don't want to digress here.)

Anyway, I really liked Jimmy Carter's crate, and I kept riding in it until one day my mom, without asking me—and I never totally forgave her for this—threw it away, because according to her it was inappropriate for a child entering tenth grade. But the point is, as a youth I spent many hours in a crate, and those were some of the happiest hours of my childhood. So when the Air China stewardess bitch put me and Horkman into the refrigerator crate, I wasn't nearly as upset as he was. It was nice to be alone for a change, and I enjoyed myself, and if you're going to tell me that you never enjoy yourself when you're alone, we both know you're a fucking liar. I actually enjoyed myself four times, including one involving Charo, before I got bored and decided to swallow the pills.

After that I don't remember anything, until I heard Horkman calling to me from the other side of the crate.

"Peckerman," he said, keeping his voice low. "Are you awake?"

"Yeah."

"I think somebody's opening the crate."

I felt the tapping on the crate, and heard voices.

"Where are we?" I said.

"I don't know," he said. "But they're talking English, and they sound like Americans."

"Thank God."

"Why thank God?"

"Because, asshole, if they're Americans, that means we're back in America."

"Right. In America, where we're wanted terrorists. Who could be shot on sight."

I'd forgotten about that. I figured the stewardess bitch must have set us up, claiming she was helping us, but really shipping us back to the U.S. to be killed. Fucking Chinese, with their lies and their fucking little soy packets.

I could hear the front being pried off the crate. I edged forward, my plan being that as soon as there was space, I'd jump over to Horkman's side and use him for protection in case there was any shooting on sight. By the time the front came all the way off the crate, I was crouched behind Horkman with my eyes closed.

I waited for shooting, but there wasn't any. Instead, there was a voice saying, "What the *hell*?" And then, "Who the hell are you?"

"Allow me to introduce myself," said Horkman. "My name is Murad Fazir. The gentleman cowering on the floor behind me is my colleague, Yasser al-Fakoob. We come in peace."

Yes, he actually said "We come in peace."

I stood up behind Horkman. Standing outside the crate, looking in, were two guys, one older and one basically a kid, both wearing khaki pants and blue shirts that said BEST BUY. Behind them was a huge industrial kitchen, with some guys in chef suits on the far side of the room.

"What the hell are you doing in there?" said the older guy.

"What the fuck does it *look* like we're doing?" I said. I don't honestly know what I meant by that, but the guy's tone just pissed me off.

"This crate is supposed to contain a commercial refrigerator," said the guy. "Which we're supposed to install."

Horkman—and even though he's an asshole, I have to give him credit for this line—said: "Clearly there has been some mistake."

There was a pause there, while the older guy pondered the situation, two guys wearing blankets in a crate that was supposed to contain a refrigerator. Finally he decided to do what guys like him have been doing for as long as there have been guys like him.

"I'm going to call my supervisor," he said. He pulled out his phone and said, "Shit. No service down here." He turned to the kid and said, "Nick, you stay here with them."

He left the kitchen. Horkman and I stepped out of the crate. Nick was looking at us, and our Air China blankets. You could tell Nick was not the brightest firefly in the forest. After a few seconds, you could actually see his head jerk back a little bit, from the unexpected impact of having a thought.

"Wait a minute," he said. "Are you those guys?"

"No," I said.

"What guys?" said Horkman.

"The Whaddyacallits," said Nick. "Of the Gnocchi."

"No," I said.

"The *what*?" said Horkman.

Nick was looking hard at us now. "You *are* them," he said. He turned and yelled toward the kitchen in general. "It's those guys! They're here!"

"Fuck," I said.

"Yes," agreed Horkman.

We looked around. There was an exit close by, with two big swing-ing doors. We trotted over and pushed through. Now we were in a long corridor lined with racks of trays and kitchen stuff. There were people to the left in waiter uniforms, so we started trotting to the right. We came to another corridor, turned left on that one, kept trot-ting. We kept going for a while, making random turns, I'm puffing and sweating through my blanket. We didn't really have a plan except get the fuck out of there.

We were coming to another corridor junction, and up ahead a sign that said PARKING GARAGE and an arrow pointing around the corner to the right. That was the good news, because a garage would be a way out. The bad news was, there were voices coming from the same direction, moving our way. In a few seconds, they'd come around the corner and see us. Horkman grabbed my arm and said, "Over here." He yanked me toward an elevator and pushed the but-ton. We were staring at the door, waiting for it to open, going "come on come on come on." Finally, just when the voices were coming around the corridor, the door opened, and we ran inside. Horkman stabbed a floor button, and now we were waiting for the fucking door to shut. *Come on come on come on . . .*

The door started to close. We exhaled.

Then a hand stuck in the door, and it opened.

Standing in the doorway were a bunch of guys in suits, including two guys the size of forklifts who were obviously security. The reason for the security was obviously the guy standing in the middle.

Donald Fucking Trump.

For a second, everybody stared at everybody else.

Then both forklifts pulled guns.

Then Donald Trump held up his hand and said, quote, "Wait a minute." Then he looked right at me and said, "Jeffrey Peckerman?"

I nearly shat my underpants. *Donald Fucking Trump knew who I was.*

"It's an honor to meet you," he said. To *me*, he said that. *Donald Fucking Trump.*

Have you ever been in one of those situations where you're thinking of two different things you could say, but instead of picking one, you say part of each one, so they morph together into a new thing that is not right, kind of like what happened to Jeff Goldblum in *The Fly*? That's what happened with me and Donald Trump. I stuck out my hand, and the two things I was thinking of saying were "I'm a big fan" and "This is an honor," but what came out was "I'm a bonor," with "bonor" sounding basically like "boner." At the same instant I realized I was telling Donald Trump that I was a boner, I also remembered that he hates to shake hands because of germs, so I yanked my hand back really hard, and my Air China blanket fell off. So I was standing there in basically my underpants. Donald Trump turned to Horkman and said, "And you must be Philip Horkman."

Horkman said, "Nice to meet you, Mr. Trump." He stuck out his hand, and *Donald Trump shook it.*

"I just want to say," said Donald Trump, "that I deeply, *deeply* admire what you two men have accomplished."

"Thank you," said Horkman, flashing me a sideways look that said *What the fuck?*

"Yes, thank you, Mr. Donald Trump," I said. I stuck out my hand again, to try to get a shake, but the timing was wrong. The handshaking window was closed. I have never hated Horkman more than I did at that moment.

"I take it," Donald Trump was saying, "that you're here to attend the convention?"

"What conv—OUCH," I said, because of Horkman elbowing me.

"Yes," said Horkman.

"Well," said Donald Trump, "I would be honored if you would sit in my box."

Which is how Horkman and I, wearing Air China blankets, ended up walking with Donald Trump into the Republican Party national convention on the night when the Republicans were going to nominate their candidate for president of the United States.

CHAPTER 53

Philip

I hate politics.

Don't get me wrong, I have strong opinions about what's going on and am very concerned about the direction our country is heading. But my frustration these days lies with the fact that it's almost impossible to implement curative policy because of self-serving partisanship.

As a concerned citizen who grew up in a Republican household that revered President Eisenhower, a five-star general who rode the wave of his WWII popularity into the White House for eight flourishing years, I learned at an early age that a person can be an effective public servant without having to be compromised by the politics it takes to get into office.

Even that night in Tampa, as Trump held the door for us to enter the St. Pete Times Forum, he expressed his own frustration that within the party itself, the lack of unity had divided the delegates' votes among six candidates, so there was still no nominee.

"Assholes," said Trump. "They should change our party's symbol from an elephant to an elephant with six assholes."

For a second, I thought Peckerman was talking.

But Trump's choice of words aside, I was curious about his take on the situation.

"If it were up to you, Mr. Trump," I asked, as he led the way to his box, "who would you like the party to choose?"

"Me," he said.

Then smiled like that was a joke. Then got serious like it really wasn't a joke.

I must say it was exciting to be inside that arena—a convention center that held concerts and where the Tampa Bay Lightning hockey team plays their home games. I mean, watching it at home is one thing, but to be where the actual delegates were, right there on the floor announcing who they were casting their votes for, was a big thrill.

And to be guests in Donald Trump's private box was an extra thrill—a glass-enclosed booth with about twelve cushioned chairs like the ones in a movie theater, as well as a TV monitor bracketed to the ceiling showing all the action down on the floor.

"You fellas hungry? Want food? Something to drink?" Trump asked, pointing to a buffet and fully stocked bar.

I was famished. I really hadn't eaten anything since that Air China flight to Beijing. But it was Peckerman, who'd had about six meals on the plane, who answered.

"You bet, Donny Boy!" he exclaimed, before picking up a plate and making a beeline from one end of the table to the other, grabbing enough food to feed the seven other people who were already seated in the booth—nicely dressed men and women whom I got the impression worked for Trump. And all of who emitted a collective gasp upon hearing the idiot Peckerman call their boss "Donny Boy."

All eyes, including ours, were now on Trump, awaiting his reaction. His face was taut and his eyebrows contracted.

"Donny Boy?" he said. "I've never been called that. By anyone."

But then, as if he had reminded himself about something, the scowl slowly started to relax, giving way to a smile.

"But I always wanted to be called Donny Boy," he said, before looking at his employees. "Didn't I?" in a tone signifying that the answer was "yes."

"Yes, Mr. Trump," they said in a single voice.

He then told me and Peckerman to come sit next to him at the front of the booth after we'd gotten our food. When he sat down with his back to everyone, the postures of the employees behind him visibly relaxed.

After filling our plates, Peckerman and I stopped at the bar to order drinks. Peckerman ordered three large gin and tonics. That's right: three. I asked for a cranberry juice with a splash of soda.

"Got a yeast infection, shithead?"

"What are you saying, Peckerman? That a person can't order cranberry juice simply because he enjoys it?"

"Nobody simply enjoys cranberry juice."

"Fine. So I'm the only one who likes cranberry juice."

While the bartender was making our drinks, we looked out onto the floor where the delegation from Tennessee was casting its votes. Since the roll call was always in alphabetical order, it meant that they were getting down toward the end of this ballot.

Peckerman shook his head and got reflective for a moment.

"You know, seeing this makes me long for my days in politics," he said.

"Excuse me?"

"There's a lot you don't know about me, Horkman. Fact is, I was president of my class in fourth grade."

"That's very impressive, Peckerman. Though I find it very hard to believe that anyone who knew you actually voted for you."

"They didn't vote for me. I stole the kid who ran for president's

bike and told him I wouldn't give it back unless he made me his running mate. So when he won, I became the vice president."

"But you just said you were president."

"Well, after the kid who was president got shot, I moved up."

"Got shot? A fourth grade kid? Who shot a fourth-grade kid?"

Peckerman looked at the bartender to make sure he wasn't eaves-
dropping.

"I did," he whispered.

"You what!"

"It was a BB gun, you dipshit. After I gave him back his bike, I hid
in some bushes, and when he rode by, I shot him about twelve times
in the stomach . . ."

"Jesus, Peckerman!"

"So when he fell off his bike and a car ran him over and he spent
the rest of the year in a full body cast and was homeschooled, I assumed the presidency."

Before I had a chance to respond, Trump was standing and calling
to us.

"Hey, come here, you two," he said, waving his hand and indicating
the seats next to him. "I want to hear all about the escapades of the
Fantasmas de la Noche."

"The escapades of who?" Peckerman whispered to me.

"I have no idea," I answered, as we grabbed our drinks and approached Trump.

"Now, Mr. Horkman, I'd like you to sit here," he said, pointing to
a seat on his right. "And Fantasma Peckerman, why don't you take the
seat on the other side of me, so I can hear your magnificent crusade
in stereo."

When Trump chuckled and then looked at his employees indicating that the stereo reference was a joke, they laughed.

"Be right there, Donny Boy," said Peckerman.

"Donny Boy," Trump repeated. "God, I love that name," he said before looking at his employees.

"Me, too!" they said in unison.

By the time we took our seats, Wyoming had just cast its votes for the very short governor of a very large state. And, once again, when the tally was announced, there was no candidate with a majority and the collective disappointment in the arena was palpable.

"Motherfucker!" exclaimed Trump, who then shook his head with the same scowl he usually has just before he fires someone on *The Apprentice*.

"Hey, we're on television," said Peckerman, pointing to the monitor that showed us on either side of Trump—the cameras had cut to him for his reaction to the continued impasse in the nominating process.

Then the oddest thing happened. Almost immediately after the camera cut away to the podium where the chairman of the Republican Party was calling for still another ballot, it cut back to the shot of us and held it. And the longer that picture of me, Peckerman, and Trump was not only on our monitor—but on every video screen in St. Pete Times Forum, including the four huge ones on the scoreboard that hung down from the arena's ceiling—the more the attention of the over nineteen thousand people in the place was drawn to it.

And as it did, the cheering grew and grew until reaching a point of sustained pandemonium.

"Boy, they really love me, don't they?" said Trump.

"Indeed they do!" said his employees.

Trump saluted in response to this commotion, and then spoke to me and Peckerman in a hushed tone.

"How would you boys like to have a million dollars? Each."

"Gee, thanks, Donny Boy!" said Peckerman.

"How come?" I asked.

"Who gives a shit how come? Could that be in cash so we don't have to pay taxes on it, Donny Boy?"

"The reason I want to give it to you is because you're heroes," Trump said, mostly for my benefit as Peckerman had already borrowed a pen and notepad from one of the employees and was making a list of the things he was going to spend the money on.

"You're heroes and you're champions of democracy," Trump continued. "In so many ways, you remind me of me."

"They remind us, too," said the employees.

"So as a fellow champion, I not only wish to personally reward you for your Trumpean efforts, but to reward our country by having you go out there and nominate me as the Republican candidate for president."

"Us? Why us? Look how we're dressed," I said, tugging on my Air China blanket.

"How much is a Bentley?" Peckerman asked the employees. "You? You? Any of you know?"

"I wouldn't worry about how you're dressed," said Trump. "I have a feeling those folks out there need to be reminded about the Blanket Revolution."

"What's that?" I asked.

"What's that, he asks," said Trump, laughing.

"What's that, he asks," said the employees, laughing.

"Well, I'm honored that you feel this way, Mr. Trump, but . . ."

"Please. Call me Donny Boy."

"But if this is for my country, that's reward enough. We don't need any money to do it."

The gash I got on my forehead after Peckerman stabbed me with the pen he borrowed from one of Trump's employees looked worse than it actually was.

"Douchebag," said Peckerman.

"I'm entitled to my feelings about things, Peckerman."

"Not when it affects my reward, you don't. Just know that if you don't want to keep your million dollars, I'd be more than happy to take it off your hands."

We were back inside the corridors of the St. Pete Times Forum, being led to the speakers' platform by Trump and the same bodyguards we'd seen earlier.

"Anything in particular you want us to say, Donny Boy?" I asked.

"Just speak from the heart, Mr. Horkman. Just say how you feel about our country and what's best for it. Except every time you get the urge to say your name, say mine instead."

We approached a blue curtain that the bodyguards parted to allow me, Peckerman and Trump to pass through first. We did and found ourselves at the back of the podium. We were still pretty much hidden from the crowd at this point, as we were behind a number of people swarming about.

Trump approached a man I recognized as the one we'd seen on the TV monitor chairing the proceedings. Trump whispered something to him and then gestured in our direction. The man looked our way, then back at Trump and nodded.

Then Trump left his side and came back to me and Peckerman.

"Okay, fellas. You're on."

CHAPTER 54

Jeffrey

Here's a tip: If you're going to do any kind of public speaking: Go to the bathroom first.

I should have thought of this on the way up to the podium of the Republican convention, but things were happening really fast. Think about it. One minute I'm in a refrigerator crate, stoned on whatever those pills were, and the next minute I'm meeting Donald Fucking Trump, in person, and three minutes later I'm calling him Donny Boy, and we're really hitting it off. I could picture us becoming friends, hanging out socially as two guys who like each other a lot but don't want to have gay sex with each other.

Then Donny Boy's bartender made me three gin and tonics the size of Slurpees. The truth is, I never had a gin and tonic in my life, but it just sounds classy, "gin and tonic," so it seemed like the thing to drink with Donald Trump. They were pretty strong, and between that and the pills, I was feeling a little out of it.

Then all of a sudden Donny Boy is asking me do I want a million dollars, and I'm, like, fuck yes I want a million dollars. Before I know it, Horkman and I are heading out to the podium to nominate

Donald Fucking Trump for president of the United Fucking States. In a situation like that, you don't think, "Maybe I should duck into the bathroom and drain the lizard first." But my point is, you should.

My plan, when we were walking out there, was for me to do all of the talking, and Horkman to not do any of the talking. Partly, of course, this was because he's an asshole. But also I happen to have, as a forensic plumber, a fair amount of experience with public speaking. In addition to testifying in court and hosting my cable show, *Forensic Plumbing!*, I am also—I believe I mentioned this earlier—on the board of directors of our national association, the National Association of Forensic Plumbers National Association. (What happened was, there used to be two rival associations, the National Association of Forensic Plumbers, and the Forensic Plumbers National Association, and they decided they should join together, but neither side wanted to give up their name.)

As a member of the NAFPNA board, I've been called upon to speak out on some important plumbing issues, including one time going to Washington, D.C., where I was scheduled to testify before a congressional subcommittee in favor of H.R. 623, a bill that would have repealed the dumbass tree-hugger federal law that made everybody switch to these dumbass low-flow toilets that don't work. I had a great statement prepared that would have torn the fucking lid off this issue, but I never got to give it because the congressmen stopped the hearing to go vote on Iraq. Bottom line, they never did pass H.R. 623, and we still have those dumbass toilets, and what the hell was the point of Iraq? Assholes.

The point is, I was going to do the talking to the Republican convention. So I made sure I was a little ahead of Horkman when we walked through the curtain.

And then, whoa.

When you think about Republican convention delegates, you don't think of hard-core partiers. Democrat delegates, yes. You wouldn't be surprised to see them smoking crack on the convention floor. But Republican delegates, you figure their idea of a really crazy wild time is putting on a Hawaiian shirt and going to see Jimmy Buffett.

But when Horkman and I walked out, those people went infuckingsane. Shouting, clapping, stomping, screaming, dancing, poking each other in the eye with their little American flags. It went on, I swear, for fifteen minutes, Horkman and me in our blankets waving at them, and them jumping around like maniacs. When it finally seemed to be dying down a little, I stepped to the microphone, and they went completely batshit again. And then the whole thing happened again. So at that point we'd been up there for nearly an hour, and we still hadn't said dick, and my head was feeling weird from the pills and the gin and tonics, and I had Lake Michigan sloshing around my bladder.

So I decided, fuck these assholes, I'm starting.

CHAPTER 55

NBC News Republican Convention Coverage

BRIAN WILLIAMS: It looks as though Jeffrey Peckerman is going to try to start speaking here, although the crowd is still cheering as wildly as ever. Tom, you've covered a lot more conventions than I have. Have you ever seen a response like this?

TOM BROKAW: Nothing even close, Brian. This is adulation. This is worship. And yet none of these delegates—for that matter, none of us in the media, either—has any idea where Horkman and Peckerman stand politically. We really don't know what message they plan to deliver here tonight.

WILLIAMS: True. We don't even know how they got here. Last we knew, they were sparking a revolution in China, and suddenly, out of all the places in the world, they appear in Donald Trump's box at the Republican convention. We have no idea why they've chosen to be here. What we *do* know is that this is an unprecedented moment in American political history, a drama unfolding live before the nation.

BROKAW: You know, the television audience for political conventions has been declining for years now. But I'm willing to bet that, as word has spread of the appearance here tonight of the *Fantasmas de la Noche*, the vast majority of the TV sets in the nation, as well as millions more throughout the world, are tuned to this.

WILLIAMS: No doubt, Tom. All right, Jeffrey Peckerman is waving his arms to quiet the crowd, and it looks as though he might actually be able to say something, so let's listen as we finally hear—as the *world* finally hears—from these two amazing men, who have brought so much healing to a wounded planet.

PECKERMAN: Thank you. Thank you. My name is Jeffrey Peckerman.

(Wild applause, cheering)

PECKERMAN: Thank you.

(Continued wild applause and cheering)

PECKERMAN: Thanks. Okay. Thank you. Really.

(Continued wild applause and cheering)

PECKERMAN: Seriously, will you people shut the fuck up?

(Gasps)

BROKAW: Did he just . . .

WILLIAMS: Folks, we remind you this is live television.

BROKAW: Well, he definitely got them to quiet down.

PECKERMAN: Okay, thank you. I'm here tonight to say a few words on . . . Excuse me, asshole, I'm talking here.

HORKMAN: Ladies and gentlemen, I just want to apologize for the lang . . . Hey! Do *not* push me!

PECKERMAN: As I was saying, I'm Jeffrey Peckerman, and I'm here tonight to say a few words on behalf of a close personal friend of mine, Donald Trump. Or, as I call him, Donny Boy.

(Laughter)

PECKERMAN: Thank you. You know, that laughter reminds me of a funny story that I'd like to break the ice with here. It seems somebody stole the commode from the police station, and now the police have nothing to go on!

(*Silence*)

PECKERMAN: A commode is a toilet.

(*Silence*)

PECKERMAN: Police have nothing to go on. Because they *can't go on the toilet*. Because somebody *stole* it. Jesus, is everybody here retarded?

(*Nervous laughter*)

HORKMAN: Okay, there is absolutely no excuse for that kind of . . . Hey!

PECKERMAN: Shut up, asshole. Ladies and gentleman, getting back to the issue at hand, Donald Trump. What can you say about this man that hasn't already been said by either himself or somebody else? But I will try. Donald Trump is a great American. Let me ask you a question. Abraham Lincoln. Was he a great American? Of course he was. But now let me ask you another question: How much was Abraham Lincoln worth? I'm talking net.

(*Silence*)

PECKERMAN: My point exactly. Now, ladies and gentlemen. Look at Donald Trump. Where is he? Okay, there he is, on the big screen. Yoo-hoo! Donny Boy! Smile!

(*Laughter*)

PECKERMAN: Ladies and gentleman, Donald Trump is richer than Abraham Lincoln, or any other president we have ever had, including John Kennedy, Benjamin Franklin, or Franklin P. Roosevelt. Donald Trump is richer than *fuck*. Do you know why, ladies and gentlemen? Because Donald Trump *demands quality*, that's why. In *everything*. His buildings, his golf courses, his signature line of chocolates, his wives, *everything*. And that's what we need in this country. Quality! Donald Trump does not settle for shitty. If something is shitty, Donald Trump says no thanks.

That's the kind of thinking we need, as a nation. We have to STOP SETTLING FOR SHITTY.

(Applause)

PECKERMAN: Thank you. Look at our toilets. Like many of you, I grew up in an America where we had great toilets. We had toilets that used 3.5 gallons of water per flush. Those toilets had *suction*, ladies and gentlemen. Those babies could suck down a mature sheep. And now look at what we have. We're using *wussy toilets*, people. Oh, sure, if you're a European, you're eating like a fucking mosquito and crapping out little molecule turds, those toilets are fine. But we don't crap like fucking Europeans! WE'RE AMERICANS, AND WE CRAP LIKE AMERICANS, AND WE DESERVE TOILETS AS GOOD AS AMERICA! People of America, ARE YOU HAPPY WITH YOUR TOILETS?

(Applause, shouts of "No!")

PECKERMAN: Exactly! And when these assholes in Washington could have done something about it, what did they do? I'll tell you what they did. *They voted on Iraq.* What kind of priorities is that? Which would you rather have, America? Iraq, or strong toilets?

(Silence)

PECKERMAN: In closing, Donald Trump. Nominate him. And I'm not just saying this because of the million dollars. Although I definitely appreciate it. I seriously have to go.

(Crowd noise, shouts)

WILLIAMS: I honestly don't know what to say.

BROKAW: I've been covering politics a long time, and I have never seen anything like that.

WILLIAMS: I don't even know if we're still on the air. But if we are, let me attempt to summarize. It appears that Jeffrey Peckerman was attempting to break the delegate deadlock here by calling on the convention to nominate Donald Trump, who as of now is not even in the running. Philip Horkman was on the stage with

Peckerman, but did not appear to share his views. In fact, at one point they appeared to get into a shoving match, and after that Horkman spent the rest of the speech standing off to the side shaking his head. It's not clear at the moment whether what Peckerman is suggesting is even within the convention bylaws. There's a lot of shouting going on down there, and at the moment the convention appears to be in a state of total chaos.

BROKAW: Meanwhile, as you can see, both Horkman and Peckerman are still on the stage, along with a large crowd of Republican dignitaries. But it seems to be an awkward gathering, Brian. My impression is, the party bigwigs initially were eager to be seen up there with Horkman and Peckerman, but now, after that speech, which can only be described as bizarre, a lot of them are not so sure.

WILLIAMS: Peckerman also seems quite agitated, doesn't he? I'm wondering if we can get a close-up shot of what he's . . . Oh my God . . .

BROKAW: Is that what I think it is?

Philip

The mere thought of what he did still horrifies me.

Jeffrey

I swear to God, I never had any intention of urinating on Sarah Palin. All I wanted to do was get the hell off the stage and find a bathroom.

But here's the thing. The stage was the size of fucking Connecticut. Also it was loud as hell in the hall, and there were all these bright lights blasting in my eyes, and I was definitely still messed up from the gin and the pills, so I had trouble figuring out which way to go. And then all these Republican suits showed up, swarming around me and Horkman, some of them wanting to shake hands, some of them wanting to talk, a couple wanting to admire our Air China blankets like they were fucking Picasso paintings. And I *could not get out of there.*

Did you ever have to piss really really bad? I mean really really REALLY bad? Well that's the situation I was in. I couldn't even *walk,* at that point. I had to do something *right away.* So I thought, Okay, I'll go behind the podium there, which will at least give me a little privacy. So I shoved past the suits, stepped behind the podium, and whipped it out.

The problem was, I got myself turned around somehow, so when I went to what I thought was *behind* the podium, I was actually going in *front* of it, to the audience side, but because of the lights in my eyes, I didn't realize this. So I basically whipped it out in front of the entire Republican convention and a worldwide TV audience.

That was bad enough. What was worse was that, by pure coincidence, at that exact moment, Sarah Palin came around the *other* side of the podium. But she wasn't looking at me. She was looking at the crowd and waving.

So there I am, just starting the longest piss of my life, the kind you can't stop even if you wanted to. I have my eyes closed, and all I'm thinking is *ahhhhhhhhhhhh*. I heard some shouting, but like I said it was loud and crazy in there anyway, so I didn't pay much attention. And then I heard a scream, right in front of me, really close. So I opened my eyes, and there she was, looking down at her pantsuit, which looked like she'd been wading in the Pee River. I real quick spun away, but unfortunately I spun *toward* the audience, so now I was hosing a whole bunch of delegates, who were not at all happy, but like I said once you get started on a whiz of that magnitude, you are basically committed to seeing it through.

At that point, things happened pretty fast. I got grabbed by some guys who I think were Secret Service, and they hustled me off the stage with my arms behind my back, which meant the dignitaries were scrambling to get out of the way because I was still basically a human geyser. I felt pretty bad about the whole thing, and I wanted to apologize to Sarah Palin, but the Secret Service assholes wouldn't listen to me.

I'll say this: You see her up close, she's still a very attractive woman.

CHAPTER 58

The New York Times, Page 1

SURPRISE GOP NOMINEE EMERGES FROM CHAOS

By ADAM NAGOURNEY

ST. PETERSBURG, FLA.—In one of the strangest developments in the annals of American politics, the Republican Party early Thursday morning chose, as its presidential nominee, the international activist Philip Horkman, who faces federal charges of terrorism and ship hijacking, and who told the GOP convention delegates, in his brief acceptance speech, that he is a registered Democrat.

The nomination culminated a strange and chaotic night that began with the convention deadlocked over the nominee, with no apparent breakthrough in sight. At about 9:20 p.m., as the delegates were preparing for yet another ballot, the convention hall was electrified by the appearance in Donald Trump's private box of Mr. Horkman and his colleague Jeffrey Peckerman, who with Mr. Horkman has engaged in a series of daring international exploits, boldly spearheading pro-democracy movements in Cuba, Somalia, the Middle East and China. The two men, both clad in the Air China blankets that have become an international symbol of their efforts, were called to the stage, where they received a rapturous ovation lasting more than 45 minutes.

It was then that the night took an even stranger turn, as Mr. Peckerman delivered a bizarre, profanity-laden speech, much of which seemed to involve toilets (Mr. Peckerman is a forensic plumber). The purpose of the speech, to the extent that it seemed to have one, apparently was to place Mr. Trump's name in nomination, although Mr. Trump later denied having any knowledge of such an effort. The speech was poorly received, both by Mr. Horkman, who stood nearby shaking his head throughout, and by the delegates, many of whom appeared shocked by Mr. Peckerman's coarse language.

The mood on the convention floor turned openly hostile following the speech. As Republican dignitaries filled the stage, Mr. Peckerman went to the front of the lectern and urinated on Sarah Palin, former Alaska governor and GOP vice presidential candidate, who was waving to the crowd. Mr. Peckerman was rushed from the stage by security officers, but not before he also urinated on a large segment of the Florida delegation.

At that point, with the convention on the verge of anarchy, Mr. Horkman stepped to the lectern, quieted the crowd and offered an emotional apology for the behavior of Mr. Peckerman, whom Mr. Horkman described as "an idiot, although to be honest, that is insulting to idiots." Mr. Horkman then delivered an impromptu speech, touching on the need for civility in political discourse, the value of bipartisanship and the paramount importance of spaying and neutering household pets. His remarks appeared to have a powerful calming effect on the delegates, who responded with enthusiastic applause, and then a sustained chant of "We want Horkman!"

As the chant echoed through the hall, growing in intensity with each passing minute, party leaders hastily met with members of the rules committee. Then, in a development that stunned political observers, Mr. Horkman's name was placed in nomination. The nomination was quickly seconded and, in what was surely one of the quickest and loudest roll-call votes ever taken in a national political convention, unanimously approved by the wildly cheering delegates, officially at 3:23 a.m. The rapid sequence of events appeared to stun Mr. Horkman, who appeared bewildered as he was led to the lectern to deliver a brief acceptance speech, which began with the statement, "I think there's been a mistake." However, this produced only louder cheers as the delegates continued to express their

Continued on Page A14

CHAPTER 59

The NBC Nightly News

BRIAN WILLIAMS: The strangest election season in the nation's history got even stranger tonight. As Democrats gather in Charlotte, North Carolina, for their national convention, it has become virtually certain that, thanks to an overwhelming and unprecedented last-minute shift in delegate loyalties, the Democrats will nominate, as their presidential candidate, none other than Jeffrey Peckerman. This comes at a time when the political world is still reeling from last week's Republican convention, where the delegates chose as their standard-bearer the *other* member of the *Fantasmas de la Noche*, Philip Horkman, apparently without realizing that he is a registered Democrat. On that night, Republican delegates were responding to Horkman's criticism of Peckerman, who delivered a profanity-filled speech before relieving himself, on the convention stage, on former Alaska governor Sarah Palin. But it is those same controversial actions by Peckerman that have made him a hero to some Democrats, who feel it's time their party was led by a fighter who would stand up to the Republicans. For more on this, we turn to NBC News political correspondent Robert Stavis. Robert?

STAVIS: Brian, that's exactly right. While most Democrats agree that the Palin incident was over the top, they feel that Peckerman was making an important symbolic point, which is that for too long their party has allowed itself to be urinated on, metaphorically speaking, by the Republicans, without having the will, as a party, to urinate back. They're mad as hell, Brian, and they're thrilled to find somebody who seems to be as mad as they are.

WILLIAMS: But what about Peckerman's speech? The language he used, and all those references to the toilets?

STAVIS: It was crude, Brian, no doubt about it, but many Democrats feel Peckerman was deliberately using shocking language to draw attention to valid issues. For example, when he asked whether Americans would rather have—and this is a direct quote—"Iraq, or strong toilets," he was graphically, yet eloquently, illustrating the fact that our involvement in foreign wars has weakened our ability to maintain our crumbling infrastructure.

WILLIAMS: What about Peckerman's party affiliation?

STAVIS: As far as we've been able to determine, Brian, he has never registered to vote, or engaged in any political activity whatsoever, although he was once charged with assault for allegedly punching a sixty-seven-year-old woman who was running for the school board and tried to put a campaign sign on his swale. Those charges were dropped when the woman refused to testify, some say because of BB gun injuries to her dog.

WILLIAMS: Fascinating. Speaking of charges being dropped, in light of their humanitarian work in Cuba, Somalia, the Middle East, and China, both Peckerman and Horkman have received full presidential pardons for any crimes involved in the acts of terrorism and hijacking that they allegedly committed. Peckerman also will not face any charges in connection with the incident involving Governor Palin, who has said she does not want to prolong the matter any further, although she has reportedly told friends in private that if she ever gets Peckerman alone, she will castrate him with a hockey stick. And so, with the legal obstacles out of the way, and the Democratic nomination all but locked up, it appears that the American voters will face one of the most unusual choices in the nation's history: Philip Horkman, or Jeffrey Peckerman. In three months, one of these men will be elected to the most powerful position on the planet. The question now is, which one will the voters choose?

Three Months Later

CHAPTER 60

The New York Times,
Page 1

BEGLEY JR., PENN WIN WHITE HOUSE IN HISTORIC UPSET

By ADAM NAGOURNEY

In a stunning rebuke to the two major political parties, on Tuesday, long-shot outsiders Ed Begley Jr. and Sean Penn were elected president and vice president of the United States, the first third-party candidates ever to win these offices.

Only weeks ago, Begley Jr. and Penn, representing the Persons of Race, Ethnicity and Gender Party, were considered extreme long shots, but they managed to eke out a majority of the electoral vote, thanks largely to a historically low voter turnout resulting from what can only be described as disastrous campaigns run by both the Republican and Democratic parties, both of which had nominated men who were popular celebrities, but also untested political neophytes.

The Republican candidate, Philip Horkman, is a registered Democrat who refused to campaign at all, stating that he was "very uncomfortable" with much of the GOP platform. He also stated repeatedly that he did not intend to vote for himself.

The Democratic candidate, Jeffrey Peckerman, did campaign enthusiastically in the early days after the convention, but his erratic behavior and profane oratory—repeatedly using such terms as "commies" and "fags," often in reference to people sharing the platform with him—quickly disillusioned the Democratic base. Party leaders tried to muzzle Mr. Peckerman by denying him staff and travel expenses, but he continued to make public appearances, often with the help of non-political sponsors, including Hooters and the video-production company Girls Gone Wild.

Movements arose in both the Republican and Democratic parties to replace Horkman and Peckerman, but these efforts were hindered by legal technicalities, as well as the feeling on each side that, no matter how bad its candidate was, the other side's candidate was worse. In the end, an unprecedented number of voters decided to simply stay home on election day, resulting in a nationwide turnout of 9 percent of the electorate—the lowest ever recorded in any Western democracy—and a narrow victory for Mr. Begley and Mr. Penn.

In declaring victory, Mr. Begley Jr. called for Americans to join him in "taking America in a new direction, with smaller cars and a lot less dietary gluten." He also announced that he would appoint Barbra Streisand to

Continued on Page A12

CHAPTER 61

Philip

I'd read somewhere that many of NASA's astronauts had trouble readjusting to life on Earth after they returned from the moon. That being in outer space, where they looked back and saw our planet as a small speck in a very populated galaxy, changed their perspective on life so dramatically that they had difficulty reconnecting with loved ones who couldn't possibly feel the way they now did.

Would the same thing happen to me? I wondered.

As I sat on that private jet for the last time, now as a defeated presidential candidate, the romantic in me was hoping for a happy ending. Hoping that Daisy and the kids would be at the door when I got to the house, and we'd go forward from where we'd left off.

Was it possible?

I had called Daisy right after my concession speech. I'd told her that I understood why she wasn't there the way wives of the losers are traditionally at their husbands' sides as a display of family support and unity. I told her that I understood that Heidi and Trace had school the next day, that I was looking forward to seeing her, and pretended to understand when she couldn't say the same thing to me.

This probably shouldn't have surprised me, as things between us had deteriorated during the campaign. At first she did make an effort to be a candidate's wife by allowing herself to be profiled on an MSNBC special about the potential First Ladies and, even though she, too, is a registered Democrat, drove around with the Republican Party's slogan ("The Other Guy Is Worse") on the bumper of our SUV.

She had even joined me at a few stops along the trail. Had her parents come over to stay with the kids while she flew to places like Buffalo and Kansas City. I could see she was trying her best, despite the fact that she was totally out of her element, and I did my best to show my appreciation.

But eventually the tumult of crowds and the intrusion of the media into what should have been our private lives made her more and more uncomfortable and she eventually retreated into a protective mode when Peckerman pulled that stunt during our third televised debate.

You remember: After I'd answered Katie Couric's question about the national deficit by saying, "No matter what your political affiliations are, I think it's fair to say that any system which allows Warren Buffett to pay fewer taxes than his secretary needs to be reexamined," Peckerman, as soon as the audience's applause in that auditorium died down, responded by holding up a picture of our son, Trace, doing a grand plié during a performance of *Swan Lake* and said, "Take a gander at this homo."

Had I changed? Well, how could I not?

Since the preceding spring, after that fateful soccer game when I called Peckerman's daughter offside (and she *was* offside, by the way) I'd been a fugitive, had fallen so deeply in love with another woman that I jumped off an ocean liner to save her from drowning, helped liberate literally millions of oppressed people, and was a candidate for

the presidency of the United States. No one could possibly experience all that and not be affected.

Were Daisy and I different people? was the more relevant question. And had we grown so far apart that our marriage wouldn't be
able to withstand the change in our definitions? Before this entire
episode, I was more than content to be a husband, father and pet
store owner. And she was happy being the wife of that guy. But now?

That was the question that hounded me during that flight, the ride
home from the airport, and the walk to the front door of what I was
hoping could still be my happy home.

And it was answered after I let myself in, and walked through the
darkened house and into the master bedroom, where I found a note
on my pillow that said "Let's take things slowly. Okay?" next to my
sleeping wife, to whom I leaned over and whispered, "Okay."

So that's what we've been doing. At home I've been slowly slipping
back into the rhythms of my family's life. And at work, I'm not only
pleased to be back selling pets at The Wine Shop, possibly due to my
national profile; business is not only booming but our plans for ex-
pansion will soon be a reality.

And to complete the picture, I've gone back to refereeing the local
soccer games. In fact, this very afternoon you'll be able to find me
running up and down the field with a whistle in my mouth in the
AYSO girls under eleven championship game.

And the best part? That Peckerman's daughter is twelve years old,
so there's no chance that I'll be seeing that moron ever again.

Yes, life is good.

CHAPTER 62

Jeffrey

You want to know what I learned from all this? I learned an important lesson about life, which I will never forget, namely: If Donald Trump tells you he's going to give you a million dollars, don't believe him, because he's a fucking liar.

That's right: He never paid me a nickel. Asshole. All the Republicans are assholes. And by the way, I am not saying that the Democrats *aren't* assholes. Oh, sure, they nominated me for president. Big whoop. After that, they totally screwed me over.

Let me ask you this: If you're the candidate for president, shouldn't *you* get to pick where you campaign? Shouldn't *you* get to decide where the motorcade goes? That's what I thought, but that's not the way it worked. I had all these dipshit little suit-wearing handlers handling me, and every day they'd give me a schedule that would say something like "7 a.m., Shake hands with workers outside a factory in Fort Wayne, Indiana, and stress the four-point plan to bring economic blah blah blah." So I'd inform the handlers that I, as the candidate, had some problems with the schedule, such as:

1. 7 a.m.
2. Outside a factory.
3. In Fort Fucking Wayne.
4. Indiana.

I'd say, how about instead I go shake hands with some workers in Vegas? And they'd say, you already did Vegas three times, you can't keep going to Vegas. So I'd say, Okay, what about the Bahamas? And they'd say the Bahamas weren't part of the United States. I checked that on Wikipedia, and it turns out they were right, but it gives you an idea of what kind of nitpicky dipshits they were.

And then there were the speeches. They'd write these *long*, bore-ass speeches for me to give, and if I didn't read every word *exactly* the way it was written on the paper, the handlers would have a hissy fit. Like one time I was giving a speech in Detroit, talking about how concerned I was about all the economic blah blah blah of Detroit, and, to emphasize the point, I kind of gestured around at Detroit and said, "I mean, *look* at this shithole." Right away I could see all my handlers making *nonono* gestures with their hands, so I pointed at the audience and said, "These people *live* here. You think *they* don't know it's a shithole?" And then the sound system went dead, which happened more and more often before they totally stopped scheduling speeches for me.

My point is, the Democrats are just as big assholes as the Republicans are. As you go through life, pretty much everybody you meet turns out to be an asshole. That was the other lesson I learned from all this.

I'll be honest: The only reason I even ran for president was I was afraid to go home. I think I mentioned this, but Donna, my wife, is Italian. She has a temper, and she knows (don't ask me how I know this) at least three ways to kill a person using only oregano. After the

Republican convention, I tried to call her a couple of times, but I could tell she wasn't ready to get back together, because of the tone she had in her voice when she told me I should fuck myself with a trombone.

So I stayed away and ran for president. I think I would have won except for the handler dipshits. Get this: On election night, they wanted me to go on television and concede, because of the Electoral College. I said I'm not conceding anything, because (a) I never heard of any Electoral College, and (b) Ed Begley Jr. and Sean Penn are a pair of—and I don't mean this in a disrespectful way, just a factual observation—faggots.

So I never did concede, but after the election the Democrats stopped paying my expenses, and I couldn't go home, so I moved into the guest house of the second-largest Hooters franchise owner in northern New Jersey, and although he and his girlfriend Traci are both lovely and generous people, after a couple of months I got the feeling that maybe they wanted me to move on, because of some remarks they made, and also they cut off my electricity. Plus I missed Donna, and I really missed Taylor.

So finally I had this idea, which seemed a little crazy, but I was desperate. I remembered that back when I first start dating Donna, I bought her this Hello Kitty stuffed doll, which was stupid but she loved it, or at least she acted like she loved it, by which I mean only minutes later I reached third base.

So here's what I did. I went on eBay and got the exact same Hello Kitty stuffed doll, used. Then I waited for Valentine's Day, and at suppertime, I went to the front door of my house and rang the doorbell. I admit I was nervous as shit, standing there, holding the Hello Kitty. It was raining, and I felt like a guy in a movie, waiting to see if his wife is going to take him back.

From inside the house, I heard footsteps coming to the door. I almost ran away, but I didn't.

Then the door opened.

And there she was, looking exactly the way I remembered her.

The cleaning lady.

I forget her name. Something like "Slubka." She's Russian or Polish or something, and she has a mustache, and we don't get along because of an issue she and I got into once involving something she claimed she found in a pair of my underwear that I'm not going to discuss here except to say she's a fucking liar.

Slubka told me that Donna and Taylor were at the mall, so I gave her the Hello Kitty to give to Donna. She took it by one corner, like I was handing her a bag of raccoon pus. I wasn't sure she would even give it to Donna. But she did, because I called the next day and Donna answered and told me if I ever gave her a used gift again, with stains on it from God knows where, she would shove it up my ass. Which was her way of saying I could come home.

So now, things are pretty good. I'm not saying great. I still sleep on a cot in the garage. But at least I'm home, and my life is settling down. The TV and newspaper assholes have pretty much stopped coming around and doing stories about whatever happened to me. I got kicked out of the National Association of Forensic Plumbers National Association, because they're a bunch of assholes, but the joke is on them, because my show, *Forensic Plumbing!*, got picked up by a major cable channel, Comedy Central, which is paying me good money to make more episodes. At first I thought, since they're called "Comedy Central," that they wanted me to make the shows humorous. But they said no, they want me to do exactly what I've been doing.

So like I said, things are pretty good. The best thing is being able to spend time with Taylor, who's a great kid, and by the way, not to brag, she's also a really good soccer player. She's a forward, and I'm pretty excited, because today she's playing in the AYSO league under-eleven girls division championship. Taylor's actually twelve, but the under-eleven team had some injuries and needed a last-minute replacement player, so I told them Taylor was eleven and gave them a doctored birth certificate. So this afternoon she'll be out there, and I'll be on the sideline, rooting hard for her and making sure her team doesn't get screwed over. Because if there's one lesson I have learned in life, it's that nothing is more important than your kid.

Buddy the Lemur was given a permanent home in the Central Park Zoo, where he was a popular attraction for several months before suffocating himself when he got his head caught inside a condom thrown into his cage by a member of a field trip from a middle school in Queens.

Denise Rodecker lost 127 pounds, got her diabetes under control, and is now a professional Zumba instructor.

Officer Barton Hempledinger, the NYPD helicopter pilot who was shot in the scrotum, made a full recovery and sold the rights to his story, which became a made-for-cable movie, *Manhood Down*, starring Erik Estrada.

Fook left Chuck E. Cheese immediately after his image appeared on the TV news. He remains undercover, working at Walt Disney World in the capacity of Pluto.

Sue and Arnie Kogen were convicted of attempting to smuggle a firearm onto the SS *Windsong*. They died in each other's arms from heart attacks during a conjugal visit.

Peckerman's Pants, the ones he wore for twenty-three straight days, are currently on display at New York's Museum of Natural History.

Maria never returned to the convent. She took her meager savings, bought a push-up bra, bleached her hair blond, and now sings the weather forecast at a local TV station in Tallahassee, Florida.

Hyo, the Korean high school student who worked part-time at The Wine Shop, is now twenty-one years old and manages one of Horkman's new stores. He is no longer Korean.

Ramon, Ramona, Roman Jr. formed a merengue band called "Carlo, Carla, and Carlo Jr."

"Secure the Radius" is now a widely used military tactic, as well as the zone defense used by both the Duke and Georgetown basketball teams.

Sharisse Fricker quietly left Cuba with a twenty-two-year-old professional bodybuilder named Miguel and two duffel bags. She settled in Central America, where, through a series of ruthless maneuvers, she acquired a secret controlling interest in the Panama Canal, for which she has big plans.

Captain Sven Lutefisk was relieved of command of the SS *Windsong* and is currently working at a Long Island Starbucks.

Charo is still performing, using a specially made bulletproof guitar.

Coast Guard Salamander Unit 9 does not exist. Please refrain from any further mention of Coast Guard Salamander Unit 9.

The Fruxnet computer virus spread rapidly throughout the Internet, where its most severe impact was a complete shutdown of both Facebook and Twitter, resulting in a spectacular worldwide increase in worker productivity.

Brian Williams resigned from *NBC Nightly News* after the Horkman/Peckerman/Begley Jr. presidential race, stating, "I've worked far too hard for far too long to have to cover shit like this."

When last seen, he answered to the name "Tuffy" and was bending balloons at children's birthday parties.

The Mickey Mantle rookie card, which was worth $250,000 before Peckerman rolled and inserted it into his anus, was eventually sold at auction for $3.4 million.

The Ed Begley Jr. / Sean Penn Administration, despite the best of intentions, wound up involving U.S. troops in four new foreign wars, including one with Sweden.

Walmart, hoping to cash in on a hot trend, ordered three million Air China blankets, of which 2.999 million remain unsold.

H.R. 623, which would return American toilets to their glory days, continues to languish, as it has for more than twelve unconscionable years, in the House Commerce Subcommittee on Energy and Power.

Jeffrey Peckerman is currently serving a life sentence without parole for crimes arising from his reaction to officiating decisions during an AYSO girls under eleven division championship game.

Philip Horkman visits Jeffrey every week, with the most benign and humanitarian of motives, which only makes it worse.

Donald Trump is still at large.